W•CLA
PUBLISHING
A STATEMENT IN LITERATURE

BONDED BY BLOOD

A Novel by

CA$H

This is a work of fiction. Names, characters, places, and incidents either are the product of the author's imagination or are used fictitiously, and any resemblance to actual persons, living or dead, business establishments, events, or locales is entirely coincidental.

Wahida Clark Presents Publishing, LLC
60 Evergreen Place
Suite 904
East Orange, New Jersey 07018
973-678-9982
www.wclarkpublishing.com

ISBN 13-digit 978-0-982841433
ISBN 10-digit 0-9828414-3-4

Library of Congress Catalog Number 2010916371
1. Urban, Contemporary, African-American, Atlanta
Georgia – Fiction

Cover design and layout by: Baja Ukweli
Book interior design by: Nuance Art*.*
Contributing Editors: Jazzy Pen Communications, R. Hamilton and M.D. Phillips

Printed in United States

Acknowledgements

As always it's a far more difficult job to pen the shoutouts than it is to pen the actual book. Because if I forget to mention one person they never let me forget it. But y'all should know it's love no matter what and it's deeper than a mention in a book. Mama (Mrs. Rosie Williams) I want to thank you for your unconditional love and unbending confidence in me. Absolutely no love compares to yours. I love you and I know that it is your greatest hope to live to see me and Darnell make it home from prison that is why I've left the other things alone and ride strictly legit these days. I wanna make you proud and I will. To my seeds Destiny, Keke, Lil Cash, Shawt, Cortez, Jakia, and the son I do not know, I do what I do to show each of you that it does not matter what your predicament is, determination and intestinal fortitude will surmount any obstacle thrown in your way. I love each of you and that won't ever change. Destiny I am so proud of the ambition you show. Keke, your vibrant personality will take you far. Shawt, it's all about making good choices and sticking them out, you are the master of ya own destiny. Lil Cash, I like your focus and i know you'll reach your goals academically as well as in the rap game. Cortez, what has happened to our communication? Get at me and sponge some of this wisdom. Ya pop got a street Phd. No need for you to travel the same road because it leads to nowhere. Jakia, where are you? It's been so long since I've heard from you. To my son whomremains unknown to me but always in my heart and thoughts, I will find you one day. To my brother and sisters, nieces and nephews, I love you all and thanx for the love back. , Jadelz, sometimes you do too damn much but I love you and we have such a great relationship which I hope will always remain this strong even when I get on that behind. ☺ A special shoutout goes to Shorty Redd, you have proven your every claim and they have withstood the test of time so all I can do is respect your heart. Kayundra, your kindness is not forgotten. Raquel, your heart is so big. Mel, you are an incomparable friend. Mo, we don't talk often anymore but that's on me. Author Dutch I thank you for the blurb on *TRUST NO MAN 3*. Author LaTonya West I see your growth and I value our friendship. WCP Authors Mike Sanders, Tash Hawthorne, Missy, Victor Martin, Anthony Fields and others we go hard for the team! To my niggaz on lock with me and all over the country keep ya heads up and remain one hunnid. Anything less ain't respected. Thanx for supporting this gutta shit I write. Midget Baby, Travis Cosby, Big Gat, Sincere, Bo Pete, Kee Boo, and Cutts Boogie Down, and my dude fa life, Manny. Toni you are a class act and your friendship is platinum lady. Misha, I haven't forgotten you. My entire fb fam much love. To my editor, Joan of Jazzy Pen Communications, you did a tight job on this, you brought out the best in me. To everyone at Wahida Clark Publishing thanx for what you do to help me succeed. Finally, to the Queen herself, Wahida Clark. Not only are you a fiyah author yaself, you're a hella publisher. Thank you for the platform you provide for me to share my stories with the world. If I've forgotten anyone my bad.

DEDICATION

THIS BOOK IS DEDICATED TO ALL MY URBAN AND STREET LIT AUTHORS WHOSE STORIES DEPICT THE STREETS AS THEY REALLY ARE. THANX FOR NOT WRITING THAT FAKE ONLY-IN-THE MOVIES GARBAGE THAT SATURATE THE GENRE.

-END-

AUTHOR'S NOTE

By the time you read this I'll have been on lock 20 years! I'm often asked how I've managed to do such a long bid yet maintain my sanity, dignity, and ambitions. All I can say is that I don't know what it is to give up. And now that I can see the finish line, I'm not slowing down. If you've read my previous two novels, *TRUST NO MAN* and *TRUST NO MAN 2*, then you already know I write that gutta shit, so you know what to expect when you turn this page. Holla at me!

On Facebook @ Cash Street-Lit author or email
WCP.cash@gmail.com or write to:
Wahida Clark Publishing
C/O Cash Fan Mail
60 Evergreen Place, Suite 904
East Orange, NJ 07018

Bonded By Blood
Prologue

Valencia Jones aka Black Girl was flat on her back, a position that she had been in many times before in her profession as a stripper and a hooker who never gave the "P" away for free. This time, however, Black Girl wasn't in a motel room or in the backseat of some baller's whip with her toes pointed to the sky; she was in a hospital bed at Grady's Memorial. The HIV virus she had contracted while tricking off with different corner hustlers for crack after the addictive drug reduced her from a boss bitch in Rapheal's stable to a clucker had turned into full blown AIDS.

The incurable disease had slowly eaten away all of the phat ass that had once been so enticing to the tricks, especially when Black Girl was young and on top of her game, strutting up and down the ho stroll like a Clydesdale or working the pole in a strip club like a pro. Her once flawless blue-black skin was now scattered with sores and held an ashen hue; those succulent lips that used to make a trick bust in minutes and come back for more head were now sunken and parched, and those pretty hazel brown eyes that had hoped to see the world were now as dull as a rotting eggshell. Death was calling.

Black Girl heard death's call as clearly as she used to hear a baller in VIP call out to her for a table dance fifteen years ago.

And just like she used to ignore the call of a broke nigga, she ignored death's persistent whisper; she needed a few more moments with her sons, Khalil, B-Man, and Quantavious, who were at her bed side.

"Mama is tired of fighting this," Black Girl said as tears of regret ran down her face onto the starched white bed sheets.

"Don't give up, Mama," pleaded sixteen year old Khalil, her first born. "Ain't that what you taught us?"

"I also taught y'all to keep it real so that's what I'm doing—I'm keeping it one hunnid," remarked Black Girl in a vernacular her sons could relate to. They were used to their mother giving them the uncut truth. She forced open her tired eyes and looked up into Khalil's. "Mama gonna leave here real soon."

"Shh Mama! You ain't going nowhere," replied Khalil.

"You sho' not. You gonna get well and get back fine so that you can get Rapheal back and y'all can stunt on haters like old times," chimed in 13 year old Quantavious. He knew that in spite of everything, their pop was still Black Girl's pride and joy.

Fifteen year old B-Man scowled at the mention of Rapheal's name. He and Rapheal had never gotten along too well and he blamed Raphael for what Black Girl was going through.

A slight smile came across Black Girl's face as she quickly reminisced back to the happier times when Rapheal was one of the most prosperous pimps in Atlanta and she was his bottom ho. Time was of the essence though—death was knocking loudly at her door and she didn't want to waste it reminiscing. She didn't have a damn thing in this world to leave behind for her sons so she wanted to at least leave them with some important mental jewels before she departed.

Black Girl understood that hers sons were born and bred in ATL's grimey inner-city and had inherited a street hustlaz mentality from both their bloodlines and the environment in which she and Rapheal had exposed them to. She had known that in life, and now that death was so imminent, she was not about to try to fool herself that her sons would choose the square life, therefore she felt obligated to prepare them for what awaited them in the streets. "Khalil," she coughed, "you a pretty nigga who the niggaz gonna envy but the girls gonna love. Neva mind the haters but don't let the girls like you for *free.* Tell those lil tricks that your mama sold ass to feed you so they gotta do the same. Make those bird bitches turn tricks and work the poles to give you what a pretty nigga like you deserve."

"Aight, Mama, I'ma mack 'em hard," promised Khalil who was already trying to chili pimp a few young broads in the hood.

Black Girl whispered B-Man's given name, "Basil," and he leaned down to hear her better.

"I'm right here, Mama," he said. At fifteen years old he was the middle son but the bond between him and Black Girl was a bit stronger than Black Girl's bond with Khalil and Quantavious because many times Black Girl had taken an ass whooping from Rapheal to protect B-Man. Now she whispered something in his ear that made B-Man understand why Rapheal had mistreated him at times.

Khalil and Quantavious strained their ears to hear what was being whispered but Black Girl's voice was too faint to carry beyond B-Man's ear, which was an inch from her mouth. When B-Man lifted his head, his mouth was a tight line and his eyes were slits. "I understand," he muttered, holding back his emotions.

"All of that don't matter now," said Black Girl tearfully, "it is what it is. Now listen to me closely. I know about you jacking niggaz. People talk Basil. That's why you have to move in silence and never do dirt where you live or revenge will come right through your front door."

B-Man nodded but his mind was on what Black Girl had whispered in his ear.

"Everything is a hustle and in the streets you gotta get them before they get *you*." Black Girl continued. "If you're gonna live by the gun, you make sure not to hesitate to do what you gotta do if a muthafucka test you." It was the type of gutter advice her sons were accustomed to hearing from her. B-Man's scowl softened, he was with that.

"Quantavious, you're gonna be the best hustla to come out of my big coochie if you can keep a bitch from being your downfall," Black Girl predicted for her youngest, who smiled. Q was proud that she saw so much potential in him. He had dreams of a crack supastar, but his mom was right . . . he had a real soft spot for chicks.

"I'ma tighten up," he promised.

"Please do, because the wrong ho will bring you down faster than a snitch can. And while you're out there pitchin' rocks on the corner don't forget to put something away for a rainy day."

"I won't," said Q.

"Another thing . . . and I'm talking to all three of you; with three of y'all gettin' money from three different hustles there's no way anybody should be able to touch y'all. By the time y'all have kids and they grow up, they shouldn't have to ever fuck with the streets. The family should be legit. Don't let money, bitches, or envy come between y'all. Believe it or not, home is often where the hate is. But I'll turn over in my grave if y'all ever allow that to happen. Remember, its family over all others. Y'all are *bonded by blood*. Promise me y'all won't ever violate that bond."

"I promise," Q said.

"Me too," vowed Khalil.

"Yeah, me too," B-Man promised.

"One final thing," said Black Girl who's every word had become a struggle to speak. "Don't hold anything against Rapheal, he didn't put a gun to my head *make* me go in the clubs and strip. He didn't make me trick off or even smoke crack. I chose to do those things because doing them allowed me to be with him, and being with him made me happy. He may not be much now but he used to be my everything."

"We understand, Mama." Khalil spoke for the three of them.

I don't understand nothin'! Thought B-Man, *Nigga fucked your life up and now his junkie ass ain't nowhere to be found. He gonna pay for this when I grow up.*

"Mama!" Q cried out when Black Girl's eyes closed and her jaw appeared to go slack.

"Yes, baby?" I was just thinking about how tired I am. I mean, what I got to fight for? Look at me, I'm nothing but skin and bones, I ain't got no ass no more and my skin looks like taco meat. I'm only thirty-eight but I look sixty and feel like I'm goddamn a hundred," Black Girl wept, allowing self-pity to overtake her emotions for just a moment. She forced her eyes open once again and saw through her tears that Q was crying too. Khalil was stoic but she felt him gripping her hand. B-Man's eyes were red with fury.

"I want y'all to bow y'all head and say a prayer with me," Black Girl requested of her sons. Though religion had never been practiced in their family all three heads bowed.

"My Father in Heaven, I ask that you hear my prayer. Lord, I know that I have forsaken you and don't deserve to enter your pearly white gates when you call me home, so watch over them and don't allow envy, hate or jealousy to destroy their bond. In Jesus name . . . amen." Black Girl's voice became as faint as the flapping of a butterfly's wings. Khalil opened his eyes when he could no longer hear her. He saw that her head had fell to the side and she was no longer breathing.

"Nooooooo, Mama, don't die!" cried Q, falling on the bed and throwing his arms around her frail body. Khalil touched his baby brother's shoulder, "she's gone lil bruh," he said consolingly while B-Man stood in the background thinking, *If it wasn't for Rapheal Mama wouldn't have died.*

When Khalil turned around and saw B-Man's expression, he reminded him, "Bonded by Blood."

"Whateva!" replied B-Man.

Chapter One
Atlanta, Georgia: Seven Years Later

Fazio sat down on the soft, butter leather, half-oval sofa in the spacious, expensively decorated entertainment room of the $2.7 million dollar baby mansion he had purchased a year ago. The 20-room adobe was only a couple of blocks away from the mansion in Fayettesville once owned by ex-heavyweight champ, Evander Holyfield.

Fazio had paid cash for the opulent home. The huge cash transaction had been cleverly concealed by his real estate agent to protect the 35-year-old black drug kingpin from the IRS, DEA, and all the other alphabet soup agencies that laid in the wings waiting to seize a nigga's properties and assets as soon as he slipped.

The fly drug supplier, who was presently that nigga in the dope game in ATL, wore silk Coogi pajamas with matching bedroom slippers. Around his neck hung a platinum chain with an iced-out medallion replica of Queen Nefertiti that was the size of a paperback book and fell to his navel. A thick platinum and diamond Rolex sparkled around his wrist and was accentuated by a 25-carat pinky ring.

There was no questioning the fact that Fazio was getting to major chips—the boy was caked up. His jewels were custom-ordered straight from Jacob's of New York, the premiere jeweler for rich mafuckers from drug kingpins to entertainers to pro-athletes. If a nigga had serious guap and wanted custom jewels, he was tryna see Jacob.

Fazio was that type of caked up nigga. He had married Selena and her family had cocoa out the ass. Her brother Francisco had put Fazio on once he had proven his loyalty when Francisco was going through a bloody war to become El Jefe or the boss of Atlanta's drug trade.

On the marble cocktail table in front of him sat a whole brick of the best cocaine to be found in all of ATL. The kilo on the table was small shit, though. Fazio had 149 more of them stashed behind a fake wall inside the kitchen's pantry, and at least 500 more hidden at his produce market out on Buford Highway.

"Yo, China, powder your nose," Fazio said to Diamond, the curvaceous stripper who was sitting to his right on the sofa, wearing nothing but a look of seduction.

"China?" questioned Diamond, thinking Fazio had forgotten her name.

Fazio explained, "It means the same as if I call you shorty or mami." He was in the habit of occasionally speaking a mixture of English and Spanish since he was around his Mexican in-laws so much and had picked up certain Spanish words and phrases from them.

Diamond accepted Fazio's explanation, along with the cocaine he pushed toward her. Turning to the naked cutie on his left he said, "You, too, baby girl. Go ahead and get your head right."

Diamond laid out several lines of the potent white powder and the three of them took turns snorting. The high quality coke sent an immediate rush to their heads, while Usher's "Confessions" played softly in the background from the

surround sound system. Bottles of Corona and tequila got popped next and the trio got real nice.

Fazio was glad that Selena was visiting family in Texas. Usually several of his people were in his company, but tonight he had given Maldanado permission to take the night off. Maldanado was Fazio's most trusted lieutenant and a cousin to Selena. Fazio didn't want Selena's people to peep his unfaithfulness. It had been hard enough gaining their respect and trust. Mexicans, besides being clannish, weren't quick to trust a black or welcome him into their family. Selena's people, especially Francisco, had put Fazio to the test numerous times before embracing him—he wasn't tryna fuck that up.

Fazio's Mexican *compadres* could understand a man having a *china* on the side, but they wouldn't have respected Fazio bringing strippers into his home. He didn't want them to see him as most men are gluttonous in their appetite for women and sex. It was okay to have an insatiable appetite for *dinero* and power, but an unappeasable thirst for women is viewed as a weakness waiting to be exploited.

Fazio couldn't afford to have his people peep any sign of weakness in him. This is why he was alone with the strippers this night.

Diamond had met Fazio at the Blue Flame several months ago when the suave drug dealer and his click of Mexicans and Blacks were ballin' in the strip clubs VIP. All the dancers had flocked into VIP that night 'cause those niggas were doing it big. Stacks were on deck and champagne was on ice all night long. They weren't just making it rain, they made it pour.

While the other dancers were busy trying to grab those dollars and looking to hook up with just any of the niggas in the crew, Diamond had focused her attention on the HNIC. She easily peeped whose plate the others ate from. Her plan had been to get herself noticed, then scheme for a permanent position in Fazio's life. Maybe become his baby mama, if not wifey.

Fuck the money the nigga and his crew tossed up in VIP, Diamond wanted to share the guap Fazio stacked inside safes. Diamond was pretty, like the singer Mya, and thick to death. With a pretty face and a bangin' body, she had succeeded in getting Fazio's attention that night. One night later she was riding Fazio's dick in the Presidential Suite at the Ritz out in Buckhead. The girl put that sweet pussy on him like she was fucking for a future of never-ending luxury; had his ass speaking fluent Spanish although he only knew a few words, normally.

That morning, waking up next to Fazio, Diamond was thinking it wouldn't be too long before she'd have the nigga open.

Tonight, several months later, she was in a different frame of mind. She had tried, but failed to pussy-whip Fazio. *The nigga all open over some wetback bitch*, Diamond said to herself. Her thoughts were full of contempt. Niggaz had been playing her sideways too damn long.

Following Fazio's direction Diamond laid back on the butter leather sofa, spread her thighs and let Vee Vee eat her out. Fazio watched while stroking his dick and urging Vee Vee on. He clapped his hands and the 103 inch plasma TV that took up half a wall in the room came on in amazing visual clarity. Scarface, the movie, played silently on the screen. Unlike most niggaz, Fazio wasn't too impressed with the character, Tony Montana. It was the character, Sosa, whom Fazio wanted to emulate.

Tony Montana was 'bout it, but Sosa was the real shit.

Bonded by Blood

"Chupe ella cuelo," Fazio instructed Vee Vee, forgetting that the stripper didn't understand Spanish.

"No comprende," she replied, nevertheless, as she continued to lick Diamond's neatly trimmed pussy. When Fazio translated his words into English, Vee Vee began licking Diamond's brown eye. She did it real nasty-like, figuring her freaky display would turn Fazio the fuck on.

Diamond moaned her appreciation for Vee Vee's oral manipulations, her cries of pleasure worked like Viagra on Fazio, who immediately got a stiff hard-on.

Fazio went over to the wet bar across the room; when he returned he was carrying a can of whipped cream. He proceeded to spray the cool whipped cream all over Diamond's 38-26-43 measurements and then he stroked his exposed erection that jutted through the opening of his Coogi pajamas as Vee Vee instantly began to lap the cream off of Diamond's body very erotically. Nothing turned Fazio on more than watching two chicks lick each other and bump pussies. The nigga was shot out over that shit. Q, one of the niggaz on Fazio's team, had put him on that girl-on-girl shit and the fuck if it wasn't proving to be as addictive as any street drug.

Vee Vee who was a five-foot-three sexual tornado with a honey brown skin tone, lots of ass, a tiny waist, and cupcake-sized titties along with a real affinity for the taste of pussy, slowly licked the whipped cream off of Diamond's 38D's tracing Diamond's hardened nipple with her tongue. Vee Vee sent heat between Diamonds luscious thighs. As Vee Vee's tongue traveled down her body, Diamond guided Vee Vee's head to her throbbing pussy and moaned when Vee Vee treated her clit like a pacifier.

"Oooh shit!"

Vee Vee placed soft kisses on Diamond's clit and fingered her sopping wet pussy.

"Make her nut in your mouth," encouraged Fazio, while jacking his seven-inch erection-then slipping on a condom and sliding deep inside of Vee Vee while she rubbed her face in Diamond's hot coochie.

"Fuck me, daddy," Vee Vee moaned as Fazio went deeper.

The more Fazio watched Vee Vee eat Diamond's pussy the more aroused he became. He gripped Vee Vee's hips and banged her pussy harder. "Oooh yes, daddy! That's it, you gonna make a bitch cum all over your dick!" Vee Vee screamed then returned her attention to Diamond.

Minutes later Diamond screamed, "I'm about to cum in your mouth!" then let out an ear-piercing wail of pleasure. Fazio couldn't hold back any longer. He pumped in and out of Vee Vee like a jack hammer until he grunted and emptied his nuts.

After recuperating from their threesome, they snorted more cocaine and drank more tequila. When Fazio was ready for another round of torrid sex, he went upstairs to his bedroom to get another pack of condoms. Getting some head, raw dick, was cool, but he knew that going up in females unprotected, especially a stripper hoe, was like playing Russian Roulette with a fully loaded gun. Fazio had survived some deadly drug wars, he wasn't about to let pussy send him to an early grave.

As soon as Fazio left the room, Diamond whispered to Vee Vee, "You got the pills?"

"Yeah, I got 'em," Vee Vee answered quietly, reaching for her purse. She hurriedly
shook two powerful date rape pills into the palm of her hand.

"Use four!" instructed Diamond.

"You sure, girl?" whispered Vee Vee. "I'm not tryna kill this muthafucka and end up with a murder charge!"

"It ain't gon' kill him. But we gotta make sure his ass is knocked out for a while."

Vee Vee shook out another two pills then dropped them into the half-empty bottle of Corona that Fazio had last drank from. Then just to be sure, they drugged a glass of tequila; Fazio was sure to drink one or the other.

When Fazio returned from upstairs both girls were sipping fresh glasses of tequila and smiling impishly.

"My two little freaks," commented Fazio, smiling back at the naked pair before picking up the half-empty bottle of Corona and draining it in one huge gulp.

"I wanna make a toast," proffered Diamond, raising her glass. "To the livest nigga I've ever met."

"I'll toast to that, "Vee Vee played along, clinking her glass of tequila against Diamond's.

Gassed up by the two strippers, Fazio picked up the unattended glass of tequila that was on the cocktail table and clinked it against Vee Vee's and Diamond's, toasting to himself.

After Diamond saw that Fazio's glass was near empty, she was certain that the two, laced drinks would soon take effect. The scandalous stripper placed her near-full glass of tequila on a coaster on the cocktail table, then she laid down on the huge bear-skin rug in the center of the floor, flaunting her nakedness, "Come and get it," she invited Fazio, spreading her smooth, shapely brown thighs, fingering herself for added enticement.

Vee Vee began stroking Fazio while he watched her partna on the rug play with herself. Though Vee Vee had skilled hands, the combination of the drugs he had consumed left Fazio half-limp. Fazio began to feel a bit light-headed at first, then dizzy. Just moments later his dick had shriveled up like a prune and spittle ran out the corner of his mouth as he collapsed face down on the bear-skin rug where Diamond lay invitingly.

"Hurry up, girl! You get his jewelry and the cocaine, I'ma search the house for money!" whispered Diamond.

Twenty frantic minutes later the two strippers drove away from Fazio's house in Vee Vee's Pathfinder. Diamond was glad the nigga didn't know where she lived. The couple of times they had hooked up before tonight, they had met up at whatever hotel they rendezvous at. She knew that she'd have to quit her job at the Blue Flame and leave ATL, at least for a while because Fazio would surely throw money around in an attempt to find her. Diamond wasn't about to play herself; she had no doubt that anyone of her co-workers at the club would sell her out for a grip.

At Vee Vee's apartment on Campbleton Road, they dumped the stolen money, coke, and jewels onto the kitchen table and tallied it up. Besides the jewels they'd taken off of Fazio, Diamond had found other expensive pieces upstairs in the master bedroom.

Neither girl realized that they had over a quarter mil' worth of customized ice in their possession. The pieces were heavy and the diamonds looked clear, even to their untrained eyes. Diamond guessed they could get a hundred stacks for it all, maybe more if they sold it piece by piece. Besides, the jewels and the kilo of cocaine, Diamond and Vee Vee counted up nearly eighty stacks. Most of the money had been found in Fazio's bedroom. Diamond was sure there had been more money and drugs hidden somewhere inside the mansion, but she had been anxious to get away before the pills wore off and he woke up.

"Girl, I'm so scared, I'm about to pee on myself," Vee Vee said breathing irregularly. She was already beginning to worry they might get hunted down and bodied over the stunt they'd pulled.

"I already told you that trick don't know shit about me other than my stage name. We'll just lay low at your place, sell the jewelry and cocaine, and then bounce out of town somewhere."

Diamond had it all planned out.

Five years working as an exotic dancer at various strip clubs in the South and having been played by different hustlas had Tynisha Brown jaded as far as money-gettin' niggas was concerned. She was known only as Diamond at the Blue Flame, but she had used a half dozen other aliases throughout her career in various clubs.

When she first started shaking her ass for the fast money, it had been exciting and fun. She was fuckin' with all types of money-gettin' niggas who came through the clubs tipping and tripping like they owned the world. After being played by one nigga after another, Diamond had grown sick of their lying asses.

Her discontent with hustlas hadn't turned her straight dyke, though. She would do the girl-on-girl thing for money, or for the occasional thrill, but she still preferred men. She had set her sight on Fazio that first night at the club, swearing to herself that if she hooked him she would treat the nigga like a king; be faithful to him, and have his back through thick and thin. The first time they hooked up at the Ritz, she had gone all out for Fazio in bed. Yet, Fazio had ended up treating her as if she was a trick—no different than other big-money hustlas had treated her in the past. So, Diamond had made up her mind to treat *his* ass like a trick nigga. Now she and Vee Vee were splitting the nigga's bread.

Who's the trick now? Diamond was laughing inside as she and her crime partner split up the eighty stacks.

Chapter Two

uantavious had been texting his connect and trying to reach him on his cell phone for the past two hours. Still he hadn't been able to reach his man. It was unlike Fazio not to answer Q's calls. Not only was he Q's supplier; they fucked with each other hard. They both patronized the strip clubs, sports bars, and other popular hangout spots.

Q had been plugged in with Fazio for a couple of years now. Fazio was hitting him off with five bricks at a time, on consignment. On the flip side, Q had been instrumental in Fazio locking down certain spots in the city. He was Fazio's link into Moreland Avenue and Thomasville Heights where Q and his brothers grew up. Q had brought Fazio business from a lot of niggas over that way.

Q's niggas in the hood, even his brother B-Man, were forever trying to get him to set up Fazio so they could jack him. No matter how they brought it to him. though, Q refused to cross his connect. Those fools were sleeping on Fazio, fooled by his handsome face and laid back demeanor. But Q knew that Fazio was a dangerous muthafucka, with a crew of crazy Mexicans that would ride for him in a heartbeat.

Q continued trying to reach Fazio for another half hour but still got no reply. Usually, if Fazio was tied up with other business he'd have Maldanado or someone call back and let Q know when Fazio would be available. Right now Q was tight because he needed to pick up ten bricks to sell to a dude over in the Bluff. He'd already had him on hold all day.

It was a little past midnight, according to the digital clock in Q's Ford Explorer. Thirty minutes later he pulled into Fazio's circular driveway and parked the SUV beside Fazio's red Ferrari. From his whip, Q tried once more to reach his man on his cell phone, but again the call went to voicemail.

Despite the late hour and the tranquility of the affluent neighborhood, Q knowing Fazio's wife was out of town, chanced blowing his horn. When there was no response from inside the house, he was left befuddled as to why his connect hadn't come to the door. *Why wasn't the laser alarm for the driveway activated?* He wondered. This was unlike Fazio.

Q went to the front door, lifted the weighted brass knocker and clanged it against the metal ball repeatedly. Still receiving no response, he rang the doorbell. It's chimes, too, went unanswered.

Fazio's custom-built Camaro was in the driveway in front of the Ferrari. His wife's black Viper was also in the driveway. Q walked back to the six-car garage, peeped inside and saw that Fazio's Escalade and box Chevy were inside; all of his whips were there. Earlier when they'd talked, Fazio had said he was in for the night. So where was he?

Q decided to check the front door to see if it was locked before he gave up and left. He was worried about his man.

It surprised the fuck out of him when the doorknob turned and the door opened easily when he pushed up against it. Stepping into the baby mansion with caution, Q pulled his Glock from his waist and called out Fazio's name. His eyes darted left to right as he tightened his grip on the burner, and his hand shook. Usher's CD played in the background, like the soundtrack to an urban movie.

Q continued calling out Fazio's name as he walked toward the entertainment room where the sound of the music was coming from. As he entered the room, he saw Fazio butt-ass naked on the rug. In the soft light of the room he spotted an empty Corona bottle on the cocktail table next to a near-empty bottle of tequila and several glasses. He also noticed traces of cocaine residue on the marble cocktail table.

"Yo, Fazio? You all right, big homey?" He could see that Fazio was breathing, so he knew that his man wasn't dead. It was strange; Q had never known his supplier to get pissy drunk and pass out. He couldn't imagine Fazio overdosing on cocaine. Fazio got his buzz on occasionally, but only in moderation. To see him in his present state sapped away a bit of the immense amount of respect Q had for him.

A nigga with Fazio's rep and stature in the game was supposed to be above such self-humiliation. Seeing his man in this condition further eroded Q's faith in idols. Weakness to a drug vice had destroyed Q's only other hero—his pop.

Q lightly slapped Fazio across the face several times, trying to awaken him.

"Yo, big folks, wake up!" he repeated with each slap.

Still Fazio didn't awaken.

Q didn't know what the fuck to do. He wondered if he should call 911. But that would bring the police along with EMS, and he knew there were drugs and illegal guns inside the mansion. *Check the stash spot inside the pantry.* He had watch Fazio retrieve kilos from there on numerous occasions.

He went to the kitchen and stepped inside the sizable pantry, opening the fake wall the way he had peeped Fazio do it.

Behind the fake wall, Q found kilos stacked from the floor up to his head, and he stood at six-two. There were several rows of the neatly stacked bricks. Six industrial-sized detergent boxes were stuffed full of rubber-banded stacks of money. Q breathed a sigh of relief that Fazio hadn't been robbed. He closed the wall and returned to the entertainment room and again tried to awaken Fazio. But again to no avail. It was then that Q realized that he could creep the entire pantry stash and Fazio would never know who had jacked him.

Q hurried back to the pantry, slid open the fake wall and began unstacking a number of kilos from one of the rows. Then he raced from the pantry to the laundry room, at the rear of the mansion, to gather a couple of bed sheets to use as a makeshift knapsack in which he could carry away whatever he stole from his man. His heart was beating faster than the bass line of a Lil' John crunk song.

With bed sheets in his hand, passing by the entertainment room as he was returning to the pantry from the laundry, Q saw that Fazio was still on the floor passed out. Once back inside the pantry, Q quickly loaded a pile of kilos onto the bed sheet he had spread out on the floor. On a second sheet he dumped money stacks from two of the industrial size detergent boxes. He hurriedly tied both loaded sheets into knapsacks, dragged the two bundles outside and hoisted them up into his SUV.

His heart was damn near pushing through his chest as he drove away from the mansion. Q felt he had done what most street niggaz would have; he had taken advantage of an opportunity that presented itself. In order to become a made man, a nigga had to seize every opportunity to come up, and never look back. Those who hesitated rarely got a second opportunity to bubble.

Still, Q felt some reservation over stealing from his man, which is why he hadn't taken all the money and drugs that was

in the pantry. Fazio had always kept it thorough with him, shit that went beyond business.

Q countered his reservations by reminding himself that Fazio had money and drugs to spare. The loss would hurt his man's pride more than it would his pockets. Since the lick was unplanned, Q hadn't thought out his next move. The Explorer was equipped with a hidden compartment that could conceal as many as ten bricks, but there was no way he could hide the two knapsacks inside the compartment. He needed to get off the road before some cop pulled him over on a humbug and lucked into the bust of a lifetime.

Taking I-85 north back into the city, Q decided that it wouldn't be too wise to take the stuff to the condo out in Scotsdale that he shared with his girl Persia. If he came under Fazio's suspicion, the condo would be the first place Fazio would search. Besides, Persia, had been acting kinda shady lately, and he didn't want her all up in his business.

Q contemplated taking the shit over to his side chick Corlette's crib, but quickly thought better of it. Corlette lived in the Thomasville Heights apartments by the federal penitentiary Po-po was real quick to pull a nigga over and search his whip over that way. Then, too, Corlette might bug out if he showed up at her crib with all that money and work. She was a down-ass chick, but like most hood rats, she ran her mouth too damn much. If word got out that Q had stashed that much shit at her crib, half the hood would be scheming to jack Corlette.

Unable to think of a safer place to go, Q got off the expressway and rented a room at one of the motels out by Hartsfield/Maynard Jackson Airport. After getting the room key from the night receptionist, he went back to his whip and drove around to the back of the motel where the requested room was located. The parking lot of the motel was less than half full with cars, and at this late hour all was quiet.

Q climbed into the back of the SUV, untied one of the sheets and counted the kilos. There were 79 of them thangs—whew! He retied the sheet and left the kilos in the vehicle, like a bundle of dirty laundry. The dark limo tint on the Explorer's windows would prevent anyone from being able to see inside. He locked the doors and carried the knapsack of money with him into the room.

Inside the room, when Q began counting the guap, it wasn't all wrapped in thousand dollar stacks like most drug dealers kept their money. So he counted it bill by bill. When he was finished tallying it all up, it came up to a little more than $250,000!

The sun hadn't peeked through the sky, yet, but Q was too amped up to sleep. Being around Fazio, he had seen way more money than 250 stacks, but never was it his. This was a big come-up.

Usually Fazio hit him off with between 5-10 bricks, at 16 Gs apiece, on consignment, and Q would flip those for whatever profit he could. In addition, Fazio would toss him a few stacks off of each deal Q put together.

Q sat on the bed in the motel room trying to figure out a safe place to stash the stolen money and drugs. *Damn! I wish Khalil was here*, he said to himself. At the moment Khalil was in prison, a few months short of finishing up a five-year bid. A prison bid Q would've been serving had his brother not taken the fall for him.

Q knew that if Khalil was home, his big bruh would come up with a plan at the snap of a finger. Khalil was built like that. Khalil wouldn't be overwhelmed by the situation. Then, too, Q figured that his big bruh probably would've handled things

differently from the start. More than likely, Khalil wouldn't have left Fazio breathing. For sho, had it been B-Man, Fazio would be flat-lined.

Now that Q had a minute to ponder what he had done, he understood that there would be hell to pay once Fazio sobered up and discovered the theft. Fazio's wrath would be hotter than an inferno. *I'll just have to play my hand right, so that he won't suspect me.*

Just for a passing moment he considered calling B-Man and letting him know the business. But just as quickly he closed his Nokia and discarded the thought. B-Man was his blood, but the butt-naked truth was that B-Man had a lot of hater shit in him. He was shady like few others, and quiet as it was kept, Q sensed that B-Man was still a little salty at him because Q wouldn't plug him in with his connect. Fuck that, Q said to himself, shit was too serious to chance telling B-Man the business. He laid back on the bed, trying to think of a master plan. It would be best to be at his crib acting as if everything was normal when Fazio discovered that he'd been jacked, and began making his rounds to interrogate those whom he believed could've been involved. Q figured he needed to be at the crib chillin' with Persia.

But first he needed to stash the money and cocaine in a safe place.

CA$H

Chapter Three

Fazio leaned over the gold-plated commode in the futuristic master bath that connected to the mansion's master bedroom suite. For the third time he stuck a finger down his throat, inducing vomit. His stomach contracted violently as a stream of bile spewed from his mouth. The rumbling in his belly continued for a full minute after there was nothing left to throw up.

Finally, his stomach settled. Fazio brushed his pearly whites, washed his face, then examined his reflection in the mirror. It was said by many that Fazio resembled Baby Face, but this morning his usually handsome face was distorted by the fury he was feeling inside.

"Fuck!" Fazio ranted.

Then betraying his usual cool, he smashed a fist into the mirror over the sink. Glass shattered to the floor, and a stream of hot blood poured from his knuckles and cascaded down his bare arm.

"You punk bitches wanna play games with me? I'll kill you nasty hos!"

What the fuck made them think that he was someone to be trifled with? Those bitches had stolen a kilo of powder from him, and his jewelry—played him like a lame. *Okay...okay...y'all wanna test my gangsta? Okay! Laugh now, cry later!*

It was another twenty minutes before Fazio discovered that he was missing much more than the single kilo of cocaine and the jewelry he'd been wearing. His infuriated scream of profanities could be heard a country block away. When he calmed down enough to analyze the robbery, what puzzled Fazio most was: why hadn't those bitches wiped out his entire stash? And how had they found out about the stash spot? Surely they should've realized that the punishment for their treachery wouldn't be lighter simply because they hadn't stolen it all? As far as Fazio was concerned, the strippers' fates were sealed. A torturous death at the hands of his Mexican goons awaited Diamond and Vee Vee.

Fazio wrapped a bandage around his bloody knuckles and tried to calm down. Unbridled fury led to missteps. The game had taught him that through the mistakes of others. Calmer now, he tried to recall who all knew of his hidden stash spot. Who amongst the few also knew Diamond and could've told her where to find his stash? He contemplated. Maldanado was the only one of his crew whom Fazio could answer yes to for both questions. He remembered that in a moment of uncustomary carelessness, he had allowed Q to peep his stash spot. But Q hadn't been rolling with Fazio's team the night Fazio had met Diamond at the Blue Flame. As far as Fazio knew, Q didn't even know the bitch.

Again Fazio's mind settled on Maldanado, his most trusted lieutenant. *It had to be him,* reasoned Fazio. No one else made sense. But Maldanado had never shown the slightest sign of disloyalty. The Mexican knew that any betrayal he committed against Fazio would, in essence, be a betrayal against, Francisco—El Jefe. Francisco would have Maldanado's entire family in Mexico murdered.

Fazio knew that if he could track down Diamond and Vee Vee, he would learn who had helped them betray him. A gun to the head of both strippers would be powerful truth serum.

The now calm kingpin took a cold shower to clear his head and revive his energy. When he was showered and dressed, Fazio checked his cell phone for voice messages and saw that there were several messages from Q. The calls from Q coincided with the hours Fazio knew he was passed out. He remembered that he was supposed to have had someone drop off some kilos to Q yesterday.

Fazio, speed-dialed Q, holding the cell phone with his uninjured hand.

"What it do?" answered Q, recognizing Fazio's personal ringtone.

"What's poppin'?"

"I need you to fuck wit' me," Q replied. "I've been tryna get at you since yesterday. I got my peoples on hold; I told you they wanna get ten of them *raffle tickets.*"

To Fazio's ears Q sounded the same as always, no stress or guilt was apparent in his tone.

"I got a little problem over here so I'll have to get back to you later," Fazio told him.

"Okay, big pimpin'. But I done had these cats on hold for two days already. Plus I need some tickets myself."

"Tell your people you'll hit 'em off tomorrow."

"*Tomorrow?*" Q clarified. "Man, these dudes tryna spend a hundred-fifty *stacks!* They gon' shop somewhere else if I put 'em on hold again." Then he added, "I know that's lunch money to you, but a po' nigga like myself need to get that lil' bit."

"Okay," Fazio acquiesced. "Tell them you'll handle it later this evening. Let me get things in order on my end. I'll call you when I'm ready to see you."

"Sound like a plan," Q said before hanging up.

Fazio hadn't heard anything in Q's voice that made him suspect that he had betrayed his trust. Still he reminded himself that *no one* is above suspicion where there's riches to be gained from betrayal. Those whom you least suspected were usually the most likely culprit.

"How in the fuck did I slip like that?" Fazio admonished himself.

It had cost him considerably, but he swore that the streets would overflow with blood until he had found and executed each and every person involved with the lick. Nothing sent a louder message than bullet-riddled bodies dumped in gutters.

Chapter Four

The house phone rang persistently, as if the caller was intent on busting up their groove. Q stopped in mid-stroke, drawing an instant complaint from Persia, who had draped her legs over his shoulders, her ass in the air. He glanced at the caller ID box and saw that it was B-Man. *That nigga's call can wait,* he said to himself. Then he got back in rhythm with Persia's rotating hips and proceeded to blow her back out.

"Ahhh! Faster, boo! Knock the bottom out, baby!" urged Persia. She was throwing that pussy up at him like she was a certified porn star.

"You love this shit, don'tcha?" Q teased.

Persia had been his girl for two years now, and he still couldn't get enough of her wet-wet. It was like shawdy's sex had him addicted. Outside the bedroom their relationship wasn't all peaches and cream because Persia was on some real materialistic shit. But Q knew how to deal with that side of his girl. He just spoiled her.

At twenty-five years old, Persia was older than Q by four years. She was a caramel brown dime piece with mad booty. What Persia looked like in a thong deserved is own reality show! The first time Q had seen that phat ass in a thong, all he could say was . . . D*ayum!*

Closely resembling a young Jay-Z, but a shade darker, Q wasn't the most handsome of the Jones brothers—that distinction belonged to Khalil—but he wasn't tore up. If a shawdy took points away from him because he didn't look like Usher, she had to give him points for the T.I. in him. Q was a grand hustla.

A few years back, when Q was still a trap star, Persia had been a baller named Travis's girl. Q used to take a glance at Persia riding through Thomasville Heights in the passenger seat of Travis's tricked-out whips, and he swore to himself that one day Persia would be *his* girl. Back then Q knew that his money wasn't grown up enough to try to holla at Persia. It was no secret how she got down for hers. A nigga had to be really gettin' to it to lock her down. But Q could dream.

When Persia's man caught two hot ones in the back of his fitted cap, Q knew it was time to step up his hustle and holla at Persia. The first time he tried to get at her she listened to his mack, but she wouldn't come off with the digits when he asked for her cell phone number. She accepted his, but never called. Then Q plugged into Fazio and began gaining more status in the hood. Fazio started hittin' him off with weight and before long Q's money grew up. His jewels got heavier; he copped a new candy-painted Chrysler 300 sitting on big rims, and with that, his stature in the streets elevated.

Persia noticed that he had stepped up his hustle and before you knew it she was giving him much more than just some holla.

"You wanna shower together?" Persia asked as she headed for the bathroom, ass jiggling and Q's semen running down her luscious thighs.

"Nah, shawdy," Q declined. "If we do that, you gon' try to seduce a playa again."

"You complaining?"

"Never dat."

"Well?" Persia cooed, showing him her tongue ring.

"Damn, shawdy," Q replied with a smirk. "You done already fucked a nigga's back out this morning. Let me get ready and go handle some business."

"I thought you said you had to wait around for Fazio to get back at you?" Persia reminded him.

"He can hit me on my cell. I need to go and try to catch up with this lil' bitch ass nigga who owes me for a half of brick."

"Since you about to get in the streets, I guess I can go to the mall and do some shopping." Persia said.

Q knew what was next, and Persia was sure that he knew. *So, why he gon' make me ask?* She was thinking as Q stood there playing dumb.

"Q, you gon' gimme some money to go shopping wit?"

"What happened to your check?" Persia worked part-time at her uncle's bails bond company across from the Pre-Trial Center downtown.

"That ain't enough to shop with!" Persia complained.

"Well, maybe you need to find a better paying job. Or maybe ya taste is too expensive."

"Or maybe I need to find a better hustlin' nigga!" Persia shot back.

"He ain't gon' fuck you like I do," Q laughed as he stepped into the shower and pulled the shower curtain closed. He wasn't trippin'.

Persia snatched the curtain back, almost ripping it off its track. Her hands were on her hips, neck rolling, the corner of her top lip turned up.

"Nigga, you gon' give me some money or not?"

"Nah, shawdy. My bank is a little funny this week. I'll hook you up next weekend." He pulled the shower curtain closed. Persia damn near ripped that bitch down!

"Oh, muthafucka, you just gon' clown me like dat?"

"Clown you like what?" Q asked, soaping his body, trying to keep his dreadlocks from getting wet.

"Think about it, ol' cheap-ass nigga, when you come home one day and find me and all my shit gone!"

The phone rang just as Persia returned to the bedroom in a huff.

"Hello?"

"What's poppin', lil' mama? Where ya boy at?"

"Hey, B-Man. Q's in the shower," related Persia recognizing Q's brother's deep voice.

"Good, 'cause I like talking to you much more than I like talking to him, anyway."

"I bet you wouldn't tell *him* that." There was a detectable playfulness in her tone.

"Girl, stop," chuckled B-Man. "My brother don't put no fear in nobody. *I'm* that nigga the streets fear. You ain't heard?" he boasted. "Q too scared to lose you to bust his gun and risk catching a bid."

"Well, hold on. Lemme take him the phone so you can tell him that."

"Don't play yaself, lil' mama. Anyway, fuck Q. When you and me gon' hook up? I won't tell if you don't."

"Why niggas always want what they ain't got no business having?" Persia sat down on the edge of the bed, holding the cordless to her ear with a shoulder, as she studied her raspberry-painted toenails and half listened to B-Man spit game.

"On the real, shawdy. When you gon' start taking a nigga seriously? I be shootin' the shit at you, but at the same time, a nigga tryna fuck wit' you for real. If I was your man, I'd keep you icy, take you on vacations to Aruba and shit—"

"Nigga, you can't *spell* Aruba," Persia interrupted him, laughing at his game.

"Real talk, shawdy, Q don't know how to treat a star like you."

"And I suppose you do?"

"Damn right. I'm serious, baby doll—you and me make a winning team. All you gotta do is say the word."

"Say the word about what, dawg?" asked Q. Persia had just handed him the phone.

"Naw...naw," stuttered B-Man, quickly recovering. "I was talking to lil' mama over here," he smoothly lied. Silently he was cussing Persia for that fuck shit she had just pulled. It made him even more determined to get those drawz.

"Yo, bruh, gimme a half hour, then hit me on my cell phone," Q told him. He figured B-Man was calling to ask if he was ready to handle a three brick deal that he had set up.

By the time B-Man hit him on his cell phone, Q had bounced from the crib and was headed to the Bluff to try to run down Lamar, the lil' nigga who owed him twelve stacks for a half of brick Q had fronted to him more than three weeks ago.

"I'ma get back witcha as soon as my people get back wit me," Q was telling B-Man. Q wanted to tell B-Man to quit pressing him; that you only press clothes and hos.

"Damn, shawdy. I done had partna and 'em on hold for three days. What da fuck, Fazio ain't got no work?"

B-Man stood to make $6,500 profit if the deal went through, so it twisted his face for Q to keep setting it off. B-Man felt that lately Q had been handling him fucked up, and was beginning to get the big head.

"Check it, shawdy. Tell them niggaz to shop somewhere else if they can't wait," said Q.

"Whateva, nigga," replied B-Man, salty. Then he hit Q in the ear with a dial tone.

Q had too much other shit on his mind to let B-Man rankle him. He knew that his brother remained salty with him because he hadn't vouched for B-Man's credibility when Fazio was considering fronting B-Man some weight. Even when Fazio said he'd be willing to drop them some weight as a team, Q had declined. He knew his brother well enough not to team up with B-Man. Not only was B-Man lazy when it came to getting his grind on, he was quick to play games with a nigga's work and Fazio would've been just as quick to send some loco Mexicano to wet 'em up. Q hadn't wanted to end up getting murked over a debt B-Man owed. Even when Q fronted his brother some work, B-Man would come short on the debt.

Q cruised through the Bluff hoping to spot Lamar, he was still amped from last night's come up, but was trying to move as normally as possible. He decided that the key to getting away with the theft was for him to keep a normal routine and not start dropping weight around the city.

He had rented a storage unit early that morning after leaving the motel, stashed the money and cocaine there, and went home. He had left the Ford Explorer parked at the crib and was now in his black 2002 Corvette 'vert; top down, T.I.'s "Urban Legend" thumpin' loud; rims spinning when he braked and put the whip in park.

Q was .38 hot over Lamar's sudden disappearing act. Lamar had promised earlier in the week to pay his debt. "I gotcha, pimpin'", but as of yet the lil' scrawny ass nigga hadn't paid Q a dime. *That's why I hate dealing with Corlette's people; there's always some bullshit in the game when I fuck wit' this hoe's grimy ass fam! If Lamar ain't got my bread when I catch up wit' him, I'ma make his ass a mafuckin' statistic!* Q vented as he pulled up to a trap house where Lamar, sometimes pushed work.

The niggaz outside said they hadn't seen Lamar in more than a week. Sensing that they were lying, Q pushed on. He stopped a few blocks away and paid a smoker to go back to the trap house and see if Lamar was inside.

Twenty minutes later the smoker still hadn't returned. Had Q not been so pissed already he would've laughed at himself for having paid a crackhead bitch before she'd completed an errand. Having dealt with crack fiends many times, he knew that the only thing a smoker could be counted on to do was smoke dope and fuck up. Q couldn't believe he had allowed a crackhead bitch to play him. Just when he was about to drive off, the smoker returned to his car. He shook his head at the sight of her size 8 squeezed into a pair of coochie cutter shorts that would've been too small even if she were a size 5. The bitch looked real stank.

"Lamar wasn't in there, baby," the smoker lied, pressing her musty ass titties all up in Q's face as she leaned inside his whip. Lamar had broke her off a nice size piece of crack to go back and tell Q that he wasn't inside. So, the slick bitch got paid from both ends. Q was too heated to peep game. As he pulled off he was fuming. *Lamar's bitch ass gon' make me dead him!*

He had told Lamar before fronting him the eighteen ounces, "Look, shawdy—I really don't fuck wit' you like this. You already owe me from the last time I fucked wit' you."

"Damn, Big Dog," Lamar popped, "I don't owe you but a stack. You wipe ya ass with that." Tryna stroke Q's ego.

"Fuck all dat. I still wants mine," Q had stressed.

"I'ma get you yours, Big Pimp," promised Lamar. "Shid, my nigga, if you hit me off with eighteen of them guys, a nigga will have room to pay *you* and get his swerve on. Last time you fucked with me, you only gave me fo' and a baby. I ain't have room to do my thing."

Lamar had been fast-talking, dick riding—the whole nine, anything to convince Q to front him the work. Q should've known from past experiences that if you allowed a nigga to short you money once, and didn't tap that head, he'd try you up a second time. Corlette, who was Q's little Keyshia Cole-looking shawdy on the side, had warned him not to fuck with her lil' cousin. Lamar was a good hustla, to be only sixteen years old but the boy loved to floss, gamble, and trick off even more than he liked to grind.

By the time Q drove over to Thomasville Heights and pulled up in front of Corlette's apartment his mouth was a tight line. Corlette's fam was testing his get down.

"I warned you not to front Lamar no work," Corlette said sitting on Q's lap on her living room couch.

Q would deny it, but he still faulted her. It seemed that Corlette had been nothing, but bad luck and an additional expense ever since he started hittin' that. What had begun as just a fuck thing had somehow turned into her about to become his baby mama. Last week she had found out that she was eight weeks pregnant. Q was catching hell hiding it from Persia because Corlette was constantly blowing up his phone. Now that she was carrying his seed she was off the meat rack.

Dealing with Corlette was problem enough but, Corlette's begging ass mama was forever hittin' him up for a grip. Shawdy's whole fam was becoming one big ass burden. When Q first started hittin' it, Corlette had served a purpose beyond giving him good pussy. He would stash work at her spot and occasionally have her to drop off a little weight to certain clientele. That was graveyard dead now. Corlette had gotten pulled over in the Kia Sportage that Q had copped for her and

the po-po found four and a half ounces of crack in her possession. Now she was out on bond awaiting trial or an agreeable plea deal after being arrested and charged with drug trafficking. So now she had to play the sideline.

Corlette did bring something else to the table in addition to her being a rider and having the body of a video vixen; she could be trusted to keep the coochie on lock when Q wasn't around. Corlette knew about Q's wifey and played her position behind her. The one thing that Q didn't like about the way she dealt with the situation, though, was that Corlette seemed to always be trying to make sure that he did as much for her as he did for Persia. Trying to take care of Corlette, her thirsty ass mama, *and* keep high maintenance Persia happy was the main reason Q's bank never matched his shine.

While Q was pondering his situation, Corlette was fumbling with the zipper of his Rocawear jeans, nibbling on his neck.

"Chill, shawdy. I'm not in the mood for that shit; it's too mafuckin' hot. Plus, I got a lot on my mind." He removed her hands from his crotch.

"You're not ever in the mood lately! I bet you don't be telling that bitch, Persia, that you're not in the mood."

"Shawdy, miss me with the drama!" Q pushed her off his lap, got up, and zipped his jeans back up. "Tell ya lil' bitch ass cousin he better handle his business before I make him a front-page story," he said walking out of the apartment and slamming the screen door behind him.

Corlette snatched the screen door open and yelled, "Nigga, while you acting like you don't have no time for a bitch, you need to know your dick is not the only one that can slide up in my shit. Trust!"

Walking to his whip Q heard that fly shit Corlette hurled at him, but he wasn't stressing; he knew that Corlette was frontin'. Shawdy had mad love for him and would not violate like that. Besides, he had bigger worries on his mind than worrying about her giving another nigga some pussy.

Q's cell phone rang as he pulled off promising himself that he would hit Corlette up later and make up with her.

"Sup?" he answered the call.

"Khalil is on the line," said Persia dryly.

"What it do, bruh?" asked Q, brightening up. He was always happy to hear from his fam.

"I'm good. What about you?"

"Tryna get at this money out here and keep the haters off me."

"I heard that," replied Khalil. Then a pregnant silence told him that Q didn't really want to chop it up with Persia listening in on their conversation. "You want me to hit you up later?" asked Khalil.

"Yeah, I'll be at the crib in an hour."

"Aight."

"Oh, I'ma shoot you a coupla stacks while I'm out in traffic today," said Q.

"Shawdy, I touch down in sixty-two days and a wake-up, what I need with two stacks up in here? I got plenty commissary already and my account is still on swole with that last grip you sent me. Just put those two stacks up so I'll have 'em on deck when I come home," suggested Khalil.

"Fuck dat, I'ma gone shoot it to you anyway. Don't worry about when you touch down. . . I gotcha."

"Oh, you got it poppin' like that?"

"You better know it," boasted Q.

When Khalil's fifteen minutes were up and the prison phone automatically ended the call, Persia cleared the line then clicked back over to Q.

Bonded by Blood

"I thought your pockets wasn't right? Lying ass nigga! How are you gon' send Khalil two-fuckin-thousand dollars *in muthafuckin' prison* and cry broke when I ask for something?"

"Like I told you before, the bid Khalil is doing was supposed to be *mine*; he took the charge for me. So shut the fuck up," he shot back then hung up on her ass.

An hour later Q pulled up in front of his condo. Fazio and two Mexicans rockin' bald- heads were waiting for him.

CA$H

Chapter Five

Khalil Jones!" Officer Wells called out in the dorm, reading the name of the inmates the letter was addressed to. It was mail call time, the only time of day a brutha on locks looked forward to other than visitation and his release day.

Khalil didn't go down to the big floor area where Officer Wells stood passing out mail; he wanted her to have to deliver his mail to his cell on the second range. From the doorway of his cell he eyed Rayne appreciatively. Her toned down beauty and athletic body couldn't hide behind her quiet demeanor or up under the ill-fitting uniform, and the ever-present windbreaker she wore tied around her waist to cover her shapely ass so as not to entice the inmates. He knew that she was a dime waiting to be shined up by the right man. "Rayne, we're gonna brighten up each other's lives," he whispered under his breath.

Her mother named her "Rayne" because twenty-three years ago, when she was born, it had been pouring down outside. Rayne's mother, at least, had been thoughtful enough to use some creativity with the spelling of her name. Rayne thanked her for that. None of the inmates besides Khalil knew her first name. Khalil knew it because she and him had a little sumpthin' sumpthin' going on.

Autry State Prison, in Pelham, Georgia, where Khalil was serving his bid, employed both male and female correction officers. With there being numerous young female C.O.'s working at the all-male prison, it made it possible for a nigga to still get his dick wet, even though he was locked up. Of course, relationships between inmates and staff were prohibited. It was only natural that more than a few female C.O.'s were attracted to certain inmates. Autry wasn't the type of violent prison often depicted in Hollywood movies. Being that it was prison, violence could occur at any moment, but it was basically a laid back atmosphere.

What made it difficult for an inmate to get at a female C.O., even when she was choosing him, was the many haters and snitches that were always hovering around with camcorder-like eyes and repeat-it-all tongues. They were quick to drop a kite to the administration, on the DL, busting' out the prohibited affair. Then there were the "jackets"; mafuckers who crept around tryna sweat the female C.O.'s, and masturbate when she turned her head. A few freak C.O.'s liked to see the dick.

Finally, there was the male C.O.'s. They were mostly lames acting tough behind a uniform and a badge. These bitch niggaz were forever blocking a playa's come up on a broad.

Most of the women that worked at Autry State Prison were bad body country hos from Pelham and other areas close by. Naïve wowen who were ripe for a slick nigga's game.

Khalil had gotten his fuck on with a counselor named Miss Chambers shortly after being sent to Autry. But she wasn't coming off of no guap, and Khalil wasn't about to keep on dicking the bitch for free. Even though he was locked up, the game didn't stop; it remained *pimp* or *die*.

After Counselor Chambers left to work at another prison Khalil couldn't seem to bag another dime. Anyway, he felt, most of the shawdies in uniform and badge were fat, out of shape, country ass rats who tried to act like they were all that because niggaz stayed drooling over them. Khalil knew that if he was to see those same nothing-ass chicks on the turf, he

wouldn't give those jump offs a second glance. So he didn't drool over 'em now.

Officer Rayne Wells was a bit of a different story, though. Shawdy had a smooth pecan tan complexion and a scrumptious body! She reminded Khalil of that chick, Free, the ex-host of BET's "106 and Park". Unlike many of the female correction officers at Autry, she always came to work in a crisp uniform, her hairstyle tight, nails manicured and polished, and lips glossed. She had a runway model's walk, and the perfume she wore made a nigga long to hold her in his arms.

C.O. Wells wasn't a flirt or a tease, though. Her femininity was all natural. She was good people; who would hold a conversation with an inmate as long as he didn't try to get too personal or come out his mouth to her sideways. If an inmate stepped to her with some dumb shit, or exposed his dick to her, she'd cut him short and would never hold a conversation with him again.

Otherwise, Rayne had some compassion for a brotha's situation; just not to the point that it made her gullible to game. She could feel a nigga but she wasn't trying to hook up with no inmate. Khalil Jones was different story.

Khalil's lame ass celly was out of the cell when Officer Wells brought Khalil his mail.

"What's up, Baby Love?" said Khalil in a whisper as he accepted three letters from her.

"Hi, Khalil." She, too, kept her voice low, mindful of big-earred snitches. When other inmates or officers were around she addressed Khalil as Inmate Jones.

"You plan on sleeping all day?" she asked in her sweet, sing-song voice. She hadn't seen Khalil outside his cell since she came on shift at 2 p.m. Her inexpensive watch now read 4:30.

"I was dreaming about *you*," Khalil said, licking his lips.

"I thought you told me you keep it real? That sounds like a game to me."

"Everything I say sounds like game to you," countered Khalil. "That's because you're *game-scared*, shawdy. But a nigga ain't always blowing smoke up ya ass; sometimes I speak from the heart."

"If you would always speak from the heart I wouldn't have to figure out when you're lying," replied Rayne reproachfully.

"I never lie, Baby Love,—not unless the truth will get me convicted or killed."

"If I had a nickel for every time a man has told a woman that same lie, I'd be rich,"

"You think I'm like them other niggaz?" Khalil feigned a look of hurt, but Rayne wasn't falling for it.

"Are you?" she asked, looking him in the eyes.

Before Khalil could verbalize a response, she pushed on, leaving only the scent of her perfume behind.

Khalil watched Rayne as she walked out of his cell. He really wanted to bag shawdy and move her to ATL once his bid was over. She had a quiet style and beauty about her that made him desire her like he had never desired a chic before.

Khalil had cut into Rayne three months ago. He kept himself well-groomed, with a temp fade, light mustache, and naturally thick eyebrows. A thrice-a-week workout kept his six-one, one-hundred-ninety pound frame in delectable condition. He did all that he could to make the prison uniform and brogans* look like Armani on him—he kept his shit creased up. Even on lock Khalil's swag remained magnetic.

More than a few female C.O.'s whispered, "That's a fine ass nigga" when Khalil passed by them. Which had been exactly what Rayne was thinking the first day Khalil stepped to her.

They didn't talk too often during the three-day cycles that she worked the dorm he was housed in. Instead, they communicated through letters that Khalil sent to the P.O. Box she had gotten specifically for that purpose. Khalil would address his letters to "Free" or "Baby Love", pen names he used for Rayne in order to keep their communication secret. When she wrote him back she would use either pen name as the sender's.

Lying back on his bunk, Khalil saw that one of the three letters was from his brotha Q; one was from "Baby Love", and the third was from Dana, Khalil's ex. He tore up Dana's letter and flushed it down the commode in his cell. Shawdy had gotten saved since Khalil had been away. Now she was trying to turn him into a Christian. Khalil wasn't feeling that; he would put the original Eve on the ho stroll and mack Mary had he lived in biblical times.

"Fuck Dana," Khalil said as he sat back down on his bunk and tore open the letter from Baby Love.

Dear Khalil,

I was just thinking about some of the things you said to me in your last letter. You're making a bunch of promises that you might find hard to keep when you're released in 58 days (Yes, I'm keeping count). Khalil, I have strong feelings for you that I'm not sure I understand myself. Oh, I understand that I'm attracted to you physically, and that your charisma intoxicates me at times. But what I don't understand is why I do feel that I'd be willing to do almost anything for you!

That is what scares me. I don't like feeling that I can be manipulated by anyone. There are too many stories of good-girl-falls-in-love-with-bad boy that have tragic endings. I'm afraid that might become my fate if we hook up once you're released. Yet, I'm willing to take a chance.

I'm not saying I don't trust you. What I don't trust is those streets that are so much a part of you. Will I be able to pull you from those streets and the fast life? Or will you pull me off into that world? The answer is unknown, and that is what frightens me.

As to the question of whether or not I'll move to Atlanta to be with you—well, that depends on a lot of things. I'll tell you this much, though: I don't want to move up there and get caught up in the fast lane. I'm just a simple country girl. Is that what you really want?

Your Baby Love

Khalil returned the perfumed letter back inside its envelope and spent a few minutes replaying Rayne's written words. A noise caused Khalil to suddenly look up. Drayton, his celly, came into the cell clutching his ever-present Bible. Khalil had nothing against religion, but niggaz who used religion as a crutch to help them through their bid irritated the fuck out of him. Drayton was that type of fake Christian.

Khalil didn't even acknowledge his celly's entrance. In fact, he hardly ever chopped it up with the lame. As long as Drayton gave him his space, Khalil didn't trip. Continuing to ignore Drayton, Khalil tore open the letter from Q and began reading it.

Whud up, bruh?

Shawdy, in 2 mo' months you'll be back out here on the streets. I can't wait 'til you touch down, fam. These hos out here are lost; waiting for a mackadocious nigga like you to come lead 'em. For real, pimp, when you touch down we gon' rape the game from all angles. You wit' the hos, B-Man wit' that steel, and me, ya baby bruh, wit' da work.

Bonded by Blood

Check it: ya baby boy done struck PLATINUM! I'm talking mil' ticket, nigga! What you know about dat? I'll give you the 4-1-1 when you get home. Right now keep it on the hush. Don't even mention it to B-Man (you know how that nigga do). I ain't frontin', fam—I'm sittin' on riches!
    N-E-way, enclosed is that bread I told you I'd send. Two stacks, shawdy. Plus, I'ma break bread when you get home. Oh, I can't forget this: When ya release date comes, I'm coming to pick you up stuntin' hard! Bruh, you done a bid for me. So you know it's all love. Real niggaz do real things.
    One love,
    Q
    Real niggaz do real things.

Khalil felt that shit. The two-thousand dollars he had just received, in money orders, from Q wasn't the half of it, though. Q had sent him money every single month he'd been down. He'd also sent CD's, pics, and had visited at least once a month. Being on lock, seeing how most niggas' family and friends abandoned them, made Khalil appreciate the love Q showed that much more.

He couldn't say the same for B-Man; it was like B-Man was always on some other shit. Still Khalil loved both his brothers just the same. Ever since Black Girl had passed away, it was the three of them against the world. Being the oldest, Khalil had felt it was on him to look out for his younger brothers. The only time they saw Rapheal was in the streets, where he'd be doing the crackhead shuffle, going out bad.

Before long, all three of the Jones boys were hustlin' to take care of themselves. They all had sold weed or crack for a minute, but like Black Girl prophesized, Q was the best dopeboy of the three. B-Man was jackin' niggaz, while Khalil was chili pimpin', too green to know how to really mack the young chics he caught.

In Thomasville Heights, where they maintained the apartment they had been living before Black Girl's death, the brothers earned a reputation for being each other's keeper. They shared whatever monies earned from their respective hustles. When a nigga violated one of them, he caught beef from all three.

Khalil was a real pretty nigga, but he was still nice with his hands. B-Man was the real threat, he was quick to bust his gun and he lived for the drama. Q was more about his paper, but his weakness was exactly as Black Girl had warned it would be.

Q was fuckin' with a little redbone named Chelsy. They were both just a few months shy of sixteen years old, but Chelsy was sixteen going on thirty. She had been fuckin' since her hair had begun growing on her pussy. By the time she turned fourteen she been passed around like a peace pipe.

When Q got with her, Chelsy hadn't too long stopped kickin' it with DeShawn, a twenty-year old corner hustla who had a twin brother named DeWayne. DeShawn was a real jealous nigga who had kept hot ass Chelsy sporting black eyes and busted lips when they were together. With Q, Chelsy didn't have to duck any punches. Q had witnessed Rapheal put his foot in Black Girl's ass way too many times to follow in his pop's footsteps. Not only was Q gentle with Chelsy, he blessed her with whatever his bank could afford at that time. At sixteen he wasn't getting' to the money as strong as "Twin" had been, but he stayed on his grind.

Chelsy had him open like a book. Hood niggaz tried to tell him that the she was nothing to hold hands with, but her wet-wet was too good for Q to listen to them. He would have to learn the hard way.

Chelsy had been creepin' with DeShawn for months before Q busted them out. Then, even after he had caught shawdy creepin', Q took her back. He forgave Chelsy, but beefed with DeShawn. Khalil told him that was some real sucka shit.

"Shawdy, I done watched my bitch, Dana, fuck another nigga. As long as the ho gets paid it's all good."

But Q wasn't built like that.

B-Man, who was always game for some brolic shit, said, "Whateva you wanna do, shawdy, I'ma ride. Fuck Twin, I ain't never liked them niggas no way!"

A week later B-Man and Q were cruising the hood in Khalil's Yukon when they saw the twins parked outside their grandmother's apartment.

"You wanna dump on them hoes, shawdy?" asked B-Man, reaching for the strap on his waist.

Q wasn't strapped, and really he didn't wanna take it that far. But he didn't want his brother to think he was soft.

B-Man was driving and Q was riding shotgun. B-Man passed the iron to Q then rolled up on the twins drive-by style. Without considering that Khalil's Yukon was known by everyone in the hood, Q opened up on the twins, spraying their car with automatic nine millimeter gunfire before B-Man mashed the gas pedal and sped off.

Witnesses identified the Yukon and both B-Man and Q. The brothers were arrested and charged with attempted murder, aggravated assault and a couple lesser-included offenses.

Keeping it gutter, the twins refused to press charges or cooperate with prosecutors who wanted to slam B-Man's and Q's backs out. Still the state wouldn't drop the charges. The assistant D.A. wanted to send Q to prison with football numbers because Q had numerous arrests for drugs. B-Man had only one prior arrest, so he was good.

Once it became apparent that the D.A. wasn't going to be satisfied unless somebody caught a bid for the shooting. Khalil stepped up to the plate and claimed he had done the shooting that night, and that Q had been nowhere around.

In the end, Khalil pled guilty to felony assault and received a straight five-year sentence. B-Man was given five years probation. The assistant D.A. knew that Khalil was taking the fall for his younger brother; all the witnesses the A.D.A. had interviewed pertaining to the case had identified Q as the shooter. But Khalil's guilty plea cleared up another case on the A.D.A.'s docket and added another conviction to his case record. That was all that mattered to the cracker.

Khalil stepped out of his cell and leaned on the guard rail. He caught Rayne's attention, but knew she would not come back up to his cell. Too many nosey niggaz were beamed in on her. "*Damn, Baby Love is finer than a mafucka,*" Khalil said to himself. He was always astonished by the feelings for Rayne that were building inside of him. Rayne had him seriously considering squaring up and making her wifey.

Chapter Six

Nearly two months passed by without Fazio having any success tracking down Diamond or Vee Vee. Nor, had he been able to detect any major upgrade in the lifestyles of Maldanado, Q, or anyone else in his clique; nothing that revealed complicity in the robbery.

Yet, Fazio knew that only someone close to him would've been able to tell the strippers about the false wall and what was behind it. He knew for sure that Maldanado and Q were aware of the stash spot, but he wasn't sure that they were definitely the only two outside of himself, who knew of it. He realized it had been uncharacteristically foolish of him to allow *anyone* to peep his stash spot.

He had already had the little Mexican who'd built the hidden wall disposed of, erasing one possible betrayer. He decided that he was going to be just as merciless on whoever in his clique turned out to be the strippers' accomplice in the robbery. Fazio believed that you had to punish a disloyal comrade twice as viciously as you would an enemy. That was the surest way to discourage others in his clique from such betrayal. Instilling fear assured loyalty within one's troops more solidly than kindness did.

Fazio figured it was just a matter of time before he caught up with Diamond and Vee Vee. The jewelry they'd stolen from him was custom designed and easily recognizable. Fazio had people all over the city keeping an eye out for those pieces.

Plus the stolen kilos had been stamped with a small replica of the Virgin Mary. The information about all of Fazio's products bearing a special stamp on the inside of the wrapper had been kept from those on his team precisely for reasons such as theft. The word had been discreetly passed on to certain drug dealers around the "A" to be on the lookout for kilos wrapped in red plastic, which bore the small Virgin Mary stamp inside. Since the theft two months ago, Fazio had not distributed any kilos in Atlanta bearing the special stamp. If some should turn up now, they'd have to be the stolen ones.

Fazio continued pushing work as usual. He hadn't let on to anyone in his clique that the robbery had occurred. Maldanado was still entrenched as his top lieutenant, and Q was still being given between five and ten bricks on consignment. All the others associated with the kingpin's legal drug enterprise were also being dealt with just as he'd always dealt with them. But all of them, especially Maldanado and Q, were under Fazio's suspicion.

Fazio was again weighing what he knew about each person in his clique when the call he'd been waiting two months to receive finally came in.

From a distance niggas might've thought she was Remy Ma, the female rapper who rolled with The Terror Squad. Whenever someone tossed that compliment her way, Vee Vee would respond, "I don't look like that bitch. She looks like me!"

The customized tag "1 of a kind" on her new 740 Beemer announced to the whole world how Vee Vee felt about herself. She believed she was the shit. She had niggas and hos all on her thong.

"My schedule stays full," she would boast to the haters. "Y'all better ask somebody!"

To the jealous bitches who tried to clown her for being AC/DC, Vee Vee simply told them, "Give your man my number,

I bet he'll like how I get down." To niggaz who hated on her, she told them to have their bitches come holla at her.

Vee Vee didn't try to deny that she bumped coochies with a chic once in a while. The way pussy made most niggas act, she *had* to find out for herself what it hit like. Wasn't no shame in her game.

"Let me call you back after I leave the salon?" she said to Moesha, a little cutie she'd met a few weeks ago.

"You better call me back or I'ma blow up your cell phone," Moesha threatened. Vee Vee had her sprung on the tongue.

"You do that anyway," she reminded Moesha. "But for real, I'll call you back when I'm done. I'm just pulling up at the salon now."

"Okay. Make sure you call me."

"I will," Vee Vee promised.

Vee Vee parked outside Bangin' Headz hair salon in the plaza on Wesley Chapel Road. She made sure that she parked where the BMW could be seen by everyone inside. *Let those bitches see how I'm livin'!*

Vee Vee was a half hour late for her appointment, but Fila, her hair stylist didn't complain—Vee Vee tipped well.

"Bitch, whose whip is that?" Fila's nosy ass asked as soon as Vee Vee was in her chair.

"Oh, that's my birthday present to myself," Vee Vee answered nonchalantly.

When Fila commenced to peppering her with a barrage of prying questions, Vee Vee deflected most of them and lied in regard to the others. Discussing shit with Fila or any of the stylists at Bangin' Headz was like broadcasting your business on local radio. Fila and the crew at Bangin' Headz gossiped so much, it was a wonder nobody had ran up in the salon and *banged* their goddamn heads.

When Fila was half finished restyling Vee Vee's hair, Vee Vee's cell phone rang. The caller ID told her that Raveion was tryna reach her. She excused herself from Fila's station and walked to the back of the shop to answer her call in private. She wasn't about to allow nosy ass Fila to overhear her business.

"What's up, baby boy?" Vee Vee said into her cell phone as soon as she had some privacy.

"I'm just letting you know I got that for you," said Raveion. "Okay. I'm at the hair salon on Wesley Chapel right now; give me about an hour and I'll swing through."

For two weeks after she and Diamond had robbed Fazio, Vee Vee had kept a low profile. Even though the night of the robbery had been her first time meeting Fazio, and he didn't know shit about her, Vee Vee hadn't returned to her job at Club Nikki's. It was better safe than sorry, she told herself. Club Nikki's was one of the hot spots for hustlers of all kind, Fazio might just happen to fall through.

Vee Vee had affected a new look, trading in the long blond-streaked tresses she'd worn that night of the robbery for a curly, black bob. Green contacts and a brand new nose piercing further changed her appearance. Despite the affected change in her appearance, she still had no intentions of going back to work at the strip club.

Vee Vee and Diamond had split almost $80,000. Diamond had held onto the jewelry and just recently began trying to sell it. *That bitch better keep it real or else!* Vee Vee was thinking every day while she waited for Diamond to sell the jewels and bring her half of the money. Vee Vee's job was to get rid of the kilo of coke.

Vee Vee wasn't stupid; she had known that she couldn't give the brick to just any nigga and expect to be paid for it.

Which is why she had sat on it until two days ago. Then Raveion had come by her crib.

Raveion was good people, not the type of nigga who's full of game. He was a grand hustla but not a street pharmacologist. Raveion hustled bootleg CDs, DVDs, "burnout cell phones", and knock off designer purses and bags. The boy got paid like he was slangin' crack. Vee Vee occasionally bought a bootleg DVD from Raveion, never any of the knock off designer shit. She wouldn't be caught dead carrying nothing but the authentic.

Raveion was her *Mr. Lover Man.* He was the only nigga she fucked strictly for pleasure. She knew that she could trust Raveion not to shit on her; he'd bring her back the fifteen stacks she told him she'd accept for the brick and he could keep the rest if he sold it for more.

An hour later Vee Vee pulled into Raveion's driveway, she was thinking she would spend the night with her Mr. Lover Man, perhaps call up Moesha and treat Raveion to double the usual fun.

CA$H

Chapter Seven

F azio's adrenaline rushed through his body like an electrical current.

Tyson, a drug dealer from the Oakland City area who usually bought weight from one of the amigos down with Fazio, had bought a single brick from a dude he met through an associate. Tyson had examined the inside of the wrapper when he was breaking the brick down to cook into crack because the amigo had told him almost two months ago to be on the lookout for kilos wrapped in red tape, and had described to him the Virgin Mary stamps inside.

The fuck if Tyson didn't get lucky. "A nigga just struck gold!" he exclaimed when he spotted the Virgin Mary emblem stamped on the inside of the wrapping. Word on the street was that Fazio must've gotten jacked for some kilos and was trying to hunt them down. Rumor had it that he was offering a big reward.

Tyson was hoping that along with the reward, maybe Fazio would let him get down with the clique. Then he could get to the money for real. Fazio and his peeps were raping the game. Tyson wanted to roll wit' them niggaz. Fuck the dude who sold him the bricks, *I don't owe that nigga no loyalty,* thought Tyson before dropping dime on the dude.

Fazio and three *eses* held Raveion at gunpoint in his own crib. The three Mexican goons with Fazio smiled menacingly at the frightened bootleg hustla.

Raveion kept trying to explain to Fazio, the three *eses*, Tyson, and even to God, that he wasn't a drug dealer, and that he had no idea where his girlfriend had gotten that kilo from.

"I was just selling it for her, tryna help the girl out," he explained.

He looked from face to face, finding no believers. When he looked to Tyson he did so pleadingly. Tyson looked away, refusing to meet Raveion's gaze.

Raveion's eyes began to water as he sensed how things would end if he couldn't convince them that he was just an innocent party. He didn't even know what the fuck Vee Vee had done. Whatever it was, he was thinking: *Why the fuck that bitch involve me in this fuck shit!*

A while later they heard a car pull into the yard. Fazio watched from behind a slight part in the vertical blinds. Vee Vee got out of the new BMW and walked up to the front door.

"Answer the door," Fazio whispered to Tyson when they heard her knock.

"Hi. Is Raveion around?" Vee Vee asked the unfamiliar face that opened the door.

"Yeah, he's upstairs. Come on in, I'll let him know you're here," said Tyson. He let Vee Vee inside, closing the door behind her.

Like a phantom, Fazio appeared. Vee Vee looked so much different than he recalled. Fazio studied her every feature for recognition. Vee Vee's recognition of him was instantaneous. Her face went ashen and her mouth opened to let out a scream. Fazio reached out with a powerful hand, choking her to silence.

"Yeah, bitch, it's me!" he gritted.

At gunpoint he led her to the back room where the three Mexican thugs had Raveion subdued amongst a clutter of the recording machines he used to produce his bootleg CDs. When they brought Vee Vee into the room, Raveion could not restrain his anger.

"Bitch, what the fuck you done got me caught up in?" he cried. Before Vee Vee could respond Raveion broke free from his abductors, ran over to her, and punched her dead in the face. Vee Vee staggered back and fell on the seat of her Frankie B jeans.

"Bitch, you better tell these niggaz I didn't have anything to do with whatever the fuck you done to 'em!" barked Raveion.

Vee Vee could taste the blood from her busted lip. *Nigga punched me like I'm a goddamn man! And you think I'm gonna spare your ass? Nah, nigga!*

She said to Fazio, "He helped me and Diamond set up the whole thing."

"You lying ass ho!" screamed Raveion.

One of the eses slapped him across the forehead with a chrome .44 magnum, knocking the bootleg hustla on the seat of his faux Sean John jeans.

"I want all of my shit back!" barked Fazio.

Diamond already had her bags packed. She was planning to hit the highway as soon as next week. The only reason she hadn't already bounced is because she was waiting around to collect her half of the money Vee Vee owed her from the brick. *If it's not sold by next week, I'm out,* she promised herself. Only greed had kept her around this long.

Diamond had decided to do Vee Vee real dirty as far as the jewels were concerned. She was jetting with all of it—fuck Vee Vee. She would sell the pieces once she reached New York, where she planned to relocate. For now, she was laying low with an old sugar daddy out in Marrietta.

Diamond's Blackberry rang.

"Hey, girl," she answered recognizing Vee Vee's ringtone.

"Hey. What are you doing?"

"Just lying around the house. Monroe's old ass is gone to play golf with his buddies. Thank God! I swear if I have to stay here and let his ancient ass lick my pussy one more day I'ma be mental."

"I got the money for that kilo," said Vee Vee without responding to Diamond's clowning, which was unlike her. They always shared a few laughs before chopping it up.

"You okay?" Diamond asked.

"Yeah, I'm good."

"You sure? You don't sound like yourself."

"I'm tired, that's all."

"Well, get some rest. I'll come by and pick that up tomorrow. And why did you just put me on speaker?"

"Uh . . . 'cause I was doing something."

The gun pressed against Vee Vee's head encouraged her to lie.

"Tell her to come through now!" Fazio whispered tersely.

"You can come through now and pick that up, "Vee Vee followed his demand. "I'm over to Raveion's."

"Okay, I'll be there in about forty-five," said Diamond.

"Sounds good," replied Vee Vee in a strained voice.

As soon as Diamond hung up she began hurriedly loading her suitcase into her whip. Something in Vee Vee's tone made her wary of going to collect the money from her. The stress in Vee Vee's voice reminded Diamond of the way her friend Simone had sounded the night she was killed by her man two years ago. Diamond was confused because Vee Vee and Raveion's relationship wasn't all that serious.

Fazio and his goons waited for hours, but Diamond never showed up at Raveion's house. Finally, tired of waiting, Fazio began torturing Vee Vee and Raveion, trying to get them to tell

him who had told them about the fake wall in his pantry, and where the rest of his drugs and money were.

"I swear…we only…took…that one kilo!" Vee Vee cried as one of the goons slashed open her right breast with a sharp pocket knife.

"Kill that bitch!" ordered Fazio.

The goon slashed her throat.

Raveion saw what they'd done to Vee Vee and guessed correctly that he was next. Had he not been duct taped to a chair, he would've tried to break free and run, even though he hadn't done a thing.

"Man, I ain't never took nothin' from no one," he pleaded for his life. "All I do is—"

Boc! Boc! Boc! His pleas got silenced by three slugs to the head from Fazio's Glock.

"Now I gotta find that other bitch," Fazio said to himself.

The bitch that he was referring to was already on the highway putting distance between them.

CA$H

Chapter Eight

Quantavious was getting tired of Persia nagging him to buy her a new whip. He didn't see anything wrong with the Toyota Cressida he had purchased for her last year. Other than it needing a tune-up, maybe. More importantly, he didn't think he should make any large purchases just yet. A brand new whip for Persia might end her nagging, but it also might end Q's life.

He hadn't spent any of the money or sold any of the cocaine he'd stolen from Fazio two months ago. Q was determined not to do anything to raise Fazio's suspicions. It unnerved him a bit that his connect had not mentioned the robbery. He'd heard a whisper or two in the streets right after he'd pulled the stunt, but nothing since, and that made him paranoid. Several times when Q was with Fazio, he half expected a bullet to the head. Fuck that, if it was going down, he wouldn't just fold up like a coward. Q didn't try to fool himself that he was a stone-cold killa, but neither did he consider himself soft.

"Q, what you gon' do? My car cut off on me three damn times on my way home from the mall!" Persia complained as she came into the condo loaded down with shopping bags full of clothes and a half dozen pair of new shoes she had just bought at Lenox Square.

Dropping the keys to the Cressida on the coffee table, she added with finality, "I'm not driving that piece of junk no more. I'll ride around on a *skateboard* before I drive that shit again!"

"Dat guy don't need nothing but a tune-up," Q distractedly replied without even looking up at Persia and continued playing Grand Theft Auto.

"Hmmmpf!" remarked Persia. Then she stormed to the TV and turned off the video game.

"Look, Persia," Q sighed. "Why you pressin' me to buy you a new car?"

"Why you being so damn cheap all of a sudden?" Persia countered with much attitude. "You used to buy me any and everything I asked for. What happened? You spending all your money on that lil' trick bitch in Thomasville Heights that I heard you be creepin' with?"

"I wouldn't fuck none of them skanks in Thomasville if my life depended on it. Gimme *some* credit, shawdy," Q lied. "And I'ma cop you a new whip if you'll just chill for a minute."

"I can't believe you're acting like a crab. Yo' ass didn't hesitate to send Khalil *two-fuckin-thousand-muthafuckin' dollars!* But when I—"

"Damn, Persia. You still stressin' over dat? That was two months ago, shawdy. Khalil about to come home now," he said.

"I know!" her voice was laced with sarcasm. "And you spending a lot of money on his welcome home party. I don't see how you can throw money away on a fuckin' party, yet, can't buy me a new car!"

"Don't even go there," warned Q.

"Why not?" Now she was all up in his grill, mushing him in the face. "You treat a nigga better than you treat your woman? What kind of sideways shit is that? You think I'm some bird-ass bitch you ain't gotta do shit for? Nigga, you better go back and check my file. I'm platinum with a capital P!"

"Girl, you betta back the fuck up before I slap ya eyebrows to the back of ya head!"

"Nigga, *please!* You put your hands on me, you better not ever go to sleep."

"Yeah, yeah—I'm scared," laughed Q. "Now you a black widow, huh?"

"Try me, nigga!"

Q didn't bite the bait. He wasn't the type to hit women. When Persia realized he wasn't going to hit her, she switched tactics.

"For real, Q, you need to get back on your J-O-B. If you can't afford a *platinum* bitch, just say so and I'll pack my shit and leave."

"So what you saying? A nigga gotta cake you off or you gon' get ghost on me?"

"What I'm *saying* is," Persia mocked, "I ain't no Reebok bitch. Don't turn into a crab or I'ma feel like you don't deserve me."

"Whateva, shawdy."

"Whose pussy is this?" he asked arrogantly as he slammed nine inches of thick, hard dick in and out of Persia's wet walls, tapping that ass doggy-style.

"Ahhh...ooohhh...shit! Beat this pussy up, nigga. You got it talking to you," Persia said.

She was throwin' that ass back at the dick, while at the same time working her vaginal muscles like a blood pressure sleeve.

Persia wanted to make sure he never got confused about where he got that good-good from. That way, he would never hesitate to come off that stack when she held her hand out.

He kept talking about how he would eventually become *that nigga* in the game, and if she would just believe in him shit would be lovely for both of them in the end. Maybe, maybe not.

Either way, it mattered none to Persia. Fuck tomorrow. She was making that pussy pop for the benefit of today.

"Tell me this is *my* pussy!" demanded B-Man.

Persia's antics were making him feel like a true stud.

"Ahhh . . . shit!" she moaned. "It's . . . your . . . pussy!"

B-Man kept right on beating up the pussy as if his intent was to give it a black eye. Persia had climaxed and was now too drained to continue throwing the ass back at him. Plus, B-Man's big-ass dick began to hurt like a muthafucka. Persia wasn't into pain.

B-Man was like a black Energizer Bunny, he kept going and going and going. *Fuck that! This horse dick nigga ain't finna rip my shit the fuck up!* She wondered why ugly niggas seemed to always have good dick. B-Man wasn't damn ugly, but he wasn't too far from it. To prevent herself from being literally fucked to death, Persia looked over her shoulder and cooed, "Take it out and let me suck it."

"Hell the fuck yeah," B-Man hurriedly complied, already picturing her pretty lips wrapped around his dick.

After B-Man withdrew from inside her, Persia removed the condom and replaced it with a fresh one. Then she stepped to her business. B-Man might've had a punishing dick game, but Persia had confidence that her head game could break his ass down. A platinum bitch couldn't rely solely on her looks and style, she had to be able to break a nigga off with that fi' head and whatever else in the bedroom. In ten minutes Persia's hot head game had B-Man seeing little green men and quoting scriptures.

After his nuts were empty and the condom was full, B-Man exclaimed, "Damn, baby girl! I wish there was some way I could sack up dat fi' head you got and sell it like weight. That shit would have the game on lock."

Persia smiled. "Did it feel good?"

"Fo' sho," he replied. "Q wasn't lying when he said you're like that chick Super Head."

"Oh, Q be putting me out there like that?" she asked.

B-Man nodded his head and smiled.

Persia hit him up for a stack and a half before they dressed and left the motel in their separate cars. Persia's Cressida took her home just fine.

A while later, Persia relaxed in a hot tub of water and scented body oil. She felt no guilt over letting her man's brother tap dat. She had initiated the tryst yesterday, calling B-Man after she'd argued with Q and he had left and stayed gone all night. If the nigga wanted to act like a crab, plus creep around on her, she wasn't about to sit around boo-hooing. Two could play games.

Persia had douched with a vinegar and water product to clean and retighten her wet walls so that if Q came home tonight with a better attitude and she decided to break him off some wet-wet, her walls would grip like always.

CA$H

1621

Chapter Nine

Q felt bad about the argument with Persia a couple days ago. Moreso, he regretted staying out all night after they'd argued. Some hater had already told her he was creepin' on her; now, he figured his staying out all night probably made his girl believe that shit.

Though he was unfaithful, Q loved Persia. She was materialistic, but he'd known that from the jump. He felt it was his job to give her everything her heart desired. Q hustled to be able to afford all the things he wanted. Well, Persia was his main "thing". He had to be able to afford her, too. He just hadn't liked hearing her spit it in the raw like that.

Q was planning a surprise for his boo boo, something that would make up for the argument. This morning he had gone to pick up the new whip he had secretly ordered for her last month. He had bought Persia a 2004 Ford Escape SUV, had it tricked out with twenty-six inch rims, sound system, TVs and DVD. He knew that what Persia really wanted was the 2004 Porsche Cayenne SUV, which cost $40,000 butt-naked. Q hadn't wanted to kick out that much then have to spend another 15-20 stacks tricking it out. At first he had thought about buying Persia the new Kia Sportage but realized Persia wouldn't have been pleased with that. A Kia was cool for Corlette, but Persia had expensive taste. The Ford Escape would be a compromise. Q hoped that his shawdy would be pleased with it.

He also hoped the new SUV wouldn't rile Fazio's suspicion. It wasn't like he had gone out and copped a Rolls Royce Cornische for his girl. He was gettin' enough dough to be able to justify the Ford Escape. Fazio was still hitting him off with work, plus he'd earned extra stacks from deals he'd put together for Maldanado.

Q figured he was good; Fazio shouldn't look at him crossways. Still, he was stressed out trying to keep Persia icy and content, keep Fazio from suspecting his betrayal, put together a welcome home party for Khalil, and find that lil' nigga, Lamar. Not to mention having to take care of Corlette and her mama. All things combined had Q smoking Newport's back to back.

It was like he wasn't sitting on 79 bricks and a quarter mil. He couldn't put the bricks out on the streets, yet, and he couldn't stunt too hard with the money. Q still hadn't told B-Man the business, because he feared B-Man might cross him.

A second voice in his head told him: *Naw, B-Man won't do no trife shit like that. Hasn't he always come ready to bust his gun whenever you needed him?* Q had to admit that it was true, B-Man always strapped up when it was time to go see a nigga. Q called B-Man's cell phone.

"What up, shawdy? What's poppin' fo' today?"

B-Man was just rolling out of bed.

"Fuck, shawdy, I'm just waking up. What da business is?"

"I just went and picked up this SUV I copped for Persia," Q related. "I had Corlette with me, to drive my car. So you know lil' mama talking a lot of shit about me buying Persia a new whip and she still pushin' the Kia."

B-Man laughed. "Mo' bitches, mo' problems."

"You got that right, bruh. Anyway, you know it's on tomorrow—Khalil comes home."

"Damn, I had forgot. You got everything hooked up?"

Q assured him that everything would be on point. He again mentioned the SUV he had just copped for Persia. B-Man laughed to himself, knowing he had just *cut* the bitch yesterday, and today Q was surprising her with a new whip.

Switching subjects Q said, "I gotta make a mover later on. These niggas over by Greenbriar wanna cop two of dem guys. I'ma need you to ride shotgun 'cause this my first time fuckin' wit' em."

"It's all good. Just hit me back when you're ready to do dat."

"Fo sho, and you know I'ma break bread."

"You betta, nigga."

"Oh," Q remembered. "Once Khalil comes home, and we get his party and shit out the way, me and you gotta find Corlette's cousin—for real, bruh."

"Damn, shawdy. You ain't done went to see about that nigga, yet?"

"I can't find that nigga."

"Shawdy, you fuckin' his cousin. Body dat bitch then catch Lamar at the funeral."

"I can't do no shit like that. Man, lil' mama spose to be carrying my seed."

"Whateva, nigga-No mercy!" replied B-Man.

B-Man was done with it. He was tired of having to help Q collect money and straighten beefs. *Khalil will be home tomorrow. He can step in and bust his gun for Q. Q is funny-style anyway! Always acting like he gotta eat better than me! If Khalil come home acting anything like Q, I'm a build my weight up and stop fuckin' wit' both of 'em.*

"Just hit me up when you ready to fuck wit' them niggas over Greenbriar way," said B-Man.

"That's what's up. Let me go surprise wifey with this new whip," Q replied.

B-Man shook his head, and laughed out loud. *A new whip? I just gutted your bitch.*

"What's so funny?" asked Gwen.

Gwen was a thirty-five year old, half-decent looking chick who had a drug habit that she couldn't admit having. B-Man fucked with Gwen because her apartment was a place to lay his head, and she knew how to treat a man when she wasn't snorting cocaine or smoking woo woos—crack-laced joints.

"What's so funny?" she asked again, wiping at her runny nose.

B-Man again ignored the question. He went into the bathroom to take a shower.

"What time will you be home?" Gwen asked when he was dressed and leaving out.

"Bout nine or ten o'clock. Why?"

"I need some money to buy groceries."

He peeled out a hundred and fifty dollars off his trap and gave it to Gwen. Then he handed her about a gram of cocaine and a quarter ounce of dro.

"Here. That's so you don't spend the grocery money on no drugs."

"Man, I ain't gon' do no shit like that," she said, making a face at him: *Don't even play me like I'm a junkie.*

"You startin' to get high every day. You gon' fuck around and become a *smoker*, "he warned.

"No, I'm not, baby. I can put this shit down anytime I want to." Clutching the gram of cocaine and the dro like she was afraid B-Man was going to call her bluff.

B-Man left the Brandywine Apartments, where he lived with Gwen, and whipped over to his partna Bed-Stuy's crib on Jonesboro Road. Bed-Stuy's real name was Marlon, but he was known in the "A" as "Bed-Stuy" because he was from the Bedford-Stuyvesant area in Brooklyn, New York.

"What's up, son?" Bed-Stuy greeted B-Man letting him into the one-bedroom apartment.

"Ain't nothing. What it do wit' you?" B-Man dapped hands with his jack partna. "What's the business on dat lick you been tryna set up?"

"Which one? You know me, B—I keep a coupla things on deck." He passed B-Man the blunt he was smoking and they sat down in two folding chairs that were in front of the flat screen television and began playing NBA Live. B-Man hit the blunt and passed it back.

"Shawdy, I got dat dro. Twist up one of these." He pulled a half ounce of dro out of his pocket and tossed it in Bed-Stuy's lap. An eightball of powder fell out of his pocket onto the floor.

"Fuck, son—you tryna hide the dust?" asked Bed-Stuy, pointing to the small package "Gimme that shit, B. I'ma roll a blunt of this dro and lace that guy," he said, incorporating Dirty South slang into his up-north lingo.

B-Man reached down, retrieved the eightball off the floor, and handed it to Bed-Stuy. They both snorted a small bit before Bed-Stuy sprinkled some on the dro he was gonna roll up in a blunt. This wasn't the first time B-Man fucked with cocaine, he'd been smoking laced joints for a minute now. Snorting cocaine, however, was a recent indulgence.

While the two partnaz got high, Bed-Stuy filled B-Man in on the two licks he was trying to set up. One was on hold because the girl whose baby daddy they were gonna rob kept wavering on setting him up.

"Ma keep changing her mind," said Bed-Stuy. "If she don't shake nothin' soon, I'm like Fuck Ma! On this other joint where we gon' flex these kids, I'm still working on that. Kid a real scary ass nigga; I gotta gain his trust."

They chilled at Bed-Stuy's for a couple of hours getting blazed, playing NBA Live, and choppin' it up. Ayesha and Jazelle, two powder monsters Bed-Stuy knew, came through and helped him and B-Man snort up all the coke and burn the dro.

Ayesha was Bed-Stuy's cut buddy, while Jazelle was free unclaimed pussy. Jazelle's coke habit hadn't had her in a chokehold long, so she was still worth running up in. B-Man took her in the bathroom and did just that. A half hour later, B-Man was on Moreland Avenue, headed to the apartments where the dro trap was located. Fifty Cent was thumpin' out of the sound system in B-Man's candy-painted bubble Chevy as he parked a few doors down from the dro trap.

As he walked down to the apartment, a few corner niggas was outside grinding. B-Man went up to one whom he usually copped from and bought a half ounce of dro and a hundred-dollar sack of dust. On the way back to his whip, B-Man's face balled up when he caught sight of Rapheal approaching him. *Fuck this junkie ass nigga. I ain't gon' even speak to his ass.*

He had seen Rapheal over this way before, but had pushed on, not even acknowledging him. B-Man's dislike of Rapheal went way back to when at age ten, B-Man tried to intervene when Rapheal was putting his foot up Black Girl's ass for coming home with short trap.

"*Don't hit my Mama no more!*" cried B-Man, wielding an aluminum baseball bat.

"*Boy, take yo' lil' ugly ass to your room and stay out of a man's business before I get mad,*" threatened Rapheal. *Khalil was off somewhere and Q was sitting in the corner of the living room acting punked.*

"*Pop, if you beat my mama, you gon' have to beat me too.*"

Rapheal laughed hard. "*She might be yo mama, but she's my ho. When she steps out of line I'ma kick her funky ass. Now stay the fuck out of it.*"

"*Basil and Quantavious go to your rooms!*" cried Black Girl.

"*No, Mama. I ain't scared of that nigga,*" said B-Man. *But Q obeyed.*

"*Basil, please?*" she pleaded, but B-Man refused to leave her alone to take another one of Rapheal's ass kickings.

When Rapheal began bouncing Black Girl off of the walls, B-Man hit him across the back with the aluminum baseball bat.

"*Leave her the fuck alone Pop!*" screamed B-Man.

Whap! Rapheal slapped the dog shit out of Black Girl! Then he absorbed one more whack from B-Man before wrestling the bat away from him and beating him with it.

As B-Man lay crumpled on the floor, Rapheal spat, "*Don't you ever get in my business again, Trick Baby!*"

B-Man swore to himself that when he grew up he would get at Rapheal. Rapheal later apologized to him for bustin' him up, but B-Man wasn't trying to hear it. He had always felt that Rapheal treated Khalil and Q much better than he treated him.

On her death bed, Black Girl had finally explained to B-Man what Rapheal's behavior toward him was about.

At the funeral B-Man had hoped to see Rapheal; he was going to spit dead in the nigga's face. Not only for those ass kickings from years before, but also because he held Rapheal responsible for Black Girl's demise. Old heads told the sad story of how Rapheal met a sweet young college girl, many years ago, and turned her into a stripper and a prostitute . . . and eventually into a fiend; whose recklessness led to her contracting HIV. Long before her death, though, when drugs became a stronger pimp than Rapheal was, he had kicked her to the curb like a discarded piece of trash; leaving her and three sons to fend for themselves.

After Black Girl was put in the ground, B-Man's anger toward Rapheal had become a toxic acid in his heart. The two ran across one another in these same apartments where they now met again. At the first encounter B-Man, who was sixteen at the time, walked up to Rapheal and punched him in the grill.

"That's for Black Girl, nigga!" he'd spat.

Rapheal had pulled himself up off the ground.

"I'm sorry about your mother. I woulda been at the funeral, but I was too ashamed to show my face. Look at me . . . this crack got me fucked up. I didn't want you and your brothers to see me like this," Rapheal had explained as blood trickled from his busted mouth.

B-Man had no compassion. Crack might've been kickin' Rapheal's ass, but Black Girl was *dead*!

"Whateva, nigga!" B-Man gritted then spat dead in Rapheal's face.

Rapheal wiped the glob of spit from his face and charged it to the game. When he turned to walk away and B-Man kicked him in the ass. Rapheal could not overlook that type of violation—he was a fiend, but underneath his addiction he was *trained to go.* He went old school on B-Man, smashing that ass with knees and elbows; beat him like he used to beat a trick that tried some funny style shit with one of his hos.

Bonded by Blood

So now, seven years later, as B-Man came face to face with Rapheal again, he still didn't like or respect the nigga, but he knew not to diss him.

"B-Man, is that you?" asked Rapheal, stopping to look him over.

"Sup?" gritted B-Man.

"Been in and out of jail since the last time I seen you, but I'm good. Dayum, you a man now."

"I *been* a man. Been one since Mama died."

"Yeah, I guess you and your brothers had to be 'cause I sho didn't step up to the plate," Rapheal half-apologized. "I sho miss Black Girl. They don't make 'em like her no more."

B-Man didn't comment, he just looked Rapheal up and down trying to assess if the nigga might have anything worth jackin' him for. Rapheal was rockin' sweats and crisp vintage Jordans, but no jewels.

"What you doing for yaself? You gettin' it up or what?" inquired Rapheal, interrupting B-Man's grimy thoughts.

"I'm making it do what it do."

"What about your brothers?"

"Q gettin' his weight up. Khalil is on lock but he touch down tomorrow."

"That's good," uttered Rapheal.

"What about you? You still fuckin' with the hard?" asked B-Man.

"Yeah, I can't lie. I'm still gettin' high, on and off. Can't seem to put it down for good, but I ain't givin' up."

Like I give a fuck, B-Man thought as Rapheal went on.

"Listen, I know we've had our clashes, and I handled 'em wrong most of the time, but it's still love. How about we let by-gones be by-gones? I got a young square chic who I'm staying with over here in 9B. Let Khalil and Q know where I'm at, and the three of y'all come through and holla at me sometime."

When snakes start wearing sneakers . . . which is never, 'cause them muthafuckas ain't got no feet! thought B-Man.

Rapheal could feel the vibe. "Aight, just remember . . . 9B," he repeated then pushed on.

By the time B-Man slid into his whip and drove off, he had already pushed Rapheal's invitation out of mind. His cell phone rang, further erasing it.

"Sup?"

"I need you to roll wit' me to make a drop," said Q.

"Aight, scoop me from the crib in twenty minutes."

"One."

Chapter Ten

Khalil tried once again to close his eyes and will himself to sleep. Unfortunately, sleep avoided him like unrequited love. He hadn't been able to sleep much the past three weeks. The anxiety of upcoming freedom had kept him awake like he had swallowed a case of *No Doze*.

Counting down the last weeks of his bid had been a slow, torturous ordeal. To Khalil it seemed that days were suddenly twice as long, and nights were even longer. But finally he was "shorter" than a mosquito's dick. When morning brought its sweet, beautiful ass around, those crackers would have to open the gates and set him free. Earlier today, following prison policy, he had been moved into an isolation cell to await his release. Before leaving the dorm he had given away all the shit that had got him through his bid: CD player and Koss headphones, an ass of CDs, two pair of sneakers (Jumpmans and LeBrons), Coogi pajamas and robe, almost $200 worth of commissary, and postage stamps.

"I wish I could take y'all niggaz with me," he had told his homies Tank, Onion Head, and Big Reese.

Khalil meant that.

Though he was happy that his bid was up and he was less than twelve hours from getting up out that bitch, Khalil felt bad for Onion Head and 'em. Only Big Reese was sure to ever get out. Onion Head and Tank both had—life sentences plus a number of years to serve.

After Khalil gave them some dap, he headed to the sallyport where the escort officer was waiting to take him to isolation. C.O. Wells intercepted him, pretending to be asking official questions.

"Is that all the property you have?" she asked, observing that the only things Khalil was carrying was a photo album.

"This is all I'm taking home from here," replied Khalil. "Unless I can take you with me?"

"I'm not your property," Rayne pointed out. Then she smiled and added, "Not yet."

Khalil said, "I'ma call you tomorrow night. You still gon' come up to the "A" on your off day, ain't you?"

"We'll see,"

"So, you already breaking your word to me?"

"Just keep your word, Khalil—I'll always keep mine."

"Check. I'ma handle mines, Baby Love. Now let's show these haters what's really happening. Gimme some tongue, let me leave these country niggaz with something to tell."

"Khalil, I am *not* kissing you right here!" her face was flushed.

"Why not? The escort officer just stepped outside, he can't see nothing. C'mon, shawdy, let me shine on these niggaz."

"No, Khalil. Don't ask me to do that," she pleaded. "Someone will tell, and I'll lose my job."

Khalil replied, "So? You can move to the "A" and roll with me. Fuck working for the state anyway."

"Bye, Khalil. Call me tomorrow night."

"Fuck that, shawdy. Show me you're real—let's stunt on these lames."

Rayne made a face in protest. Then it melted into a sweet smile. She moved closer to him, stood up on her tippy-toes and gave him a quick peck on the cheek, but Khalil wasn't about to

accept just a peck, he wanted to put on a show. He pulled her into his arms and tongued her in front of everyone in the dorm.

"Y'all haters tell *that*!" Khalil shouted out after breaking the lip lock with Rayne.

"Stunt, shawdy!" Big Reese yelled.

"Represent dat city, homeboy!" hollered Tank.

"Yeah, niggaz—*what*!" Onion Head challenged the whole dorm.

The haters rushed to their cells to write kites to the warden.

Khalil sat on the bunk in the isolation cell imagining what those niggaz in the dorm were saying now. He knew how the chain gang was; by now, he figured, the story was all over the compound. By morning, the story would be that he had fucked C.O. Wells in front of the whole dorm. Niggaz always exaggerated things.

As the hours 'til his release ticked by at a snail's pace, Khalil thought about what awaited him on the other side of the prison's fence. He had never lied to himself, like he wasn't going to hustle again. If he didn't hustle, he wouldn't know what the fuck to do.

Khalil knew that his forte was hoes. His days of chill pimpin' were over. Now he was ready to mack and take pimpin to another level. He planned to locate his pop and pick Rapheal's brain. Rapheal had once been a top-notch pimp in the city. Khalil knew that he could learn a lot from his pop. He sat up thinking of ways he would take the game to that other level; ways to mack his way to millions.

Sleep finally came to Khalil in the isolation cell as he lay planning his come up.

Khalil stood in the warden's office not listening to a word coming out of the cracker's stankin' mouth. He wished the chump would hand him his discharge papers, shut the fuck up, and let him bounce. Freedom was just outside the prison's front gate and Khalil couldn't wait another minute to claim it.

Warden Croyle was saying . . . "so it's up to you what you decide to do with your life, inmate Jones. You can—"

"Hold the fuck up, cracker!" Khalil cut him off. "As of a few minutes ago, I ain't no fuckin' *inmate* no more. Furthermore, save ya tired-ass speech for somebody who gives a fuck. We both know that you's a racist mafucka; you would like nothing better than to see me return to prison—so don't front! Just hand me my discharge papers, let me out the front gate, and miss me with the speech."

Warden Croyle's face turned red.

Khalil was still laughing to himself when he walked out the front gate into the visitor's parking lot where his brothers were waiting to pick him up. Q had sent him some new gear to wear home so that he wouldn't have to walk out the front gate in the monkey clothes the prison provided upon an inmate's discharge. Khalil was outfitted in baggy Iceburg jean shorts, an oversized white T-shirt, a crisp new pair of vintage Air Jordan's. His prison barber had tightened him up yesterday with a fresh temp fade and a razor sharp line that accentuated his deep, circular brush waves.

As soon as Khalil stepped out into the hot summer sun a Hummer stretch limo pulled up to where he stood. The chauffeur, Azure, stepped out of the limo. She was wearing coochie cutters and a sheer halter, with six-inch stilettos. When the dime-piece chauffeur opened the limo's back doors, out stepped Q and B-Man followed by six fly chicks dressed in bikini tops, thongs, and high-heeled shoes.

Q was bejeweled like the *Birdman*. He removed one of the iced-out platinum chains from around his neck and put it around Khalil's.

"Welcome home, big bruh." They hugged.

"Well, you ain't *home* yet," B-Man said, "but you're free."

"As a bird!" Khalil exclaimed, accepting a hug from his other brother. Then his eyes cut to the chicks in bikini tops and thongs.

"What's up with them?" Khalil asked grinning.

Q said to the girls, "Y'all go 'head and do y'all thang. Show my fam how it's going down."

On cue, Azure retrieved a fold-up lawn chair from the rear of the Hummer. She unfolded the chair and directed Khalil to sit in it. Grinning, he played along. Using a hand-held remote the lovely chauffeur turned on the limo's sound system and crunk music blasted from the Hummer's eighteen speakers. The six vixens surrounded Khalil and started poppin' pussy at him. They served him up right there in the prison's parking lot.

Khalil could picture Warden Croyle and the other staff members looking out to the parking lot, eyeing the stretch Hummer and the damn near naked bitches dancing to the head-thumping music. Khalil knew that those muthafuckas would rather go blind than be made to watch what they were now witnessing. Crackers can't stand to see a brutha leave prison in style. They like to send him home broken down and defeated. Khalil Jones had denied them their pleasure.

From certain spots inside the prison inmates could see out to the parking lot. Every prisoner but the haters would rejoice in seeing Khalil leave in grand hustla-style, stuntin' on those crackers up front, and those bad-body country hos who worked there as C.O.s and wouldn't give a nigga any holla. Khalil was gettin' some getback for the homies left on lock.

From the small yard outside their dormitory, Big Reese, Tank, and Onion Head saw their homey puttin' on. They were screamin' and hollerin', happy to see Khalil representing for the "A".

The Hummer limo was on the interstate highway headed back to the Atlanta. Music thumped, weed smoke clouded the inside of the vehicle, and bottles of Cristal, Remy XO and Grey Goose were being popped. Khalil leaned back in the soft butter leather seats and let purp' and cognac get his head right.

Halfway back to the "A", Q proposed a game. He offered a stack to any one of the chicks who could give Khalil some brain and make him bust in under three minutes.

"Q, let me in on that," Azure said from up front.

"You might as well break me off right now, 'cause I'ma make your brother nut in less than *sixty seconds*," predicted Creamy, a dark-skinned hottie from Virginia. She had moved to Atlanta to attend Spelman, but had gotten turned out to the fast life and the stripper's game. She and the other five girls had met Q at Teasers, where they worked.

Creamy had hella confidence in her head game. She unzipped Khalil's Iceberg shorts and stepped to her business. Khalil started to stop her before she got started. Having a mack's mentality, he wasn't down with tricking off with a bitch, even if Q was the one actually paying for it. But, it was all in fun and in honor of his freedom.

Shawdy stroked him to erection, slid a condom over it, and proceeded to do her thing. When her three minutes were up, Khalil hadn't busted.

"Who's next?" asked Q, laughing and sipping on Henny.

A shawdy who could've passed for Kelis took Creamy's place between Khalil's knees. As her head bobbed up and

down, her friends were chanting, "Go Sunshine ... Go Sunshine ... Go Sunshine!" Sunshine failed to win the prize money, too.

"Damn, nigga, what you on? Viagra?" she complained. "Q, I thought you said yo folks been locked up for five years?"

"I have." confirmed Khalil. "What's up?"

"*What's up?* Nigga, if you ain't been with a bitch in five years, you oughta be this quick to nut," said Sunshine, snapping her fingers to emphasize her point. She really wanted to win that stack; she had a mean powder habit, along with an affinity for X pills.

"Maybe ya head game is weak," cracked Q.

"Nigga please! Don't even try to clown—my head game must be *all that.* Yo' ass stay blowin' up my cell phone," she said with a smirk, putting Q on blast.

"Shawdy, ain't nothing wrong with ya skills. A nigga just gotta piss that's all," revealed Khalil.

"Nigga, no wonder you can't nut!" fumed Creamy, causing the others inside the limo to laugh.

"That shit ain't fair, Q," she pouted. "How was I s'pose to make him nut if he gotta piss? Y'all should let me try again."

She really wanted to win that stack.

Khalil told the chauffeur to pull over to the shoulder of the highway to let him get out and take a quick leak.

"Man, piss in one of those empty champagne bottles, or roll down a window and piss out dat muthafucka. We ain't pulling over; highway patrol might roll up and fuck wit' us, wanting to search this mafucka," interjected Q. They had weed, open alcohol, and X pills in the limo.

Khalil opted to roll down one of the back windows and piss out that mafucka. The force of the wind blew a spray of piss back into the Hummer, showering several of the scantily clad girls. They cussed and screamed at Khalil, Q, and B-Man. Avia, one of those who had gotten an accidental golden shower, quickly pressed a button on the door panel rolling the window up, cussing Khalil as well. .

Silk, a mocha-complected honey with a bangin' body and a cute smile quickly handed Khalil an empty champagne bottle. It blew Khalil's mind when, in the next second, the freak bitch put his dick in her mouth while he was still pissing. The shit felt damn good, but after that, Khalil didn't want the nasty hoes mouth on his dick again. He was thinking wasn't no telling where that freak bitch's mouth had been. If a hoe will drink a nigga's piss, ain't shit she won't do.

After everyone recovered from the shock of seeing Silk guzzle down Khalil's piss, a chic named Butter Cup tried to make Khalil bust in the allotted three minutes but failed. Khalil remembered that he was getting served by piss-drinking hoes, so he wrapped back up.

Only Sinnamon and Miss Tee hadn't taken a turn tryna get Khalil to bust in under three minutes. Q had been keeping track of the time with his iced-out Piaget watch. Miss Tee, a redbone stallion, declined her turn, acting like all of a sudden she wasn't a trick bitch. Q threatened to put her fake moralistic ass out on the highway and see if she liked walking a hundred miles better than sucking dick.

B-Man added, "Fuck dat ho, anyway. Her mouth look like she been chewing broken glass!"

Miss Tee self-consciously covered her mouth with the back of her hand, while the limo filled with laughter.

"Whateva!" came from behind the hand covering her grill.

A minute later Miss Tee found herself hitchhiking back to the "A."

Once the Hummer stretch pulled back into the highway traffic, Sinnamon didn't hesitate to win the prize money.

Shawdy stroked Khalil back to an erection then began slurping on the dick like it was a Popsicle. Khalil felt the back of her throat massaging him. He was close to busting when shawdy spat the dick out, straddled Khalil's lap reverse cow-girl style, pulled her thong to the side and slid down on Khalil's erection. Khalil shot off in less than thirty seconds, barking and growling like DMX.

"Fuck dat, shawdy da winner!" proclaimed B-Man.

Q hit Sinnamon off with a stack and then blessed the other girls with three-hundred dollars a piece on GP. When they arrived back in the city they dropped the strippers off at their respective apartments, then went to Lennox Mall so that Khalil could cop some gear.

CA$H

[82]

Chapter Eleven

The Jones boys were headed to the Level Three nightclub, where Q and B-Man were throwing a welcome home party for Khalil.

They had Azure at their disposal for twenty-four hours, so they were still rolling in the Hummer stretch. In the back of the limo they were drinking bubbly and burnin purp. Q had brought along Persia, who was looking sexy as hell. B-Man had left Gwen at home, but on his arm was a shawdy named Amore, whom he met through Bed-Stuy. Amore was short and thick to death, and tonight she was wearing the fuck out of a white Donna Karan mini-dress and a pair of knee-high red leather boots. Persia could've sworn she caught the weave-wearing bitch sweating Q. The night was just getting started and already she didn't like the ho.

Khalil, being fresh home from a bid, was, rolling dolo but looking to snag something to help him start up his stable. He was rocking a cream-colored Sean John linen summer suit, lightweight gator loafers, and a little shine. Upon meeting him face-to-face for the first time, Persia had commented that he looked like Morris Chestnut.

The Level Three club was crowded, but not sardine-like. The club was a popular night spot anyway, but tonight many of those in attendance were there to welcome Khalil home. Q had a growing rep in the streets, so a lot of partygoers were there out of respect for him. Thomasville Heights was in the club representin'.

There were three different levels or floors inside the nightclub. Q had rented the top level—the ballers floor—for Khalil's party. Levels one and two were open to those not attending the party but clubbing anyway.

As Q, B-Man, Khalil and 'em were being escorted to their reserved booth by the club's manager, a brown-skinned Amazon interrupted their procession.

"Hi, Quantavious," she purred, titties pressed against Q's chest. Her look said: *shake your bitch and come holla at me.*

"Whud up. Dorena?" Q spoke, tryna push on. But Dorena wouldn't move out of his way.

"You're what's up," she replied. *Fuck that bitch you're with.*

"I hear you," said Q.

Persia stopped in mid-stride, spun around and faced the bold ho.

"What the fuck? Do bitches always have to disrespect? Q, are you gonna check this drag queen, or am I gonna have to go ghetto on her ass?" Persia began removing her loop earrings.

Q just shook his head in mild disbelief then pulled Persia along to avoid that petty shit. Dorena was trying to fuck with his girl's head. He had hit it a while back; the bitch was throwback pussy. He wasn't about to allow them to start no shit and ruin Khalil's party.

A while later the party was jumpin'. Khalil and 'ems reserved booth overflowed with champagne, liquor, weed smoke and visitors'. Party streamers and banners that read "Welcome Home, Khalil—the Streets Are Yours" decorated the walls all around them. The same message flashed repeatedly across the large television screen that hung down from the ceiling.

Khalil was chillin', taking in everything. He'd been away sixty months so everything looked new to him. In addition to

the cognac and purp, he was intoxicated with freedom. He was just checking out the new styles, the new dances—the whole nine. Shawdies looked so good, and their asses were *sooo* phat, he couldn't wait to get his mack on. Hos were gonna make him rich. If mafuckaz thought pimpin' was dead they were going to be in for a big surprise. Black Girl had told him he was born to mack; he was planning to do his mama proud, elevating the game to the new millennium.

Judging from the way they were doing it up big for him, Khalil guessed that Q and B-Man must *really* be gettin' to the money. Especially Q. Bitches were acting like Q was T.I. up in that bitch; niggaz were showing him much respect.

A few seats down from Khalil in the booth, Persia was noting all the man-stealing females who were sweating Q. She stayed glued to him, not allowing any of those slick bitches the opportunity to slip Q their number. Persia had pulled that stunt too many times herself to fall victim to it. If Q needed to use the restroom, Persia planned to escort him there and back.

B-Man parked Amore at the booth with Khalil and 'em, then went off to parlay with some other hustlaz. He was using the occasion to build up clientele and scout out niggaz he might be able to flex down the line. He was determined not to play the background to Q's lead much longer.

Khalil left the private booth and drifted over to the main bar, Henny and Coke in hand. He felt a hand on his shoulder. Being fresh out the joint, he was not yet reaccustomed to being touched.

"Damn, baby, why are you so jumpy? I was only tryna get your attention to say hello and welcome home."

Khalil smiled. "Oh, what's up, April?" he was hardly able to believe his eyes. When he left the streets, April was 'bout fifteen years old, a little chunky chic. Cute, but a little round.

Now shawdy had come the fuck up; she had an hourglass figure and ass to spare!

"Ain't nothin' up," April replied. "What's poppin' with you? Can a bitch take you home and get some of that dick tonight?" She had heard that fresh out of prison dick was the shit.

"I'ma have to get back with you on that another time," Khalil declined. He guessed that April would've been some good cut, but now that he had gotten that first nut off, he planned to make the next ho he got with choose before he gave her some dick.

Khalil had just brushed off April when Sinnamon, slid up, trying to get with him for the night.

"This the business, baby girl," Khalil broke it down to Sinnamon. "I ain't knockin' ya hustle, this ain't what you think it is. Ain't nothing sweet right here."

"It ain't even like that, Khalil. Shid, I'll pay *you* to let me finish what I started in the limo earlier today," Sinnamon offered.

"Oh yeah?"

"Uh-huh."

"How much money you got?" Khalil asked.

"How much it gon' cost?"

"Ho, won't enough money fit in your purse to buy me. Don't get shit twisted because of that shit that went down today. I'm a stone-cold mack. When you're ready to fuck, suck dick, lie, steal and cheat to help me become a million dollar nigga, that's when we can finish what you started. Until then, push on."

The change in Khalil from earlier had Sinnamon fucked up. She walked away with bruised feelings, thinking Khalil had to be the only nigga in the city that would refuse to let her pay *him* to sleep with her.

The deejay was spinning *Pussy Poppin'* by Ludacris. Q asked Amore to dance. It was a way for him to shake Persia for a minute after he came off the dance floor.

When B-Man returned to find Amore on the dance floor with his brother, he knew something was up because Q wasn't the dancing type. What Q was up to, B-Man couldn't quite guess. He thought maybe Q was trying to holla at Amore, but he wasn't trippin' it. Amore was just his cut buddy, she could easily be replaced. Besides, B-Man grinned as a thought occurred to him; if Q was busy trying to get Amore, he couldn't keep an eye on Persia. B-Man would've traded five Amore's for one Persia.

"What's up, shawdy?" B-Man said, sliding in next to Q's wifey in the booth. "If you were mine ain't no way I'd be dancing with another bitch."

"Well, Amore is yours, ain't she? And *she's* dancing with another nigga. So what does that say about *you?*" countered Persia.

"That bitch don't mean nothin' to me. You already know who I want."

"*Who* do you want, B-Man? Old tired-ass Gwen?"

"Don't even go *there*. You know *who* I want. Shid, I'll give up my right arm to have you."

"That shit sounds good."

"That's real talk, girl," B-Man swore. "Just wait 'til I build my weight up. I'm coming to claim you. That's on all I love."

From the bar Khalil saw B-Man and Persia engaged in conversation, but he had no reason to suspect that something shady might be going on. As far as he knew, everything was good with his peoples. He didn't even allow the thought that B-Man might be scheming after Q's girl to enter his mind.

Khalil's visage turned hard like granite, when he saw Chyna. She was one of the lil' hos he used to chili pimp. Chyna still had that sexy walk, and when she got up close Khalil saw that she was a penny short of being a dime. The years had filled her out just right. He wasn't fazed by her looks, though. *A dime piece ain't worth a damn penny if she won't hold a playa down when sugar turns to shit, he* thought.

"Hey, Khalil—welcome home. I know you're probably mad at me for not writing and all that, but still I missed you even though I didn't keep in touch," she said.

"Shawdy, don't even waste ya breath. Fuck a letter. I ain't salty 'bout that shit. A ho gon' be a ho. But, bitch . . . you're not even good enough to be called a ho. You're sleepin' with the enemy. Back up outta my face!"

"I don't fuck with Twin no more," Chyna said.

"Still, you used to fuck with the nigga, and you knew my brothaz had beef with him. How you gon' disrespect then show up at my party? I oughta hit you over the head with this bottle of Henny!" He raised the half gallon bottle above his head.

Chyna flinched. "Why you acting like that, daddy? Ain't a bitch entitled to one mistake?"

She wanted back into Khalil's life now that he was back on the streets. She had kicked DeWayne to the curb a year ago because the nigga fell off his game. Since then, Chyna had remained unattached, waiting for a boss playa to give her a position on his team. Chyna knew that Khalil was a top-notch nigga and that he would spark.

Khalil had already decided not to fuck with Chyna ever again: if it was one thing he was unwilling to forgive it was disloyalty. He waved a bouncer over and had the ho tossed out the club.

Later Sinnamon cornered Khalil again.

"What if I tell you I'm willing to do all those things you said I'd have to do to get down with you?"

"Then you'll get yaself a boss nigga."

"That's what I need," confessed Sinnamon.

"Empty ya purse then, shawdy. Make me know I'm what you want and need."

Without hesitation Sinnamon handed him all the money in her purse, which was $1,500. It was petty cash to Khalil, but he accepted it without complaint. Because more important than the money, he had just copped the first hoe for his stable.

"Will you go home with me, daddy?" asked Sinnamon instinctively adopting a ho's vernacular.

"Yeah. Daddy gon' break you off tonight."

CA$H

Chapter Twelve

B-Man came through in his dark blue bubble Chevy to scoop Khalil up from Sinnamon's crib out in Clarksdale. She lived in the new townhouses over by the Clarksdale Shopping Center, an area B-Man was familiar with, so he had no trouble following the directions she had given him last night when Khalil left the party with her.

Khalil had tapped that ass so good last night and early this morning that when Sinnamon answered the door to let B-Man in, shawdy was walking bow-legged. When B-Man pointed it out, Sinnamon giggled like a schoolgirl.

"Damn, pimp, lil' buddy beaming like a thousand watt bulb. You must've put it on her ass real good."

"I handled mines," replied Khalil gripping Sinnamon's Victoria Secrets-clad ass.

He told Sinnamon that he would be "home" later to drop her off at Teasers, the strip club where she worked. Sinnamon had her own whip, but from now on Khalil would be using it until he copped one of his own.

B-Man and Khalil headed over to Q's crib in Scotsdale to chop it up with him about how the three of them were going to rule the streets now that Khalil was back. B-Man was bumpin' a Plies mixed tape trying to talk over the loud music as he steered the Chevy towards Q's crib. Khalil couldn't hear what B-Man was saying, so he turned down the volume.

B-Man was explaining the trouble Q was having collecting on the twelve stacks Lamar owed him. Khalil didn't know Lamar, but he knew that Q was forever trying to help his shawdy's people. He also knew that Q had been burned many times like that and should've learned his lesson by now. He reminded himself that Q was just a kind-hearted nigga who would give a mafucka a chance. The way B-Man was telling it, it sounded as if he was saying their lil' brother had turned softer than baby shit.

Khalil retorted, "You telling me all about how Q ain't straightening his business—what about you? Your gun don't bust no more?"

"Long story short, bruh; Man, I'm tired of straightenin' shit for Q." His tone disclosed a bit of hidden animosity in his heart.

"Nigga, we all fam! The three of us all came out the same womb. So it don't even go like that. Shawdy, you're ya brotha's keepa—point blank period!"

"I feel you, Khalil," conceded B-Man. "But Q ain't living by the same code"

"What you saying, shawdy?"

B-Man recounted the whole situation where Q hadn't vouched for him with Fazio.

Khalil already knew how it had gone down. He'd thought it over many times while he was on lock. In his heart of hearts he didn't believe Q had intentionally blocked B-Man's come up. The truth was the truth; B-Man was quick to fuck up money then try to juggle a nigga. Khalil understood why Q hadn't wanted to bet his life on B-Man's word.

"You can't be mad about that, shawdy. Shid, how many times you done came short with Q's money when he fuck with you like that?"

"I should've known you were gon' take his side?" B-Man said.

"Don't even try that weak shit, nigga!" Khalil snapped. "Shawdy, my love for you and Q is the same. I done a bid for him, and I duffed a nigga for you," Khalil reminded him.

Right after Black Girl had died, a well-known drag queen in the hood had tricked young B-Man into bed. B-Man hadn't realized Rachel, the drag queen was really Ricardo until they were naked. Then B-Man had to fight his way out the drag queen's apartment, 'cause the cock-strong mafucka was gonna take the dick! A week later Khalil gave Rachel something hard to suck on— a chrome nine.

"So miss me with that bullshit, pimp!" continued Khalil. "Nigga if both of y'all went blind, I'd give each one of you an eye apiece and walk around like Stevie Wonder my goddamn self. That's real talk!" he pounded his chest with a fist, emphasizing the force of his love.

Unperturbed, B-Man maintained, "Still, Q ain't doing it like dat you'll see, bruh. Just wait till we get to this nigga's condo and you peep how him and his bitch living. I mean, I ain't starvin', but we ain't eating no where close to the same."

Dayum. Is this jealousy and envy I'm hearing? Khalil couldn't help but wonder. It sho sound the fuck like it. Khalil wasn't about to try and solve any riddles or guess what was on his brother's mind. If a nigga had something on his chest, he oughta man up and be heard. B-Man was trying to say *something*, but at the same time he wasn't saying nothing at all, just talking in riddles.

Khalil cut him off, "Check this shit, pimp," he said. "If you know something about lil' bruh that I don't, spit it out. Otherwise, quit bitchin'. Maddafact, wait until we get to Q's crib then speak your piece in his presence. 'Cause the truth ain't gotta be said behind a man's back."

"Naw . . . naw," retreated B-Man. "It ain't even like dat. I'm just sayin'—"

"You just saying what? Shawdy, you ain't said shit, yet. Just droppin' salt, and spilling what sounds like haterade to me."

"You a see," B-Man maintained.

Khalil wasn't feeling that shit. He turned up the volume on the sound system and listened to 50, even though he wasn't feeling that nigga, either.

B-Man hadn't exaggerated Q's crib, Khalil realized, as Persia let them in and escorted them to the den. The shit was plush, no denying that. The cream-colored wall to wall carpet was thick, and soft as a cloud; silk-covered living room set, oriental figurines. In the den where they sat was an over-stuffed sofa with twin recliners; plasma TV, high-tech computerized entertainment console—the whole shebang.

Khalil was impressed but the splendor wasn't beyond belief. He felt that the opulence of Q's condo wasn't anything beyond what B-Man should've been able to accumulate if B-Man was doing the smart thing with his chips. So why was B-Man so envious of Q? Khalil wondered.

While they waited for Q to come down from upstairs, Persia brought them a fruit bowl full of dro and a box of Swissher Sweet cigars. *Q definitely has himself a showpiece*, ran through Khalil's mind as he watched Persia walk over to the wet bar in a corner of the den. Even in a simple tennis skirt and baby tee, Persia looked delectable.

Khalil declined a drink; it was too early for that. Besides, his head was still right from last night. He rolled a blunt of dro and fired it up. It was never too early to burn.

Persia left so the brothers were free to talk without being overheard. B-Man apologized to Khalil for those times he had procrastinated on doing one thing or another that Khalil had asked him to do. While on lock B-Man's slights angered Khalil more than a bit. At the end of the day, though, Khalil decided that it wasn't poison in his brother's heart that caused him to

procrastinate. B-Man just wasn't the type of person to handle shit promptly.

Khalil said to B-Man, "Bruh, I ain't stressin'. Y'all two niggas my blood. With mama dead, we're all we got, besides Rapheal wherever he at."

B-Man snorted. As far as he was concerned, Rapheal was just another nigga. Q, on the other hand, had much love for their pop. He hadn't been in contact with Rapheal in a while because he was embarrassed at what his pops had become. Plus, Rapheal had fucked him out of dope time and time again whenever Q gave him some *work*, trying to help him get back on his feet.

"Anyway, what's the business?" asked Khalil, changing subjects.

"We gettin' to the money," Q spoke up. "I'm gettin' five to ten bricks."

"On consignment," pointed out B-Man.

"You still working on consignment?" Khalil asked surprised.

"Q, ain't thinking large enough," B-Man suggested. "We could be *raping* da game if shawdy wasn't *scurred*."

"It ain't about being scared, bruh," Q quickly defended himself. "I ain't tryna rule the world I just wanna get *mine* and not get caught up. Plenty greedy niggas done ended up dead or in the pen for life tryna get it *all*."

"The same way plenty niggas who thought small still ended up in a hearse or with an ass of time in prison. I say if you gon' play the game, play to win it all. Be the world's champ in this crack shit!" differed B-Man.

Khalil just listened. It was apparent that there was tension between his brothers. Khalil recognized it and was determined to see that they not let it fester into something unresolvable.

He felt that they each had valid arguments. However, he told them that if he was forced to lean one way or the other, he'd *be* inclined to agree with B-Man.

"There's no way to tip-toe in and out of the drug game and be assured that you won't suffer the same consequences as those who play it to the fullest and lose. You either live it or leave it alone. Straddling the fence will just get a nigga bombed on from all sides," Khalil said, recognizing that Q was wary of shining too bright.

B-Man added, "The game ain't for the faint-hearted, lil' bruh. If you *shook*, get a job!"

"Nigga, what you know about the game? Yeah, you fuck with a lil' work, but you's a jackboy!" responded Q, getting heated because B-Man was questioning his gangsta.

Khalil listened to his brothers go at it. It was clear to him that B-Man didn't respect Q's leadership. Things would never go smoothly between them as long as that remained the case.

Khalil had his own ideas, which he believed would maximize each of their strengths, including his own, and catapult them to the top of their respective hustles. If executed properly, he believed they'd be able to walk away from the streets young, rich and free . . . in just a matter of a few years. For now, he kept his ideas to himself. He didn't want them to feel like he was coming home trying to run things.

Khalil recalled that Q had written him saying that he was *straight*! Well, getting ten bricks on consignment was okay, but it wasn't what Khalil would call being "straight". He was about to allude to that when he remembered that Q had asked him not to mention it to B-Man.

Khalil switched up, interrupting their argument and addressing their disagreements.

"B-Man, the way I see it, you don't feel you can eat good enough off of Q's plate. Right?"

B-Man stuttered something unintelligible.

"That's my point," Khalil went on, correctly interpreting B-Man's hesitancy to respond. "You can't eat at all without him. Once you look at it from that angle, and set your pride aside for a sec', maybe y'all can reach a compromise."

B-Man's face turned up. The truth was a bitter pill to swallow.

"Now, Q," Khalil continued, "when you need a nigga to watch ya back or bust his gun, who you call on?"

Q didn't need to answer, Khalil's point was made.

"So, shawdy, you need B-Man just as much as he needs you. Maybe more. 'Cause he can find someone else to hit him off with weight. Or stick to the jack game, and, instead of eating off another nigga's plate, he can *take* the whole meal. But who else you gon' trust to watch ya back and bust his gun for you like B-Man do?"

"It ain't like I won't bust my own gun."

"Shawdy, I didn't mean it like that. Still, a nigga need a second and third gun out

there in those streets. Shit was like that before I went away, so I can imagine how grimy things are now. Think about this: Q, step ya game up to, say, twenty bricks, and try to get ya bank situated to where you can pay for 'em up front. B-Man, lower your ambitions some. Instead of tryna rule the world, you might have to settle for ruling the "A". Most important, though, when Q fuck with you, don't be juggling his money," Khalil suggested.

The three brothers chopped it up for over two hours, until B-Man had to go handle some business.

After leaving Q's crib, B-Man drove to the Dec'. He was headed to the old Misty Waters apartment complex on Candler Road. The apartments, before they were renovated and given a new name, were like the projects moved in the middle of the suburbs.

Though Misty Waters had received a face-lift and a name change, the crime and drug activity that the complex had been infamous for had not been totally eradicated from the property. B-Man was over there now to holla at Shawn, the big weed man in the complex. He had parlayed with Shawn at Khalil's welcome home party last night, at which time he learned that Shawn was sitting on a lot of dro.

B-Man's mood was kinda foul after the discussion he'd had with his brothers. He felt Khalil was feeling him, but was too loyal to Q to go against him. B-Man detested the fact that Q was the one plugged in, thus the shot-caller. Not only did he not respect his youngest brother's ambition, he didn't respect his gangsta. Q was holding him back from attaining *made man* status.

B-Man parked, got out of his whip, and headed up the walk to Shawn's apartment. Before he reached his destination, he was approached by a fiend. She looked like her itty bitty ass already had one foot in the graveyard. B-Man recognized the woman who had once helped raise him and his brothers for a year or so while Black Girl was serving a short bid for prostitution and simple possession of drugs.

Sophie had been one of Rapheal's hoes. Even when Black Girl had come home from jail Sophie had continued to live with them, as Black Girl's wife-in-law, for a period of time. Rapheal had his game tight like that back then; he had his two best hos living together in harmony. For a while Sophie was a second mother to the three Jones boys.

"B-Man! B-Man!" Sophie shouted, running up to him. "Lemme get something?"

She held out a dirty palm.

"I ain't got no crack, Sophie!" he snapped. "And if I did, I done told ya a thousand times before; I ain't givin' you no dope!"

"Well, gimme some money?"

"Nah, Sophie—you can forget dat. You ain't gon' do nothing but spend it on crack." He tried to walk off but Sophie grabbed him by the arm.

"No the fuck I ain't!" she snapped, dry-mouthed. "For your information, *Mister Big Shot*, I'ma buy me something to eat! Plus I need some clothes; I just got out of the county last week, and I ain't got shit, but the clothes on my back!"

B-Man considered Sophies predicament. She had been kind to him while she was with Rapheal. Even when she was no longer Rapheal's ho, Sophie had kept an eye out on him and his brothers until crack rendered her incapable of doing so. Once, she had hid Q in her apartment when popos was looking for him.

"Gimme your phone number. I'ma—"

"Boy, I ain't got no damn phone!"

"Well, I'ma give you my number. Call me tomorrow, and I'ma have Gwen pick you up and take you to buy some clothes," B-Man said. "You remember Gwen, dontcha?"

"I know Gwen. But I don't need yo bird ass bitch to take me no goddamn where! I ain't no fuckin' child! I don't need no chaperone!"

"Since you don't know how to talk to me with respect, I'm not doing a damn thing for you."

B-Man knocked her hand off his arm.

"You ain't shit, nigga! You think you somebody? Your daddy used to think he was all dat—now his junkie ass ain't got a pot to piss in or a window to throw it out of! You just like his stingy ass. Ya mama should've flushed you down the toilet, *trick baby*!"

B-Man slapped Sophie so hard that her mind went back ten or fifteen years to when Rapheal would pimp smack her for getting slick out the mouth. Shaking off the dazing effect of the unexpected blow, Sophie attacked B-Man with both arms flailing. She ran dead smack into his fist and ended up on the seat of her itty bitty ass.

B-Man sneered down at his one-time surrogate mother. "You can cuss me all you want, Sophie. But don't ever compare me to Rapheal! That bitch nigga helped kill my mama! Even at my worst, I'm better than him."

He threw two twenty-dollar bills on the ground next to her and pushed on.

Khalil stood inside the storage bin with Q looking at the stack of bricks and two oversized detergent boxes full of guap. Q had just told him the details of how he had came up with it.

"Dayum, shawdy, why you ain't take it all?" he asked dumbfounded. "If you was gon' take any of it, you might as well took all his shit 'cause the consequences gon' be the same if ya connect ever finds out you stole from him."

All Q could say was, "I didn't want to leave him fucked up like that."

"Dayum, shawdy. Why you ain't dead the mafucka before you left out of there?" asked Khalil, but Q couldn't explain.

Khalil's head was spinning. He had no intention of getting out of jail and doing 150 mph on the freeway of life, speeding back

to the penitentiary. It was only his second day home and already shit was poppin' off.

"Alright, shawdy, this the business. We gotta knock your connects head off. Fuck you was thinking about?" Khalil shook his head in utter disbelief.

"Naw, we ain't gotta do that," Q argued. "It's been over two months and Fazio ain't mentioned anything about it. He's still hittin' me off with work, so he don't suspect me."

He fired up a Newport, Khalil's apprehension was making him nervous about it all.

Khalil fanned the smelly cigarette smoke from in front of his face, frowning.

"You can bet ya man is watching your every move, shawdy. If he ever sees anything suspect in ya game, I'm telling you, he gon' have ya bodied. That's why I say we go ahead and do him before it gets to that."

Despite the wisdom in Khalil's warning, Q stood firm on his assertion that it wasn't necessary to kill Fazio.

"Shawdy, if this what you was referring to in your letter, we gotta tell B-Man about it," decided Khalil.

Q took a long pull on the Newport, contemplating his brother's advice. After several minutes Q said, "Naw, bruh. I don't wanna tell B-Man. This some graveyard shit. You're the only one I can trust on this. Real talk, Khalil. I'm afraid that if I tell B-Man, he gon' cross me out somehow."

"B-Man wouldn't play the game foul like that, shawdy. He has a little envy in his heart, but mostly he just don't like playin' second fiddle, especially to his lil' brotha. Feel me?"

"Yeah, I feel you. But if I follow B-Man's lead he gon' lead us straight into the penitentiary. He wanna kill up everything, strong arm the game. We can't last like that," Q explained.

Khalil half-nodded. Too many reckless murders would definitely cement a nigga's fall. Still he admitted that he approved of B-Man's ambition if not his method. The streets gave you nothing worth having if you weren't willing to go out and take it from destiny's grasp.

"Whatever you think of B-Man's ambitions, we gotta tell him about this shit. 'Cause if your connect ever come gunnin' for you, best believe he gon' aim his bullets at ya peoples, too. B-Man will fuck around and catch a hot one, he could've avoided had he known the deal."

Chapter Thirteen

B-Man entered the apartment slamming the door behind him. He was still heated from his run-in with Sophie. Then, when he'd gone up to Shawn's apartment to holla at the frontin' ass nigga about that dro Shawn had claimed to have, the mafucka hadn't been sitting on nothing but lil' boy weight. It had been a waste of B-Man's time to go holla at the lame. Last night at the club, Shawn had been poppin' like he was a made man. So either the nigga had been frontin' or he had gotten spooked about dealing with B-Man. Either way, B-Man was now even more determined to put that steel in the nigga's grill.

"You okay, baby?" Gwen asked as B-Man came into the kitchen, anger etched on his face, steam literally rising from his clean-shaven head.

B-Man didn't answer; his eyes locked on the woo-woo in Gwen's hand. The pungent smell of the burning crack crushed and sprinkled over weed was unmistakable. Gwen was about to put the woo-woo out, sensing that B-Man was about to take his anger out on her. Her eyebrows rose in surprise when B-Man said, "Let me hit dat?"

"This a woo, baby?"

"I know dat. I could smell the shit soon as I walked in the door."

"You sure?" hedged Gwen.

"Just pass me the woo!" B-Man repeated harshly.

Until now he had only laced the weed he smoked with cocaine—never crack, and never in the presence of Gwen. Yet, he'd been curious about the high woo-woos produced. Now he was about to find out that the high was insatiable and would last a long, long time.

Gwen passed her man the woo-woo with some trepidation. She knew that the first hit was a mafucker, and it would have her man chasing that same high for years. She smoked woo-woos all day long chasing that high she'd felt the first time she smoked one. Recently she'd thought of taking that next step; the one of no return—smoking straight on the pipe—to reach the ultimate high. But she was frightened of becoming a crackhead, woo-woos was already gnawing away at her physical assets.

The mirror didn't lie. Gwen knew she wasn't as pretty or as fine as she used to be. If she noticed it, she figured B-Man had to notice her fall-off, too. As his bank increased so would the number of young hoes trying to get at him. Though she had reservations about seeing her man hitting the woo-woos, Gwen did realize how it could prove beneficial to her for B-Man to get hooked on the shit. The more they had in common, the more secure her position. She knew already that B-Man was creeping with young hoes. That didn't bother her; she had come to expect and accept infidelity in a nigga. As long as B-Man's infidelities didn't come knocking on her front door, she'd pretend not to know about them. She was thirty-five years old, while B-Man was a few months short of turning twenty-three; to expect his young, wild ass to keep his dick on lock would've been silly of her.

Gwen watched somewhat incredulous as B-Man inhaled the crack and weed smoke without coughing, as if he wasn't new to it. They smoked the first woo-woo then fired up

another one. The high instantly gave B-Man the feeling of invincibility. He recounted his encounters with Sophie, animatedly acting out how he had knocked her to the ground for comparing him to Rapheal. Gwen listened without comment, already aware of her man's dislike of his father. After finishing a third woo-woo Gwen began rubbing B-Man's dick through his jeans. He responded instantly.

Gwen unzipped him, got down on her haunches between his knees and then put him in her mouth. With years of experience she knew how to curl a nigga's toes. Her mouth slid up and down him the way she knew turned him on most. B-Man's hand gripped the back of her head encouraging her to take him all in; a feat that was damn near impossible because he was hung so well.

While Gwen continued to test her oral expertise, B-Man, who was seated in a chair pulled out from the table, leaned over and retrieved the last ready-rolled woo-woo from next to Gwen's purse on the kitchen counter. Simultaneous to getting his dick sucked, he fired up the woo-woo and got a multiple high.

Gwen swallowed without spilling a drop. From on her haunches she smiled up at him.

"You wanna take it to the bedroom?" she asked, looking at him like she was just getting started.

"We can do dat," agreed B-Man, passing her the lit woo-woo.

Before they could take what they had started to the bedroom, the doorbell chimed.

"Now who da fuck is that?" B-Man complained, heading to the door, dick swinging.

He looked through the peephole and saw Khalil and Q. Rushing back to the bedroom where Gwen had already gone, he hurried her to spray air-freshener in the kitchen to cover up the unmistakable smell left by the woo-woos they had smoked. While she did that, B-Man righted himself.

The doorbell chimed several more times while Gwen sprayed pine-scented air freshener throughout the apartment. When she was done, Gwen went into the bathroom to brush her teeth and fix herself up.

"What it do, shawdy?" Khalil greeted B-Man, giving him dap and inviting himself into the apartment.

B-Man dapped Q next. "What the business is?"

"Where your girl at?" Q answered with a question of his own.

"She in the back. Why?"

"Send her to the grocery store or somewhere," Q replied. "We got some serious shit to talk to you about."

Wrinkling up his nose Q added, "Damn, shawdy, smell like you been cooking *work* up in this bitch."

"Yeah, I just whipped up two *ounces* I gotta serve to this nigga Bed-Stuy be fuckin' wit," B-Man lied smoothly.

Khalil and Q sat down on the living room couch while B-Man went to tell Gwen to bounce for a minute. Khalil took in the décor of the small two-bedroom apartment, automatically comparing its modest size and furnishings to the laced spot where Q rested his head with his fly wifey. Khalil could see where at least part of B-Man's envy came from.

When Gwen accompanied B-Man back into the living room fifteen minutes later, Khalil's first thought was, *Lil' Mama about forty-years old, ain't she? She must be a ride-or-die chic for B-Man to have her as his wifey, cause she definitely ain't show off material.*

"Hey, Quantavious," Gwen spoke to Q.

"What's up," he replied. Then B-Man introduced Khalil to his girl.

Gwen had changed into a blue, pink, and white jogging suit, a pair of white and pink lady Air Max; a platinum link chain that B-Man had jacked for her last year hung around her neck, and her hair had been quickly pulled back into a ponytail. The jogging suit that just three months ago fit her ass like cellophane wrapped around a basketball, now hung off her ass as if she was sagging G-style.

To Khalil, both B-Man and his girl looked blazed, but he assumed they'd been burnin' weed.

Gwen dug the keys to her Honda Civic out of her faux Gucci purse, then told B-Man she was going over to her mama's for a while.

"Call me when you're finished handling your business," she said while fussing with her ponytail.

"I'll hit you up in a couple of hours," B-Man replied.

"Bye, Khalil, and welcome home. Bye Q," Gwen said turning to head out the door.

As Gwen left, Q was thinking: *B-Man's bitch look bad!*

"So whud da business?" B-Man asked as soon as the front door closed. He sat down in a recliner that was across from where his brothers sat on the couch, produced a bag of dro, and tossed it to Q to twist one up.

"Man, you ain't gon' believe this shit," Khalil began and then he let Q tell his own story.

Q was reluctant to spit it because he knew that B-Man was gonna be quick to judge and criticize. He expected B-Man to ridicule him for not emptying out Fazio's stash and not leaving Fazio with his cap peeled back. With several stops and starts, Q told B-Man the business.

"Why you ain't take *all* that shit, shawdy?" B-Man's words damn near echoed Khalil's.

"I just didn't wanna leave him fucked up like that."

He knew that if Khalil had't been able to *feel* his reasoning, there was no chance B-Man would. Q knew without a doubt that if B-Man had been in his shoes that night, Fazio would already be eulogized and buried.

"Damn, shawdy," B-Man interrupted Q's thoughts, "you been sittin' on all that shit for *two months* and ain't told me nothin'? Ain't broke bread on *nothing*? You playing the game raw, ain't you?" B-Man grabbed the dro off the cocktail table and rolled a blunt.

"I was just waiting on Khalil to get home."

"Oh, you can't trust me?" B-Man asked confrontationally, licking the sticky brown blunt as he waited to hear Q's lame reply.

"Dead that. What's done is done. Now what we gon' do?" interjected Khalil.

"Where the shit at?" asked B-Man.

"I got it put up," Q answered, short on details.

"You got all that shit at yo crib?"

"Hell naw! What, you think I'm stupid?"

"Shid, shawdy I don't know! You could've struck for major weight and all of Fazio's trap and you didn't! *That* was stupid as fuck," B-Man spoke with uncut candor.

"Neva mind where I got it stashed, nigga—that's my BI. I wasn't gon' tell yo ass *shit*. Thank Khalil for you knowing about it," Q shot back.

"See you's a selfish mafucka!" B-Man was up out of the recliner. Q stood up from the couch. They were nose to nose, like two pitbulls ready to lock jaws. B-Man pushed Q in the

chest, causing him to stumble back onto the couch, damn near in Khalil's lap.

"Back up out my grill," B-Man said.

Q bounced up on his feet like a jack-in-the-box. He charged B-Man, going for his knees. His quick rush caught B-Man off guard. Before B-Man could spread his legs and drop his weight down on Q's back to keep him from scooping him off the floor, Q had him off his feet and together they crashed down on the coffee table, splintering it into smithereens.

Khalil watched calmly as his brothers wrestled in the small living room, tearing it up. As long as they tussled, and no punches were thrown, he decided he wouldn't intervene. That had been the code right after Black Girl died and they finished raising themselves. There were times when the brothers had bumped heads. Usually it was B-Man and Q, or Khalil and B-Man after Khalil had come to Q's defense when B-Man tried to straight strong-arm their little brother.

Because of B-Man's unbridled fury and powerful punch, when they were younger Q hadn't been too quick to squabble with him. Like all bullies, B-Man thrived on shit like that. Any sign of weakness, and he was all over a nigga. But he wasn't quick to press Khalil after his big brother had split his head with a chair.

They'd fought earlier that day and B-Man was getting the best of Khalil. Later, B-Man was blowing trees, through with it. The chair came crashing down over his head with the force of a brick. B-Man still had the zipper in the back of his head as a reminder.

Khalil had put him in the hospital and then was the first to visit him. He hadn't apologized, though. He'd simply said, "Look, shawdy, I love you, bruh. That shit can't happen no more. We bonded by blood."

After that shit, Khalil, B-Man and Q made a pact not to ever do bodily harm to one another. If they were squabbling, it was cool to wrestle, but punches or anything more violated the pact, which had been sealed by, "I put it on Black Girl."

Now, as B-Man and Q tussled all over B-Man's living room, breaking lamps, furniture, nicknacks, and anything else in their path, Khalil watched closely to see if either of them would violate the pact. If a punch was thrown it would tell Khalil that the riff between his brothers was stronger than their bond.

Khalil was pleasantly surprised to see Q holding his own. He knew that until Q earned B-Man's respect, B-Man would continue stepping to him on that gorilla shit. In prison Khalil had seen many boar hog-ass niggas trying to run the boo on mafuckaz. You had to show those type of fools that you would go to war with 'em whenever, wherever.

B-Man was gaining a little advantage over Q as Khalil broke up the tussle.

"Nigga, *what!*" Q boasted. "You can't get with *this!*"

"Khalil saved ya soft ass," B-Man said, flexing pecs that bulged through the wifebeater he had on.

For the next hour the brothers said little; the three of them burned dro and chilled out, letting shit calm down. B-Man wanted a woo-woo, but didn't want to expose his indulgence. He settled for the dro, but the high was diminished in comparison to the way the woo-woos had made him feel earlier. Finally, B-Man went over to Q and held out a fist to him.

"It's all love, shawdy," he said.

"Is it?" Q asked, unsure, still he touched fists.

"To the grave, lil' bruh," B-Man swore. "For real, though, fool you shoulda wiped Fazio out!"

"Yep," agreed Khalil. "Cause now we gotta worry 'bout his connect finding out it was Q who touched him, then having the `eses knock lil' bruh's head off."

"It ain't too late," B-Man reminded them as he moved around the living room uprighting overturned furniture, examining broken lamps and other shit. "Gwen gon' cuss our ass out."

"Tell her I got her," Q said.

The brothers sat amongst the broken furniture and discussed the moves they'd make in wake of the stolen fortune Q was sitting on. Q's suggestions carried the most weight since he was the one who was holding the shit, and it was he who'd be the first to catch a hollow point if Fazio ever found out.

They decided that, for now, Fazio wouldn't get his head knocked off, but only because Q forbade it. Khalil and B-Man wanted to do him. They gave each other a conspiratorial look: *We gon' dead that nigga, Fazio, if shit gets lukewarm. Fuck waiting on it to get hot.*

The plan was Q would step up his game, requesting twenty bricks instead of the usual five or ten. In theory, this would give Q more opportunity to move some of the stolen kilos along with the new consignment.

Q would drop hints to Fazio that Khalil was plugged in with an out-of-town connect, which would justify the new shit Khalil needed, being fresh home from prison. Later, after they had stacked money other than the stolen dough, Khalil would make a decent size purchase from Fazio, further justifying his come-up.

B-Man would have to step up his hustle and keep it thorough, no excuses. He'd still scout out licks. Once Khalil built up his stable, his hos could put him up on sweet licks for B-Man to pull off. B-Man was good with all that, but he wasn't feelin' the way Q planned to split up what he'd stolen from Fazio.

"I'ma give both of y'all ten bricks apiece and fifty stacks," Q said. It was all good with Khalil, he hadn't expected his brother to split it evenly.

Crab-ass nigga! Always gotta end up wit' more than erbody else! He gon' have fifty-nine of dem things left, plus one hundred fifty stacks! Ain't dat a bitch! B-Man silently fumed. *What really* pissed him off, though, was that Q wasn't giving him all his shit at once.

"I'ma give you twenty-five stacks and two of them thangs off the jump. Then I'll give you the rest of the bricks two at a time, every month. You'll get the other twenty-five stacks in six months," Q explained.

"Nigga, you ain't gotta *ration* shit out to me! Either gimme the shit or don't!" B-Man said with disdain.

"Real talk, bruh," explained Q. "If I give you all that shit at once, you gon' ball till we *all* fall. Fuck that, I ain't getting' murked over your carelessness. End of discussion."

"*End of discussion?* Nigga, I ain't yo bitch!" B-Man huffed. Trying to squash the dissention Khalil said, "That's smart thinking, shawdy. Hit me with mine the same way. Better safe than sorry."

"Whateva," B-Man said. *If that nigga wasn't fam, I'd put my burner to his head and jack him for all that shit.*

"Don't tell that nigga Bed-Stuy shit about this. This family BI. Real talk," Q warned.

He didn't trust Bed-Stuy because he had heard that he bodied his best friend for a big eight of hard and ten stacks up in New York before moving south.

"Scary-ass nigga, I ain't gon' tell nobody shit," B-Man promised.

Bonded by Blood

Khalil was stretched out across the bed at Sinnamon's crib. After Q dropped him back off at honey's crib, Khalil had showered, changed clothes, and drove Sinnamon to work in her orange-sherbet colored Yukon. He'd let her out at the front door of Teaser's to go get those tricks money and bring it home to Daddy. Then he'd gone back to Sinnamon's townhouse to relax; it had been a helluva day.

After waking up from a short rest, Khalil checked the bedside clock! Seeing that it was half past ten p.m., he decided to call Rayne.

"Hey Baby Love. How you doing?" crooned Khalil when she answered her cell phone.

Rayne's heart fluttered inside her chest. She was so happy to hear from him she wanted to scream. Then she recalled that he had broken his promise to call her yesterday.

"Hello Khalil. I'm doing fine, and you?" Her tone hid her excitement.

"Better now that your sweet voice is in my ear. But you don't sound too happy to hear from me."

"What happened to you calling me yesterday?"

"My bad, but you know how it is . . . first day home and my brothers gave me a welcome home party and kept me tied up, then today I got caught up in some other shit," Khalil explained.

"Mmm hmmm!" replied Rayne. "The other stuff you got caught up in wouldn't be no other female's thighs would it?"

"I'm not gonna even justify that with a response," said Khalil, otherwise he would have to lie.

"I heard about the little parking lot show."

"Did you?" he laughed.

"Yep, everybody was talking about it today at work," she reported without sounding jealous.

"Let 'em talk. They don't have shit else to do. As long as *you* know I was just shining on those lames. Just like when I tongued you in the dorm before I left."

"Don't remind me! The captain called me into his office today to question me about it. Of course I denied it and acted insulted that such a rumor would be connected to me," laughed Rayne.

"That's right, Baby Love, never admit anything."

Rayne asked if he was enjoying his freedom. Khalil told her that there was nothing sweeter but the smell of her perfume.

"I'm going to have to watch you because you know exactly what to say to make me blush," she confessed.

They talked for an hour and Khalil had Rayne dreaming of blue skies and eternal sunny days when they finally ended the call.

Whew! A nigga ain't been home, but two days and already shit is about to jump off, Khalil thought as he browsed around Sinnamon's crib checking things out. *Let me see if this bitch got anything up in here that could get a nigga cased up, anything some fool might run up in here after. Cool, everything looks legit. Now I can really relax. Shit is crazy. Already got me a ho; my lil' bruh sittin' on hood riches, and Baby Love will be coming up to the city to spend a weekend with me soon.*

Mexicans were gunnin' for the Jones boys night and day. Everywhere Khalil turned Mexicans were bustin' guns at him; even brothas in the hood were trying to knock his head off and collect the blood money that Fazio had out on Khalil's head. He and B-Man had dumped on a Trans Am full of 'eses just yesterday. Q was missing, and Khalil feared that his baby bruh

might be dead. Fuck! Here come two muthafuckas with choppers . . .

The ringing of the cordless phone on the nightstand awoke Khalil from the dream just when he was about to wet some shit up. Even in his sleep he wasn't letting muthafuckas put him in no body bag.

"Hello?" he answered, glancing at the bedside clock. It was two o'clock in the morning, not yet time to pick up Sinnamon.

"Baby, uh . . . I got this guy who wants me to go home with him for the rest of the night and maybe spend tomorrow with him, too. He's a big spender, baby. What—"

"Stop!" Khalil cut her off putting his hand up as if Sinnamon could see the gesture. "What did you just call me?"

"Huh?" she asked, confused by Khalil's question.

"Did you just call me 'baby'?"

"Uh . . . yeah," she stuttered.

"Check this, and file it in your memory so you won't allow your tongue to violate again. *Baby, honey, sugah . . .* those are pet names for tricks."

"Okay, daddy," Sinnamon agreed. "I'm sorry."

"You good, shawdy. Now, how much money this nigga spending? He better be spending real good to keep you with him overnight and all day tomorrow, too."

"Yeah, daddy, his money is official, he plays for the Hawks."

"That's all good and shit, but we ain't accepting no shopping spree or VIP tickets to none of that nigga's basketball games. Make sure you let him know up front that it's gonna cost him a couple stacks."

Sinnnamon listened dutifully, muttering her understanding. Last night they had talked and she already understood what was expected of her.

"I'll see you in a day or two, daddy. Don't worry, I'ma come home with a purse full of that NBA dough," she promised.

"All right. Get that money, shawdy."

Chapter Fourteen

 pulled up in Thomasville Heights in his Ford Explorer, fresh out the shop with a new cotton-candy green paint job and brand new twenty-four inch Blades. Riding shotgun with his lil' bruh was B-Man.

Several months had passed since they'd tussled in B-Man's living room. Q had broke his brothers off as promised, plus he had upped his consignment from Fazio to twenty bricks and had been showing B-Man love. Q didn't realize it, but he'd made the wisest move of his young life when he'd changed the wrappings on the stolen bricks he'd put in the streets. He hadn't known of the small Virgin Mary stamp on the inside of the original wrappers, he'd changed them just as a precaution against the bricks being identified by the color of their wrappers. It had been four and a half months since he'd touched Fazio's stash, and he was beginning to relax.

The summer sun shined down on the SUV, accentuating the new paint job. When Q parked in front of Corlette's crib and stepped out the driver's door, he was sporting a Gucci shorts set, customized Gucci Air Force Ones, and a Gucci sunvisor turned to the back. His locks was down to his shoulders and freshly oiled—with the platinum chain and iced, saucer-sized pendant that hung down to his belly, Q was flossing like the hood celebrity he had become.

B-Man was sportin' baggy Dickie khakis, wifebeater, and a crisp pair of Forces. He left his Desert Eagle under the passenger seat of the Explorer before stepping out. Letting Q go inside to holla at Corlette, B-Man leaned against the whip, just chillin'.

"What's up, boo?" Q spoke to Corlette as he entered her apartment unit without knocking. He was paying all the bills up in that bitch, so he felt he was entitled to come through like he lived there. Corlette never tripped it; she loved Q's ass more than he seemed to appreciate.

Q flopped down on the sofa next to where Corlette sat eating hot wings and cheese French fries, watching BET videos on the flat screen. He rubbed her swollen belly, causing the baby inside to shift around. Corlette was due to drop her load in a couple of months.

"How's my baby doing?" Q inquired.

"Which one?" asked Corlette cuddling in his arms, inhaling the scent of the Gucci for Men cologne he was wearing.

Q gave her some quick tongue, then he replied, "I'm asking about both babies—you and this one, too." Patting her belly he said.

"The baby is good, me too," Corlette replied.

Q snatched a handful of her fries and stuffed them in his mouth.

"Q, you know when I have this baby we gon' have a responsibility for a lifetime," Corlette said.

"No doubt, shawdy, I'ma handle mine, don't even worry 'bout dat. No matter whatever happen between me and you I'ma always take care of my seed."

"That ain't what I'm saying, Q. Your name ringing louder than when we first hooked up. I want you to get the money and get out the game so our baby don't have to grow up without a father."

Born and bred in the hood, Corlette had seen many hustlaz and ballers living large one minute, cased-up or dead the next.

Before getting pregnant she hadn't really contemplated the many pitfalls in the game Q faced on the daily. Now that she was carrying his unborn, Corlette realized that she had to think beyond the hood glamour and material gifts she received being Q's side chic. She had to think of what was best for the baby she was about to bring into this world.

"Lil' Mama," replied Q pensively, "I know the game spares few. Many better hustlaz than me have crapped out in this shit, so I ain't tryna make it no lifetime occupation. Two or three more year's max, and I'm out the game. Just roll with a nigga while I stack a few mil tickets, okay?"

Corlette nodded her head.

"You know I'ma hold you down, nigga," she vowed.

Quiet as it was kept, Corlette was the most thorough chic Q fucked with, including wifey, Persia. Just last week Corlette had went to court and copped out to a seven year bid for the case she had caught dropping off work for Q. Shawdy had stayed down, refusing to flip on Q, even though she'd faced the possibility of being sent to prison while six months pregnant, having the baby in prison, then being separated from her newborn. An uncharacteristically, sympathetic judge had shown compassion, suspending the prison time in favor of Corlette serving fifteen years on probation. Before dismissing Corlette from her courtroom the judge had stared down and given her a stern warning.

"If you violate your probation in any way, I won't have mercy on you the next time."

Now Corlette was playing the bench as far as putting in work for Q. Her willingness to be sent to prison instead of flipping on him should've proved to Q that Corlette was a down -ass shawdy. He valued her more now than when he'd first started hittin' it. But Persia had him too sprung to fully appreciate Corlette.

"Oh, Q, guess who I saw yesterday?" Corlette said.

"Who?"

"My lil' cousin Lamar. That nigga ridin' around in a brand new Mustang, acting like he hood rich and shit. He had two lil' ashy hos wit' him. He was flashing stacks, tryna impress them."

"Oh, yeah?" Q's face was twisted.

"Uh-huh. I told him he need to pay you your money before you catch up with him and do something to his stupid ass," Corlette relayed.

"What he say?"

"He talkin' 'bout you ain't hurtin' for nothing. I told him that don't matter, pay you your money."

Q's anger swelled with each word Corlette recounted. Lamar was really testing Q's gangsta. B-Man had been urging him to ride. Now it was at that point where he was gonna go ahead and knock the lil' nigga's head off.

He gave Corlette a grip and promised to swing through later.

When Q got outside, B-Man was already inside the whip. Q got behind the wheel, noticing that his brother had the Desert Eagle in his lap, gripped like he was ready to bust off.

"What's the business, shawdy?"

"The twins just walked by, mean-mugging and shit. They went up in that apartment over there," B-Man said, pointing with the sizeable burner.

"Put that shit up!" Q said. "Nigga, you know popo be rollin' deep over here."

B-Man lowered his arm.

"I oughta wait on those pussies to come out and body both of 'em—a real twin killing," he cracked.

"Fuck them bitch ass niggas; they ain't worth the lead it'll take to body 'em, remarked Q, as he pulled away from the curb. Boc! Boc! Boc! Boc! B-Man squeezed off four shots, up in the air, when they passed by the apartment the twins had gone into. Just to let Deshawn and DeWayne know that they could get it any day of the week.

Khalil was kicked back at the apartment where Rapheal lived with his young, twenty-six year old girlfriend named Elisse. A month ago, Khalil had finally gotten B-Man to admit that he knew where Rapheal was resting his head.

Accompanied by Q, Khalil had shown up at Rapheal's door, hoping he wouldn't find their pop tore the fuck up from the ravages of crack. He'd guessed that Rapheal couldn't be doing too bad if he had a roof over his head and it wasn't a crackhouse. Rapheal had been surprised to see his sons being led into the front room by Elisse.

"What's up, pop?" Khalil had been the first to speak; his smile was genuine.

"*Goddamn!*" Rapheal exclaimed, standing up to bear hug his sons. "I been wanting to see y'all for a long time! Where B-Man?"

"He ain't wanna come," admitted Q. Keeping it real was how they were taught to be with fam.

"He still salty wit' me, huh?" asked Rapheal. "Well, anyway, it's good to see you two."

That first day they spent hours reminiscing about Black Girl and catching up on each other's lives. Rapheal didn't front he admitted that he still got high occasionally.

"I'm ready to leave it alone, though," he'd said with conviction. "It's just a matter of *doing it.*"

Since that day, a month ago, Khalil had visited his pop two or three times a week, being schooled by Rapheal on all the complexities of macking bitches. The game had changed since Rapheal's heyday, but the fundamentals of macking remained the same. Each day they spent together, riding around the city or chillin' at a Bar & Grill, where they'd go to grab a bite to eat and discuss Khalil's ambition. When they drove around the "A" with old school jams, by artists like The Isley Brothers or the OJay's, crooning in the Yukon, Rapheal recounted many of his days in the game when Atlanta's ho strolls were where his women plied their trade. He recalled his years pimping hos up and down the legendary Auburn Avenue so that Khalil could digest the morals of those stories and apply them to his game.

Rapheal told Khalil that 'cop and blow' was a given in the profession, as surely as night follows day. "Son, there's not a playa alive that has never lost a ho. That's just part of the game. So when it happens, don't lose no sleep over it. Go out and cop another one. Now ya first ho, she'll set the tone for your entire stable so work that bitch hard and never accept short trap from her," he advised. Khalil sponged up the wisdom so that he could apply it to Sinnamon.

"What about this Rayne chick you been tellin' me about? What you got planned for her?" asked Rapheal as Elisse passed through the living room, rolling her eyes.

"Man, I don't know," Khalil wavered.

"You gon' mack the bitch or what?"

"Real talk, I don't want to. Rayne is something special. I know I sound like a square but I'm just keeping it real."

"Boy, you ain't no pimp. Not when you start catchin feelings for a ho." Rapheal schooled him.

Bonded by Blood

By the time Khalil left a few hours later, he had soaked up some boss game, but he was still having trouble shaking what he felt for Rayne.

CA$H

[1124]

Chapter Fifthteen

Driving away from Raphael's apartment, Khalil wondered if he should just let Rayne go. Raphael had warned him that he was going to lose Sinnamon catching feelings for Rayne. "A ho ain't gonna sell pussy and bring you trap for you to blow it on another bitch."

Khalil understood his pop's warning but Rayne was hard to let go of. Every week on her off days she drove up to Atlanta and they spent time together, doing everything from going to the movies and visiting the Martin Luther King Jr. Center to making love out on the balcony of the penthouse apartment Khalil had recently leased. They talked about their childhoods and shared their dreams with one another.

Khalil's cell phone rang, interrupting his reverie.

"Hello."

"I'm at the apartment waitng for you and I'm in my birthday suit," said Rayne in a sultry tone. Khalil had given her a key to his crib but it had slipped his mind that she was coming today.

"I'll be there in twenty minutes," he promised.

Two days of blissful love-making, shopping sprees and dining at different upscale restaurants is how Khalil and Rayne spent the weekend. For both of them time went too fast and before they knew Monday's morning sun peeked through the venetian blinds. Rayne groaned in protest, she absolutely hated to remove herself from Khalil's embrace.

"Is it time for you to go already?" he asked, stirring awake.

"Unfortunately." She kissed him quickly and crawled out of bed.

"Hold up I need to ask you to do a favor for me," said Khalil sitting up and reaching in the drawer of the nightstand by the bed.

"I want you to give this to my nigga Onion Head." He was holding a plastic Ziplock bag containing two ounces of purp. Rayne didn't know that it was exotic but she recognized that it was weed. *Why would he compromise me like that?* She wondered. She would lose her job and more than likely be arrested if caught smuggling drugs to an inmate in prison.

Khalil correctly read Rayne's apprehension.

"Baby Love, if it wasn't important I wouldn't ask you to do it. My homie got an ass of time to serve unless he can get his conviction reversed on appeal. To even have a chance, he needs to hire a top notch lawyer to file the appeal. He'll be able to flip this purp and get himself a good attorney, so handle this for me."

"Okay, Khalil, but just this once," agreed Rayne, sympathizing with Onion Head's predicament.

"Just this once," promised Khalil. "And thank you, baby." He handed her the purp and told her to be careful.

Awhile later after Rayne had showered, she stood in the bathroom mirror, wrapped in only a towel, fussing with her long bangs. Khalil, wearing only boxers, came up behind her and wrapped his arms around her and began sucking on Rayne's collarbone. She felt his dick pressed up against her ass and it made her whole body heat up. It was pitiful, she thought, how she had become a nympho for his touch.

"Damn, I hate when you have to leave me," he whispered. His bass voice moistened her pussy.

Bonded by Blood

"I hate it, too," Rayne cooed. His tongue in her ear was sending tingles up and down her spine. His strong, masculine hands were gently rubbing her taut nipples, causing them to ache with desire.

"Umm," she moaned, dropping the towel to the floor then reaching behind her and sliding her hand inside of Khalil's boxers.

"You gon' miss me?" he whispered into the crook of her neck as Rayne stroked his engorged dick.

"Baby, you're so thick," she moaned.

Khalil's hands cupped her breast as she continued to stroke him, then slid down and traced her moist, swelling pussy lips. Rayne's knees weakened and she felt faint as Khalil lightly rubbed her clit while she caressed his huge dick head.

"K-Khalil, *please, baby*! Please don't turn me into an addict for you," she begged through her moans.

"Why not?" putting three fingers in her wet pussy, taking them out then letting her see him lick her moistness.

"Just . . . don't," she cried.

Khalil turned her around, lifted her up, and sat her on the sink's counter. Then he pulled her to the edge of the counter, leaned her back, then went down to his knees. He gently peeled back her wet folds and traced them with his tongue to spell "Baby Love" on her clit over and over again until Rayne exploded. Her honey poured down into his mouth and her breathing became irregular. When she recovered from the intense orgasm Rayne panted, "Khalil, I want you inside of me."

Khalil dropped down his silk boxers and his thick seven inches stood tall. Rayne eyed every inch appreciatively while licking her lips in anticipation.

"You like the way I spread you wide open?" asked Khalil as he slowly penetrated her tight fit.

"Ummm!" was the only reply he got. Rayne was feeling too damn good to say anything more. She wrapped her legs around his waist and pulled him real deep inside of her.

"Dayum . . . oh fuck! Baby you feel so goddamn good," exclaimed Khalil.

He struggled not to bust yet, but looking into Rayne's eyes while he grinded into her made it difficult to hold back. He tried to think about something else, which would've helped him last longer, but Rayne's hot grip held his attention and would not release it.

"Don't hold back. Give it to me. I wanna feel you come inside me," she moaned.

Khalil's nuts erupted like a volcano. He sucked on Rayne's tongue and steadied his legs.

"Khalil, I'm falling in love," admitted Rayne after hopping in and out the shower again.

"That makes two of us."

As soon as Rayne left, Khalil went over to Sinnamon's crib to check his trap.

A couple hours later his cell rang. "Khalil, I'm in jail!" Rayne sobbed into the phone as soon as he said hello.

Khalil went into another room to get some privacy away from Sinnamon. "Try to calm down, baby, and tell me what happened." His voice was full of concern.

"You know what happened!" she screamed.

"No, baby, I don't. Does it have something to do with that thing I asked you to do for my man?"

"Yes!" she cried.

"Dayum, Baby Love, I'm sorry. That bitch nigga must've dropped a dime!"

"He had to because as soon as I showed up for work, the lieutenant asked me to step into her office. When I did, she patted me down and found the stuff," explained Rayne sniffling.

"I shouldna told that nigga when you was gonna bring it, but I never thought Onion Head got down like that?"

Rayne didn't respond. She was so mad at Khalil she could kill him.

"What jail are you in, baby?" he asked.

"Mitchell County."

"Aight, I'm on my way to bond you out."

"Please hurry, Khalil. It stinks in here."

After Khalil posted bail for Rayne he waited in the jail's reception area for her to be released. An hour later she came rushing into his arms, burying her head in his chest and crying, "I'm so embarrassed!"

"It's gonna be okay," he said soothingly. "Don't worry about anything. I'm gonna take care of you. I'm gonna move you to the "A" with me. Fuck country-ass Pelham, Georgia."

Rayne offered no protest. She didn't have a job anymore and she would've been too ashamed to remain living there anyway. Her arrest at the prison had made the evening news.

"Just take me by my apartment so I can pack my clothes. I never wanna show my face down here again."

She planned to call a friend and ask if they would put her furniture in storage. At Rayne's apartment Khalil shook his head in mild amusement as she tip-toed in and out like a cat burglar.

Khalil kept his promise to take care of Rayne. He moved her in with him and introduced her to his people. The love and attention he gave, helped to ease Rayne's anger at him over what happened. Khalil spent every minute of the day for a month making it up to her until finally he had to hit the streets and get money for them to survive on.

"I can go look for a job," suggested Rayne.

"No, baby, your job is to look beautiful for me," Khalil said, punctuating it with a kiss.

"Khalil, I don't want you out there selling drugs," she would say when he'd come home with pockets full of trap money.

"I don't get down like that, Baby Love. My hustle is gambling," lied Khalil he was not ready to tell her the truth.

In just a short time Rayne learned to accept what Khalil told her he did to put food in their mouths but she still worried about something bad happening to him.

Rayne's worries heightened when a whole week passed without Khalil coming home or calling to let her know that he was okay. Crazy with worry, Rayne called Khalil's pop. *You have reached the answering service of Rapheal Jones; unfortunately I am unable to answer your call. At the sound of the beep . . . you know what to do,* the prerecorded message inpersonably told Rayne for the fifth time.

Rayne decided to call Q. She was near hysterics when he answered.

"Have you seen Khalil? This is Rayne." Worry laced her voice.

"Naw, not since last week. Why? Whud up?" Q asked.

"He hasn't been home or called in a week," Rayne cried. "I'm worried something has happened to him."

"Let me hit the streets and see if I can find out something," replied Q, concern in his tone.

Rayne called Q every hour, on the hour, for two days, but each call brought the same reply.

"No one has seen him," he told her.

When Rayne wasn't calling Q, she was calling all the local hospitals, and all the jails. She didn't know whether to be happy or more alarmed when she was told "no" by each hospital and jail she contacted.

Rayne couldn't eat or sleep. She could barely breathe; she was so worried about Khalil. All she did was cry, envisioning her boo dead somewhere in a gutter his body rotting. *Please, God! Please, let him be alive. I don't care if he's maimed, crippled or gone crazy, just let him be alive,* Rayne prayed.

When she was on the edge of insanity her prayers were answered. She heard the door unlock; in stepped Khalil. He looked as if he hadn't shaved in all the time he'd been away. His hair, usually in perfectly neat circular brush-waves, was unkept, and he had on the same clothes he'd had on the night he'd left home. In short, he looked a mess. But he was a *beautiful* sight to Rayne's sore eyes. She ran to him and hugged him so tight, had he been wearing the platinum chain he'd normally have on, Rayne's desperate hug would've surely snapped the link chain.

"Where have you been, Khalil?" I thought something bad had happened to you," cried Rayne.

Khalil disengaged himself from her arms and sat down on the couch, his head in his hands.

"What's wrong?" Rayne asked, taking his hands in hers.

For a while Khalil didn't respond, he just shook his head.

Finally he said, "I fucked up bad, baby."

He again hung his head.

Rayne kept pleading with him to explain, but all Khalil would say was, "I fucked up, baby. I fucked up bad."

"No matter how bad you messed up, Khalil, we have each other. Together we can get through anything," pledged Rayne.

Finally he said, "Can I get you to run me a bath? That might help me feel better about my predicament."

"It's not *your* predicament, Khalil, it's ours," Rayne corrected him. "Whatever it is, we're in it *together*. You stepped up to the plate for me when I got arrested and the whole deal; I'll do the same for you."

While Khalil bathed in silence, Rayne sat on the edge of the bathtub rubbing shampoo into his hair and wondering what Khalil could've possibly done so terrible. She tried to imagine the absolute worst thing he could've done. Murder? She asked herself. If so, she would remain by his side through trial, prison time, or on the run. It didn't matter, as long as they were together.

If he's been with another woman, I can forgive that. Love weathers any storm, Rayne was thinking as she helped Khalil rinse the shampoo out of his hair. *Damn, I love this man so much! I'm so happy he's home and in one piece. Anything else, anything, absolutely anything, I can deal with. I'll stand by his side . . . no matter what.*

When Khalil was finished bathing, and shampooing his hair, he asked Rayne to cook him a quick meal. Like most country girls, Rayne could get *down* in the kitchen, but Khalil didn't want her to spend a lot of time on the meal.

"Microwave something for me, Baby Love. Anything at all; I just wanna put something in my stomach."

After a quick dinner, they retired to bed. Khalil was still being unusually quiet, but Rayne didn't want to press him to talk about whatever had happened. He'll tell me what's going on when he's ready, she told herself. Wanting to help ease Khalil's mind, Rayne molded her body to his; her tiny, neatly trimmed patch of pubic hair pressed against Khalil's thigh.

Rayne's delicate hands caressed his chest then moved to his manhood, stroking.

"Not right now," Khalil rebuffed her, causing a pang of heartache to shoot through Rayne. He had never refused her before. It was so unlike him. Rayne worried that he may have lost desire for her. *Of course he still desires me,* she assured herself, *it's just that he has something on his mind.* The thought made hella sense, yet the insecurity of new love made Rayne imagine all types of reasons for Khalil's distraughtness. It was another sleepless night for her, though she thanked the angels in heaven for delivering her man home safely.

For two days Khalil sat around the apartment in silence, seemingly weighed under by his troubles. After much prodding Rayne was finally able to convince him to open up to her.

"Please talk to me. We'll handle it together," she kept promising until he gave in.

"I fucked up, baby," Khalil began. "I wanted to win enough money gambling to be able to take care of you and buy you all the fly shit you deserve. I—"

"Khalil, I don't care about the material things," interrupted Rayne. "As long as I have you, nothing else matters."

"But it matters to *me*," Khalil said with emphasis as he held his head in his hands as if the weight of the world was on his shoulders.

"I'm a street nigga," he continued. "I never had much, that's why I want so much now. I don't feel like a man if I can't give my girl the world on a silver platter."

"All you have to give me is your love."

"Nah, Baby Love. I wanna give you that and much more, and I almost had it right in my hands. I was at the skin house, tryna stack my chips, come home and dump a quarter mil in ya lap . . . show you that your man is a winner. I was only a hundred stacks short of my goal . . . then the cards turned on me," he sighed. "Over a two day period I lost everything, plus I owe a hundred fifty."

Rayne's eyes got big; she couldn't comprehend men gambling for such large sums. When she was a CO at the prison she had seen inmates "skinning", so she was familiar with the fast paced card game and its addictiveness. More than a few inmates had bottomed-out playing Georgia Skin.

"I lost everything, baby; my jewelry included. And I had to pawn the Yukon." Khalil went on, shaking his head in disbelief. "The niggas I owe the hundred fifty stacks . . . they held me hostage, threatening to kill me if someone didn't bring them the money that I owe. I called Q, but he wouldn't fuck with me."

"Why not? Has he forgotten that you went to prison for him?"

"That nigga just dirty like that."

"Well, what about B-Man or your father?" asked Rayne.

"Nah, they not caked like that."

"Baby, I have fifteen thousand dollars saved in an account, will that help?" Rayne offered.

Khalil shook his head.

"It would help, but I'm not taking your savings. I'll go out and rob a bank or body a muthafucka before I'll accept your savings. Nah, baby. I got myself in this shit. I'ma get myself out of it," he declared, getting up out of bed and going to the closet.

"No, Khalil!" Rayne shrieked when he turned around with a Glock in his hands. "What are you about to do with that?"

"Go lay some niggas down."

Rayne jumped up and threw her body in front of Khalil. He tried to push past her but she would not move out of the way to allow him to leave.

Rayne withdrew her savings and gave it all to Khalil. "They're giving me one month to come up with the rest," he said. "I still don't know how I let you talk me out of bodying those niggas."

"Please, Khalil, don't talk like that," Rayne pleaded.

They were rolling in a rental returning from the bank and Khalil was counting the $15,000 withdrawal Rayne had just made.

Later, while Khalil was out in the streets trying to get up some more cake, Rayne placed a desperate call to Q.

"Quantavious? Uh, this is Khalil's girl, Rayne."

"What it do, shawdy?"

"I'm calling to ask if you will please loan Khalil the rest of money that he owes. We have no one else to turn to."

"Hell no! I ain't loaning that nigga shit. I done broke bread with him when he first came home. He shouldna fucked that up. Them niggas can kill him for all I care!"

"How can you just turn your back on him like that? I know what Khalil did for you. You owe him!" she cried.

"Shawdy, you got it twisted. Don't nobody owe a nigga shit! Nigga gotta stand on his own two," Q replied coldheartedly.

"But he's your *freakin'* brother!" she screamed in his ear.

"So! You're his girl. You help him pay off his debt! Shid, you're the reason he went broke gambling, tryna get his bank up to take care of you. Fuck no! I'm not givin' him a damn thing."

"Wait one minute! I never asked Khalil for anything, but his heart and I've given him all of my savings to help him out of this. What else can I do?"

"Ask Khalil. He knows what you can do to help him get the money up," said Q and ended the call, leaving Rayne wondering what he was talking about.

Rayne sat quietly, with her legs folded under her on the bed next to Khalil as he counted up the money he'd been able to bum and beg off of everybody he knew. Counting over his shoulder, Rayne had totaled it up to exactly eight thousand dollars, well short of what he needed.

She knew that her man was stressing because he'd suddenly taken up the bad habit of smoking cigarettes. Rayne couldn't stand cigarette smoke. She covered her nose and mouth with a hand.

"Khalil, baby please don't smoke," she said gently from behind her hand.

Khalil took another two puffs on the Newport then smashed it out on the nightstand.

Rayne said, "Baby, if I tell you something will you promise not to be angry at me?"

"I'll try."

"I called Q today," she blurted. Khalil had told her not to call his brother begging him to do shit for him.

"You did what?"

"I was desperate, Khalil, please don't be upset," she cried, wrapping her arms around his neck.

"It's okay, Baby Love."

He kissed her tears.

"Why won't he help you?" she sobbed in frustration.

"Fuck him, Rayne. It's dog eat dog out here in these streets. A nigga can't depend on nobody, but his damn self. Even fam will sell you out. You see how Q do it."

"I'll never sell you out, baby," she sobbed into his chest.

"I know you won't, Baby Love."

"Khalil?"

"Yeah, baby?"

"What did Q mean when he said *I* can help you come up with the money?"

Khalil took a minute to contemplate her words. Finally, he told her to forget about it.

"I'm not asking you to do that."

"Do what, Khalil?"

"Let's talk about something else," he said but it was obvious to Rayne that the question bothered him.

He unwrapped their arms from around each other, stood up and went to the window to look up into the sky for a solution to his dilemma.

Rayne came up behind him and put her arms around him. Her head rested in the center of his back as she spoke.

"Baby, just tell me what it is Q was referring to. Baby, I love you. I'll do *whatever* I have to if it will help us out of this situation."

"I can't ask you to do that."

"Well, how bad can it be? I won't have to kill anyone, will I?"

"No, it's nothing like that."

Rayne breathed a sigh of relief.

"Then I'll do *anything* else," she proclaimed.

Khalil kept repeating that he couldn't ask her to put herself out there like that for him, while she kept professing her unconditional love and her willingness to do whatever it was going to take. After much prodding from Rayne, Khalil explained that he knew some major ballers who'd hit females off with stacks, jewels, and gear for "dating" them. "That's what Q was talkin' about but I'm not asking you to do that bullshit." His voice was heavy with disgust at the thought of her sleeping with other men.

"Dating them?" Rayne asked.

"All night dates," Khalil clarified. "In other words, sleeping with them."

Rayne was silent. She almost gagged at the idea of it, but she knew that she'd do anything to help him out of the predicament he was in.

After a while she asked, "Two questions, Khalil; One, will it get you out of debt if I do it? Two, will you still love me?"

He turned to look into her eyes.

"Baby Love, I'll forever love you, no matter what you do. So that's not even relative. And, yes it could pay off my debt and get us back on our feet."

"I'll do it then," she cut him off "But, Khalil, please don't stop loving me."

Tears slid down her face. Khalil pulled her into his arms. For a woman with her morals she was making the ultimate sacrifice for him.

"I love you, baby."

He kissed away her tears.

"I pray that you mean that."

"I do, baby," he swore.

Rayne asked how long she'd have to "date" these men, and how many? Khalil estimated she'd have to do it for six months. "Just a couple dates a month," he said, dropping his head in shame at having to put her out there like that.

"You'll have this girl named Sinnamon with you," he said.

"Who is she?" Rayne inquired.

"Someone I used to kick it with," he lied. "She's gonna help me out, too. Just remember it's all about you, Rayne, and you won't have to do it for long."

"Khalil, will I have to kiss these men? I can't do that. It would be too personal."

"Never, Baby Love. Save your kisses for me."

"Khalil?"

"Yeah, baby?"

"Make love to me, please," Rayne cried.

CA$H

Chapter Sixteen

B-Man was on those woo-woos hard today; he'd been blowin' 'em since rolling out of bed this morning. Gwen had woke him up with a face full of smoke. Lately, he didn't even want a blunt or joint unless it was laced with crack.

After blowing three or four woos with Gwen he left the crib, smoked another on the drive over to Bed-Stuy's crib. Then, he and Bed-Stuy got rawed and burned purp all day. With B-Man on those woos and Bed-Stuy on the raw, they both were borderline junkies.

"We gon' do this shit tonight or what, B?" Bed-Stuy asked, looking geeked.

His big, thick lips were chapped the fuck up. He looked like JJ from the old black sitcom *Good Times.*

"It's goin' down, shawdy," confirmed B-Man, locking one in the chamber of his burner.

"Q gon' lace a nigga's pockets proper for this, ain't he? I know he ya fam' but I ain't slumpin' niggas fo' sneaker money, yo."

"He gon' break bread," B-Man assured him. "Plus, I'm hoping this lil' stuntin'-ass nigga, Lamar, got some bread and some work where we touchin' him at."

"Word," cosigned Bed-Stuy.

Q had finally grown tired of Lamar shittin' on him about those twelve stacks. The fool was stuntin' all over the "A", like he was daring Q to bust his gun.

Q wasn't the violent type of drug dealer who was out to turn the city into a cowboy movie; he finessed the game. Niggaz all wanted to be *Scarface*, but how did the movie end? Q repeatedly pointed out to B-Man. Bodies brought heat and that was something a nigga didn't need.

Had Lamar stayed out of sight, he would've been out of mind. But the fool was putting his come up on display, which irked B-Man more than it did Q. *I'm my brother's keepa*, B-Man would say when Q told him not to trip Lamar.

B-Man was on some murder shit, though. Woo-woos had him crazy in the head. Tonight, he and Bed-Stuy were geeked up and ready to put in work. Bed-Stuy kept checking his cell phone to make sure that he hadn't missed Adina's call.

Adina was a shady chick from Hollywood Court whom Bed-Stuy gutted from time to time. At the moment, she was at a club on Memorial Drive where Lamar liked to hang out. Bed-Stuy had pointed Lamar out to Adina last weekend in the parking lot of the same club. He hadn't smashed Lamar that night because Q had been wavering on whether or not he wanted Lamar bodied. But, tonight it was going down.

Adina had been told to play the parking lot and to hit Bed-Stuy on the hip when she spotted Lamar. The call seemed to take hours to come through, but then Bed-Stuy's phone vibrated.

"Speak," he answered.

"He's here," said Adina.

"You sure, Ma?"

"Yep, I just got done hollering at him. He showed me the new tat on his stomach. It's nice; it says STREET SOLDIER," she blabbed on.

"Fuck all that! What that nigga rollin' in? His 5.0?"

"Uh huh."

"He dolo?"

"Yeah."

Bed-Stuy nodded to B-Man, who was sitting on an ottoman in Bed-Stuy's living room, and they both strapped up.

"Where son at now, yo?" Bed-Stuy asked Adina as B-Man followed him outside where they hopped into a plain black old school Cutlass.

"He's here in the parking lot parlayin' and shit."

"Keep your eye on that nigga, I'm on my way. I'ma keep choppin' it up with you while I drive so you can let me know if he leaves. I'll be there in fifteen minutes; don't let him out of your sight."

"I won't," promised Adina, whispering into the phone from the back seat of another niggaz whip.

"Shawdy, get off the phone and come holla at my people," a voice called from the background.

"Tell him I'll holla at him in a few," she called back.

"Who dat, Ma?" asked Bed-Stuy.

"Nobody. Just this dude from N.O. tryna get me to holla at his boy," Adina replied with a *tssk!*

"You doing it like that?"

"What you mean?"

"Hollerin' at other niggaz. I thought I had that pussy on lock?"

"You do," she giggled.

In the passenger seat of the Cutlass, B-Man sparked up a woo-woo while half-listening to his man kick the bo-bo with Adina. Him and Bed-Stuy had tag-teamed that pussy on numerous occasions so he knew his man hadn't caught feelings for the ho.

By the time B-Man finished smoking the woo-woo, they were turning into the club's parking lot. Adina described the box Chevy that she was now standing outside of. She nodded at them imperceptibly as they drove by.

"I'ma get at you tomorrow, Ma," Bed-Stuy said into the phone. "One."

It was time to put in work.

"You see his whip? It's over there where all those hos are posted up," B-Man pointed.

"Yeah, I see it," said Bed-Stuy inconspicuously parking amongst other whips a few car lengths away.

After several hours of stuntin', Lamar chose one of the thirsty females who were sweating him and mashed out. The chic was giving him slow neck as he headed down Memorial Drive to a motel. The whip was swerving like the driver was DUI.

"Stupid ass nigga gon' fuck around and get pulled over," B-Man worried as they followed Lamar at a discreet distance.

"I think shorty braining him," said Bed-Stuy. "I don't see her head."

"We bodying the ho, too?"

"You know how I rock—no witnesses."

They followed Lamar to the Motel 6 further out on Memorial Drive, where he parked and dashed inside to get a room while the chick waited in the car.

"Dayum! I was hoping he took her to his crib, I know the nigga got some chips wherever he rest at," said Bed-Stuy. A frustrated frown was etched on his face.

"It is what it is," remarked B-Man. He was ready to nod Lamar and get it over with.

"Let's go do this nigga," he said as soon as they saw Lamar come back toward his whip.

Bed-Stuy moved in sync with his man as they both slid out of the vehicle and crept up on their target, catching Lamar just as he was pulling open his car door.

"Get on in, nigga!" growled B-Man with his strap pressed against Lamar's temple. Bed-Stuy ran around to the other side of the whip and yanked open the passenger door.

"If you even let out a sound I'ma push ya wig back!" Bed-Stuy warned the chick.

He forced her into the back of the vehicle and pressed her forehead to the floor.

In the front seat, B-Man forced Lamar to do the same, then searched his waist for a strap. Not finding one, B-Man made Lamar clasp his hands together behind his back in case he had a strap stashed somewhere within arm's reach. He went inside of Lamar's pockets and removed the stacks he was carrying.

"Yeah, lil' bitch-ass nigga, you thought this shit was a game didn't you?" he taunted.

"Nah, man. I was gonna pay your brother!" cried Lamar, recognizing B-Man.

"Too late!"

The two gunshots that followed sounded like loud claps of thunder. In the back seat Bed-Stuy didn't hesitate to silence the scream that filled the car after the girl realized what had just happened to Lamar.

Boc! Boc! Boc!

Q was in bed spending the night with Corlette. He had told Persia that he had to make a run out of town with Fazio. Corlette was cuddled up under her man, sleeping contentedly. Earlier they had gone out to dinner and the movies then came back to her place and devoured each other's bodies. Q had torn that pregnant pussy up.

Corlette was in LaLa Land, dreaming about eternal bliss with her man. Q, however, could only feign sleep; he was amped because he knew what was supposed to be going down tonight. He peeked at the digital clock on the nightstand near the bed and saw that it was nearly 2:00 A.M.

He was laying there imagining all the shit that could've gone wrong. He hoped B-Man and Bed-Stuy hadn't fucked up. Just when he was about to worry himself sick, his cell phone rang. He leaned over the edge of the bed and snatched his cell phone off the floor.

"Hello."

"It's a done deal, shawdy," B-Man informed him.

Q was quiet; he was trying to picture Lamar dead. *Damn, all you had to do was pay me my dough.*

"You heard me, shawdy?"

"Yeah, I heard you," Q finally replied morosely. "I'ma get at you tomorrow."

"What time?"

"I don't know. I'll call you."

"Get at me," said B-Man.

Click.

Q pretended to still be talking, just to cover his ass with Corlette if she became suspicious of the call, after she learned of her cousin being killed.

"Man, I ain't getting out of bed with my girl just to serve you *four and a baby*. You gon' have to get at me tomorrow, I done told you that three times."

Corlette rolled over, sat up and mouthed, "Un-uh, you ain't goin' nowhere!"

"Man, my girl just laid down the law; for real, though, I'ma get at you tomorrow," he said to no one.

Q stayed in bed with Corlette a few hours longer before getting up, showering, and getting dressed. He was tryna dip before Corlette's mama woke up and put the beg to him like she always did. But luck wasn't on his side, Miss Jean, Corlette's mama, came out of her bedroom, almost bumping into Q in the hallway as he was about to bounce.

"Good morning, Quantavious."

"Good morning, Miss Jean. You looking good; how much weight have you lost?" Q replied, gassing Corlette's mom.

"Oh, I done lost a lil' bit," she smiled, sucking in her stomach. "Can you tell?"

She profiled for Q, front, back and side, knowing she hadn't lost one single pound and was just as plump as ever.

Q continued gassing her up.

"Yeah, I can see it in your face, too," he complimented her then tried to push on.

"Quantavious, can you gimme some money to go play Bingo tonight? I feel kinda lucky?" Corlette, who was handing Q his cell phone he'd forgotten said, "Mama, why you always asking him for money? I know he gets tired of everybody always tryna hit him up for something."

"Nah, it ain't no trip," Q intoned, clipping the cell phone on his waist. He pulled a couple hundred dollars off his trap and handed the money to Miss Jean.

"Thank you, baby,"

"Here you go, boo," Q said, offering Corlette some guap. "Go buy yourself something pretty."

Corlette turned down the money.

"I'm good, baby."

"You sure?"

"Uh-huh."

Corlette kissed Q goodbye.

As Q drove off he was thinking about how much Corlette was changing since getting pregnant. Before, she had always had her hand out, begging. But lately he had noticed a profound change in her; it was as if carrying his child had given her the security she'd craved; the assurance that she was more to Q than a piece of ass. Now she was no longer fixated on trying to get as much money out of him as she could.

Q was taking notice of Corlette's new and improved attitude, but right now he was more concerned with what her and her peeps attitudes would be like once they learned of Lamar's murder. He wondered if Corlette would suspect him of being involved.

When Q got home, Persia wasn't there. He assumed that she'd gone in to work at her uncle's bails and bonds company, but just to reassure himself that Persia wasn't off somewhere creeping he called her at work.

"A and A Bonding, how may I help you?"

"*I wanna make love to you all night long,*" Q whispered into the phone, disguising his voice.

"Excuse me?" replied Persia.

"*I wanna make love to you all night long,*" repeated Q.

"My man might not like that," giggled Persia, playing along.

"*Who is your man?*"

"Quantavious Jones, the same man who's trying to disguise his voice," Persia laughed.

In his natural voice, Q said, "I still meant what I said."

"We'll see when I get home," Persia challenged.

"It's on, shawdy," Q promised.

"Nigga, you'll be in the streets by the time I get off work,"

"Nah, I'ma chill wit' my boo tonight. What time you gettin' off?"

Persia told him she'd be home by eight o'clock; it wasn't even noon yet.

"Damn, your uncle gon' work you to death, ain't he?" Q quipped.

A few hours later both B-Man and Corlette were blowing up Q's cell phone. Q answered his brother's call, telling B-Man to come on over; he knew that B-Man wanted to pick up the pay for nodding Lamar.

"Don't bring ya partna with you," he reminded B-Man, who already knew that Q didn't fuck with Bed-Stuy like that.

B-Man could fuck with Bed-Stuy all he wanted to, but Q wanted no direct dealings with the nigga. He was gonna break B-Man off for slumping Lamar, and leave it up to B-Man to break bread with Bed-Stuy.

"Gimme 'bout an hour before you come through," Q told B-Man.

He needed to make a quick trip to his stash spot to pick up some work; he was going to pay B-Man with half coke, half money.

Disconnecting from his brother, Q dialed Corlette's number. She answered on the first ring.

"What's up, shawdy?"

"Can you talk?" she asked, thinking he was around Persia. Her voice was somber.

"Yeah, I can talk. What's the business? You miss me already?"

"Lamar is dead."

"Huh?" replied Q, feigning surprise.

"Somebody killed him last night."

"*Dayum!*"

There was a long silence on the phone.

Q broke the silence, "You know I was salty with Lamar 'cause he owed me money; still I hate that the lil' nigga done got himself killed."

"I told that boy a million times, somebody was gon' do something to him if he kept playing games wit' people's money," recollected Corlette. If she suspected Q it didn't show in her voice.

Q didn't know how to respond to that, guilt had his tongue in a knot. He was glad he wasn't face to face with Corlette. Finally, he offered, "I'm sorry about your lil' cuz, boo. You good? Or you need me to come through later?"

"I'm okay," Corlette said, and then began sniffing back tears.

Lamar had been tempting death for several years, running off with work different niggaz had fronted him, so his death wasn't a huge surprise. Still, he was fam'.

"He's in a better place," Q added consolingly. "Just look at it like that, shawdy."

He promised to fall through Corlette's crib later, then he said goodbye, and went to get the cocaine he had to give B-Man.

While en route to his stash spot, Q hit Khalil on the hip.

"What's up, shawdy?" Khalil answered.

"Shit," replied Q. "What you up to?"

"Taking Sinnamon to get her hair styled. Why?"

"Nothin' I was just asking. Handle ya business, pimp."

"I'ma always do that," vowed Khalil.

Q couldn't dispute it, his big bruh was macking the fuck outta Sinnamon, Baby Love, and a new hoe named Cha Cha who Khalil had just caught two weeks ago. Q had to give his brother props for pimping with the utmost finesse. Until he'd seen the stacks with his own eyes he would've never thought

pussy could clock them type of dollars. He still couldn't understand what made those dumb ho's sell pussy, strip dance, and suck dick for money, then give the money to a nigga. But he knew that their pop was schooling Khalil well and whatever game Rapheal was giving Khalil was damn sure working.

"Oh, guess who got slumped last night," said Q.

"Who?" asked Khalil.

"Remember I told you about my lil' shawdy Corlette's cousin owing me for a half brick?"

"Yeah."

"Well, somebody slumped him last night."

"Somebody?"

"It wasn't me," Q declared, laughing. "Lamar must've owed somebody else, too."

"Just don't be doing no stupid shit, shawdy," warned Khalil. "Keep your focus on the big prize."

Q was keeping the truth from Khalil because he knew that Khalil would've told him that if he was going to slump anyone it should be Fazio. Khalil had told him before that Lamar was small shit that could certainly wait, while Fazio was the most serious threat.

"I'm focused, bruh," Q assured Khalil, who was just pulling up in front of Bangin Headz beauty salon.

Khalil wasn't slow, by any means. Instinct told him that Q wasn't being straight up with him, but he'd holla at Q about that later. He damn sure wasn't discussing it over a cell phone.

"Hit me up later, shawdy. Let me run in here with Sin, I just pulled up at the beauty salon."

"I'll holla," said Q.

When Q got back home, B-Man was parked out front waiting for him.

"What it is, shawdy?" Q touched fists with B-Man as they walked toward the condo.

Inside, Q tossed B-Man the half of brick he was paying him, plus ten stacks.

"How much is this?" asked B-Man, indicating the tightly wrapped cocaine.

"Eighteen zones," said Q. "Plus ten stacks."

B-Man looked disappointed. "I was expecting at least a whole brick and twenty five stacks."

"*Nigga please!*" Q snapped. "Shid, Lamar ain't owe me but twelve stacks. What da fuck I'ma pay you twenty-five and a whole brick to slump him fo'?"

"It ain't like you can't afford it."

"Don't try to count my trap, shawdy. You be on some next shit."

"Nigga, you just stingy as fuck," B-Man said.

Q brushed off his brother's remark. "How did that shit go down last night?" he asked.

B-Man gave a blow-by-blow replay, enjoying the recounting as much as he'd enjoyed the actual hit.

"*Dayum!* Why y'all do the bitch?" Q questioned him.

"Wrong place, wrong time," replied B-Man.

When B-Man left, Q dipped over to Corlette's crib.

The vibe at Corlette's crib wasn't accusatory or distant, so Q felt at ease with that. He offered fake condolences to Corlette's mom, sounding so sincere Miss Jean cried on his shoulder.

Chapter Seventeen

"Y o, B, fuck is this?" spewed Bed-Stuy, frowning at the two thousand and five hundred dollars in his hand as if it was a food stamp card.

"That's what I said when Q handed me only five stacks. That's your half, though," contended B-Man.

Bed-Stuy sensed that B-Man wasn't playing it square with him. He peeped game because in his own sheisty heart he knew that he would pull the same stunt on B-Man if the tables were turned. They had both cuffed money from each other numerous times in the past. *I ain't gon' get mad, I'ma get even.* Bed-Stuy promised himself as he fought hard not to let his feelings show on his face.

B-Man pulled a half a brick out of a shoe bag that he was carrying and placed it on the coffee table in the living room of Bed-Stuy's apartment.

"At least he showed some love on this," said B-Man coming clean in regards to the work, which they split evenly.

The cocaine calmed Bed-Stuy some, but he was still tight about receiving only $2500. *These country niggas got me fucked up, yo!*

"Son, we gotta break bread with Adina. She put in work, too," Bed-Stuy reminded B-Man.

"Call her up. When she gets here I'll give her a stack and a zone, and we'll both give the lil' bitch some dick," suggested B-Man.

When Adina came through they broke her off as B-Man had suggested. Adina was a Reebok bitch so she was good with what they gave her.

Bed-Stuy tapped the pussy but whispered to her, "Don't let B-Man hit it, ma. I'm salty with that nigga."

"What you gon' do, lil' mama?" B-Man asked when he entered the bedroom to find Adina getting dressed after being dicked down by his partna.

"I'ma holla at y'all later," Adina said, finished dressing, then mashed out.

B-Man wasn't fooled; he knew that Bed-Stuy had blocked him. *Fuck him and that punk ho,* he silently vented.

"Shawdy, I'm 'bouta bounce; I'll get back at you later," he said to Bed-Stuy then jetted.

The hair stylists at Bangin Headz were sweating the fuck out of Khalil as he lounged in the waiting area of the beauty salon while Sinnamon got her hair done by Fila, the self-proclaimed best stylist of the bunch.

Today was the first time Khalil had accompanied Sin to the beauty salon. Khalil was stylishly casual in cream-colored Armani summer wear; his wrists were heavy with ice, diamonds in both ears. No introductions were forthcoming or necessary; Like in most salons gossip ran rampant and unmitigated at Bangin Headz. All the stylists there had heard that Sinnamon was selling pussy for a nigga.

When gossiping behind Sinnamon's back, Fila and 'em derided her for being weak and gullible, allowing a nigga to pimp her. That shit was played out, they all had agreed. None of the stylists spoke against Sinnamon for stripping and tricking, but to sell ass to support a nigga? *Ain't no freakin'*

way! Was the consensus up in the salon before the stylist laid eyes on Khalil.

Now seeing him for the first time and quickly becoming intoxicated by his swag, the opinions of Fila and 'em weren't as strongly opposed to how Khalil put it down. They were more than a little curious to know what made a nigga worth selling your pussy so that he could live the life of a balla. They guessed that Khalil must've had a sick dick game. They didn't realize that mackin' is all between the ears, not between the legs.

Khalil peeped their wide-eyed curiosity, but he had no time to appease it. He answered his vibrating BlackBerry.

"What's good, baby doll?"

"Hi, daddy," replied Cha Cha a thick, ghetto booty redbone he had bagged a month ago.

"Where you at?" he inquired because last they spoke she was going on an all-nighter with a balla she had cut into at the ESPN Zone bar in Buckhead.

"I'm on I-285; headed to Riverdale. I just left ol' boys spot. Is Rayne expecting, me?"

"Don't question me, girl," he lightly scolded. "I told you I would handle it, and I will. The question is did that nigga break bread?"

"I was only able to get a stack out of him, daddy. He's tight with his trap."

"A stack? Ho, either you're tryna play *me*, or you let that nigga play *you*! Either way, it ain't happenin'—you hear me? What did I tell you to get for an all-nighter?"

"Nothing less than three."

"Well, ho you better turn that whip around and go get my other two! And don't bring yo dumb ass nowhere around me until you have my trap right!" Khalil gritted and pressed the END button.

When he looked up he realized that he had an audience. He glanced at his bejeweled Jacob and quipped, "Pimpin' ain't easy."

"I'll always make it easy for you, daddy," chimed Sinnamon.

"I know you will, baby," he replied, taking a seat to wait for her to get her hair done.

Khalil closed his eyes in deep thought. If every ho in his stable was cut from the same cloth as Sinnamon, pimpin' would be as easy as toasting bread. That wasn't the case, though. So the game was as complicated as the evolution of man.

Khalil was doing the damn thing, putting the "P" back in pimping. A couple of months ago he was checking out different strip clubs, trying see if he could come up with a new addition to his stable. These days it was rare to find a girl in the strip clubs who was being "managed" by a pimp. Most strippers were in the clubs on their own. Their men were usually dopeboys who were like rest havens for a ho. But a few girls in the clubs were the property of macks.

One of the bouncers at the Blue Flame, a cat Khalil knew from the joint, put Khalil on Cha Cha. He told Khalil that Cha Cha's man was a pimp named Roco a big, brolic nigga from over the old Eastlake Meadows way.

"What's up with the ho?" Khalil had inquired, watching her shake her phat ass on stage.

"The bitch a million-dollar ho, homeboy," said the bouncer. "And she ain't happy with that nigga she wit'."

"Why she with him then?"

"Cause she scared to leave him. He's one of them gorilla pimps. Niggas wanna fuck wit' Cha Cha, but they fear Roco."

"The nigga a killa or somethin'?" asked Khalil.

"They say he'll go *all out* about that ho."

Any nigga could see that Cha Cha was a potential gold mine. She was a tall mocha-skinned stallion, the type of phat ass and build that Dirty South tricks loved. The girl had a cute face, too. So with the right nigga macking her, Cha Cha could definitely get paid. The only drawback was trying to bag her without having to slump Roco, or without him slumping you. Khalil wasn't pussy, but there were too many hos choosing him for him to have to go through that. Rapheal told him, "You gotta be willing to kill to protect *your* women, but you don't ever wanna kill a nigga about his. The game is finesse, baby."

Cha Cha approached Khalil one night at the club.

"I hear you know how to treat your ladies," she began.

"Well, hi to you, too," Khalil smiled.

"Hi, Khalil," she retracked. "They call me Cha Cha."

Khalil nodded.

"Girl, I know who you are. I would have to be blind *not* to. You're the finest thing up in here, and I been checking you out for weeks."

"I've been checking you out, too."

"Now why would you be checking me out?" he asked with a wink. "Other than the fact that my swag is way up there. What? You looking to make some changes in your life?"

"Maybe," Cha Cha admitted.

"Now I have the answer to a question that's had me puzzled since I first laid eyes on you," said Khalil, throwing her off balance.

"Huh?"

"Nah, see, I've been wondering why a boss bitch like yourself ain't already got the world at her feet. At first I figured it had to be bad *management*. No disrespect to Roco, but sometimes a nigga is simply out of his element. I still believe that's part of it. But now I see that the other thing that's holding you back is *indecisiveness*. You know how it is in these streets, baby. You hesitate and you miss out on your blessings."

"Is that right?" Cha Cha tested him.

"Rule number one, baby girl: never hesitate. Me? I came home from the joint and hit the ground running full speed. I just needed me some thorough hos to help me exploit these tricks. My stable is real small right now, but it's solid. If you wanna make some changes in your life, I would love to have you in *mine*. You're a top-notch ho, no doubt. And I'm a top-notch nigga. What gon' stop us if we hook up? We can play these streets and these trick-ass niggas for a couple of years. Then we can ride off into the sunset—you and me. 'Cause that's what it's all about, baby girl. In the end, I wouldn't just wanna end up with the riches. I'd wanna end up with you, too."

"Do you tell all your ladies that?" Cha Cha asked.

"Of course," admitted Khalil. "But I only mean it to the thoroughest one. Can you be the best? If so, *you're* the one I'm being honest with."

Cha Cha indeed envisioned herself as the best ho to ever put on a thong. She also envisioned how much sweeter life would be if she had a man who had a goddamn plan; one who'd stack their chips and plan for tomorrow. She desperately wanted to make changes in her life, but she was deathly afraid of Roco. He had made it clear to her that he'd see her dead before he'd see her with another nigga.

"When you're no longer so indecisive, baby girl, I'd love to have you as mine," Khalil told her.

Some hatin' ass bitch told Roco that Cha Cha had spent more than an hour kicking it with Khalil. Roco beat her so bad

she couldn't work for a week. When she was able to return to work, her mind was already made up, she wasn't returning to Roco.

Khalil told her, "I'ma keep the nigga off ya ass, as long as you keep him off your mind."

"He ain't on my mind, daddy," Cha Cha promised that first night as they left The Blue Flame together.

The next day Khalil had Cha Cha to call Roco up and tell him that shit had changed. That was the code of the game. If you're thorough enough to take a nigga's ho, you had to be thorough enough to tell him. That way he wouldn't waste time looking for the ho. Time is money.

Also, once you took a nigga's ho, and had paid him the courtesy call, you then had to be thorough enough to face the nigga, which was inevitable. Khalil had faced Roco, flanked by B-Man and Q. The nigga saw that Khalil was 'bout his business, ready to bust his guns if need be. Roco could punk a ho, or a weak ass nigga, but he peeped that Khalil was of a different breed. The night they bumped heads at the club, Roco folded like a lawn chair.

Cha Cha became Khalil's third ho; he let her crib with Sinnamon at first, so that his top money maker could hip shawdy to the way shit was done in their "family." Now, he was changing arrangements for Cha Cha to move in with Rayne for two months.

Shit was going lovely for Khalil. Shortly after Cha Cha hooked up with the family he had pulled a snow, a white girl named Emily. That gave him four prize hos in his stable. They each had a four thousand-dollar a week quota to fill, and Khalil took no shorts.

After leaving the beauty salon Khalil and Sinnamon went shopping. He bought her gifts reflective of her title in his stable. When he suggested that she take the night off, Sinnamon replied, "If it's okay with you, daddy, I'ma go to work. I'll rest when we accomplish our goals." Khalil had sold her that pie-in-the-sky dream, too.

Sinnamon was dumb, but she wasn't plumb dumb. She knew that Khalil had spat the same game to his other women. He professed to love Rayne and 'em just as he professed to love her. And she was sure that the others believed, just as she did, that at the end of the day it would be them walking down that aisle, in a beautiful wedding gown on Khalil's arm. But she was his top ho, the one who never failed to fulfill her weekly four thousand dollar quota *and* more. If an all-nighter was supposed to bring in three stacks, she got at least four out of the trick, knowing that she earned extra points with Khalil by bringing home extra dough. Every week Sinnamon made sure she out-hustled her wife-in-laws. Largely due to the money she brought home, Khalil had been able to order a customized Humvee that was due to be picked up in a week.

After dropping Sinnamon off at work Khalil whipped out to Riverdale to spend some time with Rayne, whom he'd given the night off. It was a Tuesday night, one of the slowest nights of the week at the club, so Rayne wasn't missing out on many dollars. Tonight, she was in sexy lingerie cuddled up in bed with Khalil. Such moments made everything else bearable to her.

"Do you love me?" Khalil whispered in her ear, while easing a hand under the sheer nightie she was wearing and caressing a nipple.

"More than life itself," Rayne moaned. Khalil's gentle touch always sent tingles through her body, heating up her pussy instantly.

"For always?"

He sucked her nipple as his hand moved slowly down her smooth body to the center of her growing moistness.

"For . . . eternity . . . daddy."

He lightly traced the soft, wet lips of her pussy, feeling sticky deliciousness of her passion on his long, gentle fingers. As Rayne's breathing announced her desire, Khalil eased a finger into her steaming valley, while his tongue danced around her nipples. His finger found her clitoris, and gently he rubbed the center of her, causing her thighs to quiver.

"Kiss . . . me . . . daddy," she moaned, needing to taste his tongue deep inside her mouth.

Giving her what she wanted, Khalil traced her sensuous lips with his tongue, which she desperately craved to taste. Rayne loved deep kissing Khalil; it was the one thing she associated with sacredness between the two of them; she never kissed the tricks.

Rayne sucked her man's tongue as she climaxed from the manipulations of his fingers. Khalil let her ride out the pleasure, then he removed her teddy and eased her down on top of the silk sheets, all the while looking deep into her light-brown eyes. He stared down at her and drank in her total nakedness. He understood why niggas spent their hard-earned or hustled money to sleep with her.

Khalil removed his Coogi robe, tossing it across the headboard. Now it was time for Rayne to drink up his nakedness. Involuntarily her tongue ran across her lips in anticipation. Though they'd seen and shared each other's bodies many times, they were both always impressed by what the other possessed.

Shawdy fine as hell. No wonder them trick niggaz be fiendin' for her. Khalil was thinking.

Damn, this nigga make me wanna eat him up, thought Rayne, running her hands across his muscular chest and well defined six pack.

Just for a brief second Khalil felt a twinge of remorse at having turned the sweet, naïve, country girl out. Here she was wifey material and he had her stripping and tricking. He could not envision keeping her in the life too much longer. He just needed to get his bank proper and figure out something else to do for a living, with Rayne by his side.

Quickly his thoughts went back to the task at hand. He knew that the first orgasm he gave her had left her aching to feel him deep and hard inside her honey walls. She was a junkie for his dick. He teasingly kissed her body, from head to toe, spending more time on those spots that drove her crazy with desire. By the time he kissed her neatly trimmed vulva, Rayne was crying out, *"Please, Khalil. Don't...tease...me!"*

When he sucked her throbbing clit, Rayne knew that heaven *had to be* here on earth. Khalil took her to her peak, then a little bit higher, again and again. Finally, she cried, "Ahhh...ahh...oh...god...damn! Here...it...comes, daddy!"

The intense orgasm left Rayne as limp as a rag doll. Khalil let her rest in his arms for a while then began kissing her breasts again. The fuck if he wasn't driving her out of her mind! Now she was dying to feel his dick deep inside of her, filling her up as it always did. She coaxed him on top of her after he'd slid a condom over his hardness, then guided him into her sweet center, wrapping her legs around his waist and kissing him deep.

An hour later they were still at it. Finally, Khalil released his ecstasy. Rayne had wanted to feel her man's hot seeds splashing up inside of her, but Khalil didn't roll like that. He always wrapped it up, and he vehemently demanded that his hoes require their tricks to do the same. He'd be damned if AIDS was gonna blow his spot up.

After pleasing Rayne, Khalil sat on the edge of the bed feeding her grapes.

A short while later, after they had showered together and were back in bed, chillin Khalil said, "Baby Love, there's this chick named Cha Cha who's been putting in work for me. You know, adding to the stash I'ma need to do all the things I got planned for me and you. Anyway, I was letting her stay with Sinnamon, but I need to move her in with us. I need you to keep an eye on her and make sure she don't play games with *our* guap."

"Move her in with us? Here with me and you?" Rayne asked, alarmed.

"Yeah, baby girl."

"I don't think I'm going to like that, Khalil. Why do you need her?"

"Because, baby I got big dreams. Me and you going into some legit business. I'm talking real estate and chain stores. But first we gotta hustle up enough cake to get started. At the rate shit is going—with just you, Sinnamon and Emily—we'll be *forever* tryna get start-up money. Most of the money coming in is going toward paying off that gambling debt. I still ain't cleared that all the way up, yet."

In a moment of contemplation Rayne asked, "Don't you think we're going about this the wrong way? What pleasure will we be able to take from life if we gotta sell our souls in order to achieve our dreams?"

"Rayne, don't be so naïve, girl. The end *justifies the means.* Fuck what you heard, baby. If we get to the top, ain't nobody gonna care how we got there."

"But Khalil—"

"No 'buts', he cut her off. "Either you with me or not. Do you believe in me?" he held her hands in his and looked into her eyes.

"Yes."

"Now that's my Baby Love," smiled Khalil. "See, I can't make it if you don't believe in me. Baby, I can be happy hustling in these streets. But I know it's your wish for us to be legit. So I wanna make that happen. Just hold me down."

A moment of silence passed, then Rayne asked, "How many, Khalil?"

"Come again?" he replied.

"How many women will you have to use this way for us to get what you're after?"

"As many as it takes. 'Cause it's all about *you and me*, baby. You think I like having you strip? You think I enjoy having you lay with other niggaz?"

"I hope not."

"I don't, shawdy. That's why I'm recruiting other girls to put in work. I wanna get my baby out of the business as soon as I can."

"Two questions, Khalil. One, will you have to sleep with Cha Cha when she moves in with me? Two, did you have this whole, uh...lifestyle, uh...planned before you left prison? Give me honest answers, Khalil."

Khalil admitted that he would have to sex Cha Cha occasionally; otherwise he'd have a hard time keeping her.

"She's important to what we're tryna do, baby. But me fucking her is nothing but business. You're the only one I make *love* to—so don't trip the small shit."

Does he tell Cha Cha and them the same thing? Wondered Rayne. But she didn't voice her thoughts; she had decided to roll with Khalil for better or for worse. Though, an inner voice was warning her that she was being gamed.

Khalil said, "As to your second question—see, I'm not even gonna respond to that. If you think I planned all this while locked up, then you don't trust in me like you claim."

"I trust you, Khalil," Rayne backed down.

Two days passed before Khalil heard from Cha Cha; he'd begun to wonder if the ho hadn't gone back to Roco, a nigga who accepted whatever coins she brought home. Khalil wasn't built like that, he'd rather have no hoes at all than let one reduce him to chili pimpin'.

Khalil was having lunch alone at *Justin's* when his Blackberry chirped, displaying Cha Cha's number.

"Hi, daddy," she said when he answered his phone.

"What's crackin'?"

"Can I come home?"

"You got my trap proper?"

"*Proper* and then some."

"C'mon home to daddy, then. I'll meet you at the spot in Riverdale. You remember the apartment number don't you?"

"Yeah, daddy."

Khalil was already there when Cha Cha arrived. He helped her bring her things inside then introduced her to Rayne. The two spoke, then Cha Cha handed Khalil five stacks and an iced-out platinum Rolex.

"Is this watch *hot*?" he asked, inspecting the piece.

"No, daddy. I know better than to bring my man some stolen jewels without putting you up on it."

Cha Cha had spent the past two days with a rich lawyer down in Miami. The lawyer was a well-known criminal defense attorney, with high-end clients all throughout the South and Southeast. She'd represented some of Miami's biggest drug kingpins, and she was paid out the ass.

Eva Padevoni was one of Florida's most-esteemed in her profession. She was of Italian and Spanish descent, married, with two adult children. Her husband was a judge, who didn't know that Eva was a closet lesbian. Cha Cha had met her while in Florida several months ago. They had exchanged numbers and calls a few times, but their schedules hadn't allowed them to hook up until two days ago.

Eva paid for Cha Cha's round trip airline tickets to MIA, put her up in a suite at the Inter-Continental Hotel, in Coconut Grove, and spent two whole days sucking Cha Cha's chocolate pussy, pampering her, and buying her things. Cha Cha had explained to Eva that she was in desperate need of five thousand dollars. No sooner had she asked she was given the money.

In addition to the five thousand dollars and the clothes the attorney bought her, the Rolex had been a bonus.

"Something to hold on to for hard times," Eva said when presenting Cha Cha with the man's timepiece. "It was given to me by one of my clients, who's on trial for trafficking two hundred kilos of cocaine. He had to use the watch as a part of his retainer because he's short of money. The government seized over five million dollars worth of his assets in Fort Lauderdale."

Cha Cha smiled as she explained all this to Khalil, who was appraising the Rolex.

"Did I do good, daddy?"

"Yeah, baby girl, you did *hella* good," Khalil pulled her into his arms and kissed her.

Rayne fought back the urge to snatch Cha Cha's expensive weave out! *Kissing*, she thought, was supposed to be sacred between her and Khalil. If her eyes had been knives, two blades would've been sticking out of Cha Cha's fuckin' back! The bitch hadn't been there a hot twenty minutes and Rayne already wanted her gone.

Cha Cha wasn't being catty when she asked Khalil in an impish tone, "Since I did so good, daddy will you make love to me?" Cha Cha asked Khalil.

Rayne wanted to slit her throat.

"*Pleeeze*, daddy? After two days of strictly tongue, I need some dick, and not no trick dick," Cha Cha added with a laugh.

"I might hook you up a little somethin' somethin'," Khalil said. "Rayne, baby, go tidy up the bedroom while I give Cha Cha a bath."

Releasing Cha Cha from his embrace Khalil peeped the intensity of Rayne's gaze and noted it as something he'd have to keep an eye on. *She'll get used to it*, though, he was convinced.

The following day Khalil dipped by his pop's crib. Rapheal was just chillin' at the crib with Elisse.

"What it do, pop?" Khalil spoke as Rapheal let him in. "Hi, Elisse, Rapheal treating you okay?"

Elisse replied, "He's treating me *superfantastic!*" she beamed, looking like Fantasia, thick, juicy lips and all. Elisse loved her some Rapheal, and now that he hadn't smoked crack in more than a month Rapheal was regaining his swag. Q had begun fronting Rapheal, a brick at a time, and so far Rapheal was keeping his business square.

Khalil had worried that their pops might have a "slip up", selling the same drug that had been his downfall before. "Why not dust off ya pimp game and get back that way?" Khalil had suggested.

"Nah, that's over with for me. You gotta love it to live it; I pass you the torch."

Khalil was taking the torch and running with it, tryna reach the pimp's Hall of Fame.

As for Rapheal, he was doing alright. He didn't sell crack, he only sold powder. Mostly to old heads that he knew from back in his heyday. He didn't fuck with young jitterbugs, they had no respect for the game.

Khalil surprised Rapheal with the iced-out Rolex he'd gotten from Cha Cha yesterday.

"You're blingin'," Elisse teased Rapheal.

"Go on, girl!" Rapheal busted a smile.

"Yo, pop, I gotta bounce, man. I gotta check on Emily, my lil' snowbird. I just stopped by to drop that Rolex on you, nigga. You straight on everything else?"

"Yeah, I'm good. I hooked up with Quantavious earlier. You good?" inquired Rapheal.

"Pimpin' hard pop, pimpin' hard."

"Remember if you ain't gon' play to win, don't play at all," Rapheal reminded him. "The world is yours, make them hos bow down to dat."

"Nothing less, pops."

They touched fists and Khalil left to go check on his snow bunny.

Emily was a tall, blonde haired, blue-eyed white girl Khalil had picked up one day at Lennox Mall—picked the ho up and

added to his stable just like he'd pick up new gear for his wardrobe.

Khalil had taken Sinnamon and Rayne to Lennox Mall, rewarding them with a shopping spree to break the dull monotony of work, work, and work.

Emily saw the handsome black dude with two dimes on his arm, in the Gucci store, and figured he had to be an entertainer or a ball player; she had seen dozens as a flight attendant for Delta Airlines. Through eye contact she made it known that she was interested in him. Khalil flashed her a smile that said, *I don't discriminate.*

Emily didn't snag herself a rich entertainer or star athlete, instead she got snagged by a nigga that was out to pimp or die. In a matter of weeks Emily belonged to Khalil's stable. However, he made a concession for her; she would not have to become a stripper. Emily's job as a flight attendant served up plenty enough tricks for her to fulfill her weekly quota. The Maria Sharapova look alike, with the Angelina Jolie sex appeal, was already tricking with airline pilots and wealthy businessmen who frequently flew Delta.

"Hi, daddy!" Emily beamed pearly whites. "I missed you so much." She cooed, letting Khalil in her crib.

"I missed you, too, baby," said Khalil, "You got my trap proper?"

"Yes, daddy, always. I'm a good ho," she replied.

"Indeed you are" he agreed. And later when he counted the trap money and saw that it
was a stack more than quota, he promised, "Daddy is gonna give you a little treat." He scooped her up in his arms and carried her to the bedroom where he put an exclamation point on his mack game.

CA$H

Chapter Eighteen

Summer swung into fall, but the temperature in the "A" remained sweltering. Though it was deep into September it was almost ninety-five degrees outside. In the hoods, people were hanging out, doing what they do in the Dirty South, damn the heat.

Q and Khalil were steadily tryna master their respective hustles, while B-Man, was tryna hide his increasing drug habit from his brothers. The woo-woos, along with his envious heart, laziness, and foolishness with his chips was beginning to bring B-Man down.

Khalil's stable was still at four. But Sinnamon, Rayne, Cha Cha and Emily were official moneymakers, more guaranteed than government insured bonds. Had Khalil been a thirsty or impatient nigga he could've been added more hoes to his stable. Khalil was careful and particular about the additions to his family. One bad apple could spoil the whole bunch. Life was too sweet to fuck up with a false move.

Khalil had already got off of the ten bricks Q had blessed him with, and then stepped away from dealing drugs. If a nigga had to push dope to supplement his pimp money, that meant he wasn't pimpin' hard enough. *I'ma leave the dope game to baby bruh,* he wisely decided.

As for Q, he was doing it large now. He had locked down the Thomasville Heights and Moreland Avenue areas. And he hadn't had to beef with these niggaz to accomplish it. He had simply served weight to niggaz at a sweet price, sacrificing some profit to win their business from other dealers. He'd earned a rep for being reliable and trustworthy—his product was always on time and on point.

Life is lovely, Q was thinking as he whipped through Thomasville Heights bumpin' Young Jeezy in his Explorer. Niggaz were outside, in the projects, on every block. They tried to flag Q down when they spotted his gleaming whip pass by, but he just honked his horn, threw up the deuce from behind tinted bubble-windows, and mashed on. He had love for his homies, but too many of 'em had shitted on him when he'd gave 'em a chance. Fuck tryna help a man that won't help himself. Q was taking prison chances er'day; his homies needed to get their own hustles and quit tryna eat off of him.

When Q pulled up in front of Corlette's crib, lil' kids bum-rushed his whip as if he was Santa Claus. They all knew they could hit Q up for ice cream and candy money; the bigger kids might even walk away with a dub.

"Calm down," Q said, smiling down at the little hardheads. "Get in line, I'ma give all y'all some money."

The dozen or so kids jumped up and down with excitement.

"Vashon, why you cutting line? Go to the back or I ain't giving you nothing," Q lightly scolded a twelve year old.

"Gimme some sugah, Dayja," he said to a cute six year old girl who lived two doors down.

Dayja kissed Q's cheek, then she skipped off clutching the ten-dollar bill he gave her.

Q passed out ten-dollar bills to eight other children, and then gave five older kids a twenty a piece. When Vashon was the only one left in line Q slid him a hundred dollars.

"Make sure you buy some groceries for you and your little sister," he said.

Bonded by Blood

Q knew that Vashon's Ma Dukes was strung out on crack and neglected her children; it was a wonder nobody had called DFACS on her.

"Y'all got school clothes?"

"Nope," Vashon answered honestly, "Fuck school anyway."

Q rubbed the top of the boy's head and laughed. " I'ma have Corlette take you and your sister shopping for school clothes," he promised.

Q went inside Corlette's apartment and found her feeding their month and a half old daughter, Alize, milk from a bottle.

When Q had suggested "Alize" as the name for their baby, at first Corlette wasn't having it.

"You ain't naming our daughter no ghetto name like dat!" she had scoffed.

"Why not, shawdy?"

"Cause it's *tacky*."

"No, it ain't. I was on dat Alize the night I pumped you up," Q had revealed. So Corlette had conceded.

Q bent over Corlette and kissed Alize's little cheeks. "Oh, before I forget," Q said, "I want you to take Vashon and little Val shopping for school clothes."

"Huh? Vashon's little bad ass ain't gonna go to school."

"It don't matter just take them shopping, those kids ain't got shit. You know their mama is a clucker," said Q.

"Okay when you want me to take 'em?" asked Corlette.

"ASAP."

Q gave her a stack and a half. "Buy 'em name brand shit. And tear the tags off the clothes before you let 'em take 'em home—Gloria might try to take the clothes back to the store and exchange them for money."

Corlette wiped away a tear that she hadn't felt coming until it was already wet on her butter-colored skin. Motherhood was softening her emotions. It touched her to see Q do things for others, just from the heart. It proved to Corlette that her baby's daddy was worth the infinite love that she had for him.

"They was shooting over here last night," said Corlette.

"Who was shootin'?"

"I don't know; I didn't look outside, but I heard 'em."

"I'ma move you away from here," he said.

"When?" asked Corlette, hoping that she didn't sound conniving.

Q promised her that it wouldn't be long.

A few minutes later Q's cell phone rang. "S'up?"

"I'm ready," Fazio informed him.

"Gimme about an hour," Q said.

Q kissed Corlette and the baby good-bye, and headed outside to his whip. When he got to the crib Persia wasn't there. Q knew that she didn't have to work today, so he wondered where the fuck she was at. *She betta not be nowhere creepin'!* He thought to himself. Lately, she stayed gone some muthafuckin' place or the other. He was gonna have to lock that ass down, 'cause she was indeed a slick bitch.

Right now, he didn't have time to call around and hunt Persia down. He'd called her on her cell phone, but apparently it was off, or she was ignoring his call. *Fuck it! I'll check her ass when I get back tonight*, he told himself.

Q heard the car horn. He looked out the window and saw that it was one of Fazio's people. Q grabbed a backpack from the bedroom closet and carried it with him outside.

"Sup," Q spoke, sliding into the backseat of the nondescript four door Buick. Up front was Jimmy, Fazio's nephew and Hector, one of Fazio's boys. Hector was behind the wheel.

"You got the money?" asked Jimmy.

"Yeah, it's all here," Q said, holding the backpack up.

When Hector pulled off Q asked, "Sup, amigo?"

Usually Fazio's people made the exchange right there in the parking lot. Obviously, something had changed.

"Sup, amigo?" Q asked a little louder while trying not to act alarmed.

Hector pretended like he didn't understand English all of a sudden.

Jimmy explained, "My uncle told us to pick you up and bring you to him."

His tone sounded ominous.

"*Bring me to him?* What da fuck going on?"

"I don't know, folks," replied Jimmy.

Hector said nothing.

The ride out to Fazio's mansion was heavy with silence. Q had no idea what Jimmy and Hector were thinking. *Damn, I ain't got my strap with me, and these muthafuckas acting all funny style and shit. Like I'm in a world of trouble with Fazio. Which can only mean one thing!*

I oughta jump out this muthafucka.

But they were already on the interstate; if he jumped out of the car now he was sure to be ran over and killed by trailing motorists.

Fuck it, I'ma let the situation play itself out. If Fazio has found out I clipped his stash I'd already be stomped. Then, too, if he was sending the Grim Reaper at me, that fool-ass Mexican, Maldanado, would be in the front seat, I'm sure. Q was thinking all the way out to Fazio's crib.

"Have a seat," Fazio said.

Q had just been escorted into the large den. He sat with the backpack of money between his feet.

Fazio sat next to Q on the half-oval sofa made of soft butter leather. Maldenado sat on one of the long sofas; Hector took a seat at the other end, while Jimmy sat down in an end chair. Four other `eses and two other Blacks stood around the room. Nobody's visage was friendly.

I'm going to die! Q was thinking.

"Several months ago I was robbed," began Fazio. "The details don't matter. I know that the snake who set the robbery up is here in this room tonight."

He looked at Maldenado, then to Q, his eyes fierce and piercing.

Q felt a sudden urge to swallow and avert his eyes away from Fazio's penetrating stare, but he didn't dare. He just maintained his game face.

"I believe I know who the guilty one is," Fazio continued. The even keel of his voice was more intimidating than had he been shouting. He stood up from the couch and nodded imperceptibly to Jimmy.

Jimmy left the den.

Minutes later Jimmy returned holding a sawed-off shotgun, which he promptly handed to Fazio.

Fazio cocked open the shotgun and loaded both barrel with double-aught shells. When he snapped the weapon closed, the sound itself would've caused Q to jump had he not been willing himself to remain still and expressionless.

As Fazio paced back and forth, from one end of the long sofa to the other, saying nothing, Q was feeling his underarms begin to perspire. Suddenly Fazio stopped at one end of the half-oval sofa, where Hector sat, leveled the shotgun at the Mexican and pulled the trigger.

Kaboom!

Bonded by Blood

The unexpected blast caught Hector square in the chest, lifting him up and nearly flipping him over the back of the sofa. Blood sprayed all over the place.

Kaboom!

The second blast decapitated Hector.

Fazio said, "I never really trusted that muthafucka."

He handed the shotgun back to Jimmy.

"We just found out Hector stole from my associates in Mexico a few years ago when he worked for them."

The den was as quiet as a library after business hours.

"It took a few years for Hector's thievery to be discovered, but as you all can see," Fazio waved his hand over Hector's mutilated body. "Once his guilt was established, punishment was swift and merciless. The same fate awaits whichever of you stole my shit."

Fazio looked from one face to the other. "Return all the stolen cocaine and money to me. I don't care how you get it to me, or who you get to deliver it—I won't harm them. But as soon as you return my shit, you better get out of town, and never come back. If you do it that way, I give you my word I won't come looking for you. But if you make me have to sniff out which one of you robbed me, you get what Hector got."

Q wasn't a *damn fool*. There was no way he was buying that bullshit Fazio was tryna sell. He concluded that Fazio didn't really know which one of them had robbed him; tonight's brutal display was an attempt to scare whomever had robbed him into returning the stolen loot.

Jimmy drove Q back to his condo. During the drive he informed Q that Fazio planned to have them all polygraphed, but Jimmy did not say when the tests would be administered. Jimmy liked Q, and he didn't believe that Q was the culprit.

"Be easy, dawg," said Jimmy as he let Q out at his front door.

Q had smoked five Newport's to calm his nerves. When his heart rate returned to normal he realized that wifey still hadn't come home. *Where the fuck she at?* He wondered. He didn't need Persia stressing him out, not with the stress he was already under.

Chapter Nineteen

Persia and B-Man were at the hotel. Yesterday he had called her up and dropped dime on Q about Corlette and the new baby.

"The nigga over there right now if you don't believe me?" he snitched.

Persia had gotten out of bed to go see for herself. When she drove past the apartments where B-Man said Q would be and saw his car parked outside, that was all the confirmation she needed. He had told her that him and Khalil was going out of town on business. PAYBACK IS HOW I GET DOWN, she'd said to herself as she drove away steaming. And today she was paying him back in the worst way! She smiled with no regret as she felt B-Man slide out of bed.

He went in the bathroom, locked the door, and lit a woo-woo. The sensation was unbelievable. He closed his eyes and thought about how good sex was with Persia. She had that wet wet. A soft rap on the bathroom door interrupted his pleasurable thoughts.

"Hurry up, B-Man. I gotta pee!" Yelled out Persia.

He put out the woo and let her in. She nudged him out of the bathroom and closed the door. She wrinkled up her nose as the lingering scent from the woo-woo assaulted her nostrils when she sat down on the commode.

"Damn, nigga, what were you smoking in there?" Persia asked B-Man when she came back into the room.

"Some new weed, from the Bahamas," lied B-Man.

"It smells like *crack*."

B-Man didn't respond. He was admiring Persia's body; she was so damn fine. Sitting on the edge of the bed, he pulled Persia to him. He took her by the hips, pulled her closer, and ran his tongue up the length of her slit. Persia's knees wobbled but her pleasure was interrupted by Q's ringtone.

"Damn, yo pussy taste good," he mumbled.

Persia's knees had just stopped wobbling when her cell phone rang. She retrieved the phone from inside her purse and sat down on the bed, pulling the bed sheet over her nakedness.

"Hello."

"Where da fuck you at?"

"Don't you wanna know?" she responded sarcastically.

"What da fuck that's supposed to mean?"

"Ask your bitch!"

"What?"

"You heard me, nigga! What you calling me for? Call Corlette!"

The ensuing silence exclamated Q's guilt.

"Look, baby," he finally spoke. "Come home and we'll talk about it."

"*I'm* not your baby! Your bitch just gave birth to your *baby*!"

"Boo," Q pleaded, "I need you right now. Don't do this shit."

"Trust! You haven't seen nothing yet! I just got my pussy ate and it felt damn good. Now I'm about to suck his dick until that muthafucka get real hard then I'ma let him run up in my wet pussy. I don't get mad, nigga, I get even—you got the wrong bitch!"

She hung up before he could respond.

Bonded by Blood

A few seconds later Persia's cell phone rang again. She ignored the persistent ringing letting the call go to her voicemail.

"I guess that was ya boy, huh?" B-Man said, tryna put his arms around her.

"You think?" Persia replied. Her tone was sarcastic and suddenly cold. She looked at B-Man like he was retarded.

Persia removed B-Man's arms from around her.

"Oh, it's like dat?" he complained. "Don't let my brother fade you shawdy. He's out there doing him; you need to do you. I keep tryna tell you to leave that nigga and become *my* woman."

Persia wasn't tryna even consider that. B-Man had a big dick, and he was a determined, if not skilled, pussy-eater, but he still couldn't measure up to Q. Now that Persia took a good, long look at B-Man—to her, he looked like he was on dope. *This nigga has gotten skinny as hell.*

Persia wondered if B-Man might have HIV or something. Sweating his diminished physique, she asked him why he had lost so much weight.

"Stressin', shawdy," he told her.

Saying that she suddenly felt ill, Persia was able to get B-Man to leave. Before leaving he had broke her off a stack. Persia added the thousand dollars to the other money she had in her purse. She had more than enough money to see her through until she decided to go back home. Q always kept at least eight stacks at the condo; before leaving Persia had taken all that, plus she'd already had money of her own.

Three days after he'd been with his brother's wifey, B-Man sat at the crib with his own girl, Gwen, smoking woos and tryna figure out how he had fucked up so much money the past few months. He had spent the entire fifty thousand dollars Q had given him. What the fuck he spent it on, B-Man couldn't clearly recall. He knew he'd been tricking off a lot of guap lately, but *dayum*!

The thousand dollars he'd given to Persia didn't fade him, though. B-Man would've gave his last dollar to his lil' brother's fly ass wifey—he desired her just that much. He had convinced himself that he would eventually have Persia, especially if he could drop just a little bit more salt in the mix.

"Hook up another woo, baby," B-Man instructed Gwen.

"We ain't got no more weed," she informed him.

"Damn, what happened to all the weed?"

He had just bought two ounces the other day.

"Dat shit gone, boo," Gwen said reminding him that they'd been smoking woos damn near 24/7, for three straight days.

B-Man and Gwen searched their apartment for weed that they may have accidentally hidden from themselves. Usually a joint or two could be found under the couch cushions. But today the search under the cushion was futile; B-Man and Gwen were too high and paranoid to go out and cop more weed to twist up a woo. So they just sat there looking at one another, like two fiends.

Gwen said, "Baby, let's try it without the weed."

B-Man knew what she was proposing.

"I don't know about that, shawdy," he hedged. "Fucking wit' it like that is a whole 'nother level."

"We ain't gotta do it all the time; just this once, since we don't have any weed."

B-Man pondered it for a minute; he had been curious about smoking crack for a while. He wanted to feel that high that made others neglect their children; that high that made bitches suck a dog's dick for a five-dollar crack rock. That shit had to be dat helluva helluva!

"How we gon' smoke it? You got a pipe?"

"I got a straight shooter," replied Gwen, dashing off to get it.

When she came back from the bedroom, B-Man was thinking: She been smoking it like this already. Why else would she have a muthafuckin' straight shooter around?

B-Man had the bloodline of a hustla, from both parents, so he could've been focused on getting at the money, like Q and Khalil. Together, the trio would've made a formidable team. He also had the bloodline of a junkie. So once he let Gwen talk him into putting that glass dick in his mouth, the end of his story was written.

B-Man put the pipe to his mouth and inhaled. "Hold the smoke in for a minute, baby. Then let it out slowly." Coached Gwen.

He followed her instructions, and within seconds it felt as if his whole body was busting a nut. The feeling was better than any other he had ever experienced. He felt he had the ability to pimp harder than Khalil and hustle better than Q. With each hit he became more confident, more unstoppable. But this was only in his mind. Reality would prove to be much different.

CA$H

Chapter Twenty

R apheal was one of the few who was strong enough to get that crack gorilla off his back. It had taken him damn near fifteen years to do it though. Still he knew better than to think that the gorilla was dead. Like all reformed addicts, Rapheal could only count one day at a time, hoping he'd continue to have the strength to stay clean.

It had been a little more than three months since Rapheal had gotten high. Things were looking up for the old school playa. The same shit that brought him down, was bringing him back up.

Rapheal had bought himself a brand new Escalade and tricked it out with some rims.

"Pop, you stuntin', aintcha?" Joked Q when Rapheal pulled up in front of Corlette's apartment bumpin' Levert.

"Just doing me, young jit."

Q smiled at Rapheal's swag; he was glad to have been able to help his pops regain his pride and dignity in the streets.

"Where's my granddaughter?" asked Rapheal.

"She's inside."

"S'up, Elisse," Q spoke to his pop's girl, who was in the passenger seat of the Caddy.

"I'm superfantastic," beamed Elisse. "How are you?"

"*Superfantastic, too!*" Q playfully mocked.

Rapheal laughed.

"I don't know where she got that country ass shit from," he said, shaking his head.

"You don't be saying that when I'm putting this *superfantastic* nookie on you," teased Elisse.

"Puttin' it on me? Girl, I be having your young ass climbing the wall."

"Nah, I be having your *old* ass climbing the wall."

"Old?" Rapheal laughed. "Shid, ain't *nothin'* old about me. Even my money new!"

He flashed a roll of crisp new bills, held together by a gold money clip.

"He jammed on you, Elisse," laughed Q.

"Yeah, he got down," she conceded with a smile, then leaned over and planted a kiss on Rapheal's cheek, leaving lipstick on his neatly- trimmed goatee.

Rapheal reached in the back seat and grabbed the presents they had brought for his granddaughter. Elisse lovingly wiped the lipstick smudge off of his face with a tissue before they went inside.

"Hi, Mr. Jones," Corlette greeted Q's pops. "Hi, Elisse."

"Lemme hold my precious granddaughter," Rapheal cooed as he gently took little Alize from across Corlette's shoulder.

"I just burped her, so she shouldn't spit up on you."

Still she passed him a small blanket to lay across his lap. Ten minutes later Alize was asleep. Corlette laid the baby in her bassinet. Then she oohed ahhed over the presents.

Miss Jean came through the front door. Q introduced her to Rapheal and Elisse.

"His *girlfriend*?" Miss Jean shrieked in exaggerated disbelief. "Chile, you look young enough to be his *daughter!*" she commented, hatin' on Elisse's youth.

"I like my women like I like my steaks—tender," Rapheal said. "Never well done."

His proclamation cooled Miss Jean's thighs.

Bonded by Blood

Rapheal and Elisse left, Miss Jean couldn't stop talking about how "fine" Q's father was.

"If I can just get that fine nigga in bed one night, I bet he'd change his mind about not liking his steak *well done*," declared Miss Jean.

"Mama, you need to stop your stuff!" laughed Corlette.

The next day when Q and Khalil fell through Rapheal's crib, the three of them had a good laugh at Miss Jean's expense.

"I'm telling you, pop, she gon' rape you if you ever go over there without Elisse," Q warned laughing hard as hell.

"Boy, I know that's your shawdy's mother, but real talk, I wouldn't hit that unless she's paying five figures," Rapheal let it be known.

Miss Jean, who resembled Oprah wasn't Rapheal's cup of tea.

"Oh, guess who I ran into the other day," said Rapheal.

"Who?" asked his sons simultaneously.

"Y'all's step-mother."

"Sophie?" asked Khalil.

"Uh-huh."

"Where at, pop? Damn, I ain't seen Sophie in a minute," Q said. "

"Where she living at?" Q asked.

"In different crack houses."

"She fucked up like dat?" Khalil further inquired.

"Yep. Got that crack gorilla on her back," Rapheal informed them. "I gave her my cell phone number; when she calls I'ma help her if I can."

"You getting soft, old man," Khalil teased tryna make light of the disconcerting news about Sophie. He didn't really consider Sophie his step-mother, but he liked her well enough.

Q, true to his character, had a soft spot for Sophie. He recalled Sophie being as kind to him as if she had pushed him out of her own pussy.

"When Sophie gets in touch with you, pops, let me know. I'ma put her on her feet," said Q. Rapheal reminded him that he couldn't "lift" a junkie up, all he could do was offer her a helping hand.

"She gotta lift herself up," Rapheal explained.

Q nodded his understanding.

"Anyway, what's up with your wifey? She still ain't come back home?" asked Rafael, changing the subject.

"Nah, shawdy still trippin' bout Corlette and the baby. I be talking to her on the phone, but I can't talk her into coming back home, and she won't tell me where she's staying. I know she's coming back sooner or later, though," Q added. "Cause she left a lot of her things at the crib."

"Yeah, she'll be back, she's just fuckin' with his head for a minute," guessed Khalil.

"Never let 'em see you sweat," advised Rapheal.

"Neva dat," Q said frontin'.

He was damn near going out of his mind with worry. Every single day since Persia had said that slick shit he had constant thoughts of some nigga running dick up in his wifey. If he only knew the half!

Rapheal could tell that Q had it bad. He had met Persia and wasn't impressed.

"Quantavious," Rapheal said, "some shit you just gotta live and learn. So I'ma just say this: A spoiled woman is like a rotten tooth—you just get rid of 'em. I'm a leave it at that."

"Pimpin' ain't easy," added Khalil, patting his lil' brother on the back.

Rapheal laughed.

It was a week later when Rapheal received a call from Sophie.

When he and Elisse picked her up from outside a crack house, Rapheal was horrified by what had become of his ex-ho. Having been on drugs himself for the past decade and a half, before finally bouncing back, Rapheal had seen up close and personal how crack could turn the flyest muthafucka into a hollow-faced zombie. Still, it appalled him to see Sophie. "Hey, daddy!" Her smile was missing four front teeth.

"What's up, girl," Rapheal spoke.

"Missing *you*, daddy."

Tears fell from Sophie's eyes.

Wasn't shit romantically nostalgic about her past life as a ho in Rapheal's stable. Pimps use, abuse, and destroy their women. Rapheal had done exactly that to Sophie, but her reality since then had been even worse. Her naturally long and curly hair was now short, stringy, and unwashed. That ass of hers that once could balance a cup on its mounds had diminished into two bee stings. Her skin, which used to be radiant and smooth, was now blemished with dark spots. Most of all, Sophie's dreams had turned into nightmares. Though it defied logic, she longed for the days when she was walking up and down the stroll, turning tricks for her pimp.

"Cut the tears, girl, and get in the back seat." Rapheal told her. "This my woman Elisse. Elisse that's Sophie."

At their apartment Elisse fixed dinner while Rapheal and Sophie sat around reminiscing about the past.

Later, after they had eaten, Rapheal told Sophie that he'd help her get herself together if she'd enter a drug rehabilitation program. "But I'm not going to help you until you prove to me you're willing to help yourself," he said.

"Okay, daddy. I'ma call around and see what I can find."

When they dropped Sophie back off in front of the house where they'd picked her up, Rapheal was doubtful she'd stick to the plan. Despite his misgivings over it, he gave Sophie some money before pulling off, knowing she'd most likely spend the money to get high.

Two nights later, Rapheal was at the crib in the bathroom trimming his newly grown goatee. Elisse was asleep on the couch, having dozed off while watching television. There was a knock on the front door, which awakened Elisse.

"Who's there?" she called out, going to answer the door.

"Excuse me, ma'am. May I please use your phone? My baby is sick, and I need to call her daddy to come take us to the hospital. I live over in the next building; I just moved in and I can't find my cell phone."

Elisse looked through the peephole to see if she recognized the woman whose anxious voice resonated from the other side of the door. It was dark out so Elisse tried to switch on the porch light to get a better look at the woman, but the light did not come on. She tried the switch again, but to no avail.

Elisse engaged the door's security chain then opened the door just wide enough to pass the woman her cell phone.

"I'll let you use my cell phone, but I'm sorry, I can't allow you to come inside," she explained politely.

"That'll be fine."

"Who you talking to, baby?" asked Rapheal, walking up behind her and putting his arms around her waist.

"A lady who—"

The door was kicked violently inwards, slamming into Elissa's face. She screamed slipping from Rapheal's arms and falling to the floor, blood pouring from her broken nose. Rapheal stumbled back and fell.

Bonded by Blood

Two men rushed the apartment, both wearing black ski masks and brandishing burners. One stood over Rapheal; the other stood over Elisse. The girl, who'd knocked on the door, now closed it and went back to the get-away car to wait for her accomplices. Inside the vehicle she tossed a bundled baby doll on the back seat.

Inside the apartment, one of the armed, masked men ordered Rapheal to take him to the drugs and money. The other robber remained silent, but the gun he held to Elisse's head spoke loud and clear.

"Yo, old school, you make a country move, I'ma nod you! Then, son over there gon' do your bitch," threatened the masked robber with the burner trained on Rapheal.

After they had robbed them of all the money and drugs at the apartment, the robbers took the couple's jewelry, too including the iced Rolex that Khalil had given Rapheal. One robber hadn't spoken the entire time. As he and his partna prepared to leave, the silent one pointed his burner at Rapheal and shot him in the stomach.

Elisse was still screaming as the robbers ran outside, hopped in the awaiting get-away car and mashed out.

"Damn," one of the robbers said to his partnas. "Why you shoot him?"

"Fuck dat nigga."

CA$H

Chapter Twenty One

Khalil was .38-hot! He wanted to nod somebody for what happened to his pops. But with Rapheal in critical condition in ICU at Georgia Baptist Hospital, and unable to point a finger at anyone, Khalil didn't know who to slump.

Elisse had not recognized the one ski masked robber's voice when he'd spoken, and the second robber hadn't spoken at all.

"What about the girl who knocked on the door?" Khalil and Q questioned Elisse after she explained how the robbers were able to gain entry into the apartment.

"I can't recall ever seeing her before," she answered. "And now that I think about it, that wasn't a real baby she was cradling because she held it like it might have been a doll or something."

Elisse mentioned that they'd just had Sophie over for dinner a few days prior to the incident.

"I'm not saying that she had anything to do with it. It could just be a coincidence."

Khalil was saying to himself, *I bet that crackhead bitch did set dat shit up!*

"Na, fam. Sophie would never violate Rapheal like that." said Q.

"Fool, a clucker don't love *nobody*," Khalil snapped. Q was too quick to give people the benefit of the doubt.

When they told B-Man that Rapheal had been shot and robbed, B-Man couldn't have cared less.

"What, you want me to fake kick it? Come to the hospital and *act* like I'm concerned whether Rapheal lives or dies? Real talk, I hope he dies," B-Man stated, with no compassion.

"You ain't shit, shawdy!" Khalil spat back.

"Whateva, nigga—you already know how I feel about that dude; his being shot don't change shit."

Khalil was peeved with B-Man, and it was clear that he couldn't count on him to ride once he and Q found out who had violated. It wasn't a question of whether or not the shit would be avenged. Whoever had touched Rapheal, Khalil figured, had to know that he was fam. If the streets was tryin' Rapheal, they were tryin' them, too!

Q was feelin' Khalil on that, but he wasn't letting B-Man's callous disregard for their pops condition stress him. Rapheal had made his bed, if B-Man refused to soften it, well, a hard bed is what their pop had to sleep on. Q knew firsthand how coldhearted B-Man could be. If you wasn't paying B-Man, you couldn't count on him for shit. One good thing had come out of it though. As far as Q was concerned, Persia had come back home.

The night Rapheal got shot, Q called Persia and informed her of his pops condition.

"I need you by my side now, shawdy," he said.

In a rare moment of concern for what anyone, other than herself was going through, Persia sat aside her anger over Q's infidelities and drove to the hospital to be with him while he worried over his pops condition. At the hospital he hugged her as if he never planned to let her go again.

"I need my baby back," he'd said, kissing her face.

Persia was ready to come back for sure, but she had to let Q's side bitch know *her* place!

Q was crashed out in Corlette's bed; he had been up for a couple days straight, without sleep, worrying about Rapheal, and stressing over what had went down with Persia at the hospital. Plus, he had taken one of the strong sleeping pills he now kept with him 24/7. The sleeping pills had been suggested to throw off the polygraph test whenever Fazio summoned him out to his crib to be tested.

Q had told Khalil about the shit that had gone down at Fazio's estate, and that Jimmy, Fazio's nephew, had told him that one day soon they all would be polygraphed. It occurred to Khalil that if anyone would know how to outfox a polygraph exam, it would be that lawyer bitch, in MIA that Cha Cha tricked with. Cha Cha made the call to Eva Padevoni and posed the problem to her.

"Well, strong sleeping pills will slow your system down. Your heart rate, blood pressure, all of that—which can screw the test results up some," the attorney explained.

Cha Cha passed the scheme to Khalil and he put his brother on point.

Q knew a pharmacist, who hooked him up with the proper pills in exchange for a little cocaine. Now Q kept the prescription pills with him at all times. When that fateful day arrived for him to be polygraphed, he would take a triple dosage of the sleeping pills and hope like hell the scheme deceived the tester.

Today, he had taken a pill just to put himself to sleep for a minute. He was sleeping hard, and dreaming good, when he was awakened by a loud banging on Corlette's door. He jumped up, groggy, but definitely awake. *Can't be no jack boys them stick up kids don't knock. Sound like po-po! Shit!*

"Corlette, who da fuck bangin' on your door like dat?"

"I don't know," she replied, frowning as she got up out of bed and stomped to the door.

"*Who is it?*" she asked with mad attitude.

"Tell Quantavious I said to bring his ass out here . . . right now!"

Corlette couldn't believe her eyes when she snatched open the front door to confront the crazy bitch who was banging on her goddamn door.

Persia stood in the doorway, arms folded across her chest like she planned to stay rooted in that very spot until her man brought his ass outside. Corlette started to slam the door in the disrespectful bitch's face, but she knew that would lead to a scene, exactly what Persia wanted. Corlette wasn't going to give her the pleasure.

"Who da fuck is that?" Q asked when Corlette returned to the bedroom.

"That's your wifey, or whatever you wanna call her," replied Corlette even-toned. "You better go handle your business before she creates a scene and some fool calls the police."

Q quietly stepped into the Iceberg jeans he'd thrown across the bedroom dresser before crashing out. Then he pulled a baggy jersey over the wifebeater he was wearing, and stepped into the crisp new LeBron's at the foot of the bed. He wasn't about to go to the door half dressed and give Persia more ammunition.

"You asking me to come back home to your ass and you over here laid up at your bitch house?" Persia ranted as soon as Q stepped out onto the porch.

"I was visiting my daughter."

"Nigga, please! Do I look like Suzy the Fool?"

What could Q say to that?

"Who you want, Q? Me or your bitch?"

"Why you gotta call her a bitch, baby?"

"I call it like I see it! What, you defending her *honor* or something?"

"I'm just saying, Persia."

"No, I'm just saying, *Quantavious*! Who you want, me or your rat BITCH?"

"Girl, you know I want *you*," Q whispered.

"Well, let's go tell your bitch that."

"We ain't even gotta do it like dat. Believe me, shawdy already know what time it is," Q tried, not wanting to be forced to clown Corlette. But Persia insisted.

Q started to get in his whip and drive off; Persia could follow in her car if she wanted, or she could stay there and have it out with Corlette since she was so intent on starting drama. Just as Q was about to follow his mind, Miss Jean pulled up. If Q left now and Persia confronted Corlette, she was sure to get her ass whipped. Miss Jean, alone, would probably get on that ass.

"Good morning, Quantavious," Miss Jean spoke, eyeing Persia with instinctive dislike. Dressed in tight capris and a t-shirt Miss Jean pushed on into the crib.

"Let's go home, boo," Q reached for his Persia's hand.

"I wish I would nigga! Get your hands off of me," Persia snatched away from him.

"Damn, baby, why you gotta be so difficult? Ain't it obvious who I love? Who pushin' a tricked out SUV? You! Who I rest at the condo with? Who I shed tears over, huh? You, girl! Now, damn, why you don't know who it is that I want?"

"Never mind all that," Persia snaked her neck. "I wanna hear you say it to your bitch, point blank, period, nigga."

Reluctantly, Q led Persia to Corlette's bedroom. Corlette lifted her face up off the pillow when she heard them enter her bedroom. Tears streaked her face but Persia had no sympathy.

"I'm going to need you to tell your rat bitch what time it is!" she demanded of Q who didn't want to diss Corlette. But neither did he want to lose Persia again.

Swallowing hard before speaking and feeling a little punked, Q said to Corlette, "Shawdy, you know Persia is wifey. I told you that from the jump."

"Tell her you're done fuckin' with her! And you better mean it!" hissed Persia at his elbow.

After Q said those words, Corlette held in tears and simply replied, "It's all good. I would appreciate it if y'all would leave now."

When Q and Perisa left, Corlette laid across her bed and cried her eyes out, holding baby Alize in her arms. She knew Q's wifey came before *her*, but it hurt like hell for her baby's daddy to do it like that.

Khalil drove through the spot where Elisse had told him she and Rapheal had picked Sophie up from. He called the first smoker he spotted over to his whip. "You know Sophie?" he asked with a twenty-dollar bill in hand.

"I might," the crackhead replied, sensing a bigger bribe if he held out for a minute or two.

"Check this, old school," Khalil said. "I ain't got time to play games. Go inside and get Sophie and I'll bless you with fifty."

"What if she ain't inside?"

"Tell me where I can find her."

"She ain't inside, but I'll tell you something I bet you're interested in."

Khalil handed over two tens, which the crackhead clutched in his palm in a death grip.

Then he promptly sold Sophie out.

"Man, that ho ain't around no more. I heard she done hit a lick for a whole lotta money—*thousands*! And dope, too! She ain't rob you, did she? Oh well, I don't owe that bitch nothin'. She ain't sharing her riches wit' *me*!"

Across town B-Man had been smoking his back out. For a couple days he and Gwen had been doing the *Bobby and Whitney* like crack was going out of style. But today he'd only smoked a ball. He hadn't intended to get high today, but Gwen kept on pressing him. *I'ma have to cut this junkie bitch loose or I'ma end up a goddamn Junkie*, he told himself now. *I gotta get back on point.*

B-Man knew he was slippin', and not just by smoking crack. The recklessness he'd shown with his chips had him desperate and doing dope-fiend shit, just to keep up the appearance that he was handling his business. Of the ten bricks Q promised him, B-Man had fucked up the money off of four of 'em. Two other bricks had been flipped to cop the Chevy drop he had parked out front. Some niggas Bed-Stuy had vouched for had got ghost with another two bricks B-Man had fronted them. *I know Bed-Stuy was down wit' dat shit*, he'd said to himself. *I'ma check dat when the time is right.*

That was eight of the ten bricks. The last two, Q hadn't given him, yet. That, in itself, had B-Man pissed the fuck off. Had his money funny! So, like the jackboy he was, B-Man picked up the steel and got his pockets right. Just the night before he and Bed-Stuy had jacked Shawn, the weed man. It was their second lick in the past week, and B-Man had fifty racks to show for it.

Three nights later he and Bed-Stuy was up in the strip club partying like rap stars. Teaser's was packed. VIP was off the chain. B-Man was making it rain in VIP, tossing bills up, letting the money shower down on the strippers who were entertaining him and his man.

Two strippers were poppin' pussy two inches from B-Man and his man's faces. The deejay was playing Jeezy's whole CD *Let's Get It.* The whole VIP room got crunk when "Soul Survivor", the fourteenth track from the CD started thumping through the club's speakers. Sinnamon walked past in a g-string, pasties and stilettos.

"*Dayum! Look at the fleas on Fluffy!*" he remarked.

B-Man was mesmerized. He wanted to hit that. He saw her dancing for another nigga in VIP. As he watched Sinnamon slow grind her hips he recalled how she rode Khalil's dick in the limo. When the record ended he intercepted her as she strutted across the VIP room.

"What it do, Sinn?"

"Hey, B-Man. You ballin' ain't you?"

"You know how I do it."

"Live it up," encouraged Sinnamon, 'bout to push on and get after them dollars other niggaz had in their pockets.

"Hold up, baby girl," B-Man stopped her. "Come over to my booth and serve a nigga a little love."

"We're kinda fam, baby boy, but you gotta be spending for me to serve you—you know how it goes."

"I gotcha."

Sinnamon hit B-Man off with a lap dance that had his shit boned up like a muthafucka.

"Say, lil' mama, what it gon' take for us to cut something."

With no hesitation Sinnamon asked, "How you tryna do it? We can go out to your car, if you got tinted windows. That won't cost you but this much."

She held up three fingers.

"Three hundred?" B-Man clarified.

"That's all, baby boy."

"Let's do it."

"What you riding in, and where are you parked?"

B-Man told her.

"Give me fifteen minutes, I'll meet you outside by your whip."

Down in the dressing room, pulling on her street clothes, Sinnamon called her man on his cell phone to tell him how it was going down. She wanted to make sure Khalil didn't have a problem with her tricking with his fam.

"Hell, no, I ain't trippin' it," Khalil reassured her. "My brother's money spends, too. Get that money, baby."

"Okay, daddy. I was just making sure."

"How it poppin' tonight?" Khalil inquired.

"Stacks on deck, daddy," she replied.

B-Man went outside in the parking lot. He sat on the hood of his whip, zoning. Besides the crack he had smoked today, he had smoked a coupla woos, then before heading to the club he had popped an X pill and a Viagra. Add to that, he was on that bubbly *and* that Hypnotiq. With the mix of all that, it's a wonder the boy was as lucid as he was. Though that wasn't saying much, 'cause he was high as a giraffe's pussy.

B-Man was anticipating the feel of Sinnamon's wet walls. There was something about fucking his brothers' bitches that stroked B-Man's fragile ego, even if he did have to pay for the pussy. He couldn't wait to stick that cobra head up Sinnamon.

Instead of reveling in the anticipation of running up in Khalil's ho, reminiscing about cutting Q's wifey, B-Man should've been paying attention to the shit going on around him—the niggas inside the club, and their movements.

Inside the club, a couple of nemesis had been paying much attention to the shit going on around them. They had peeped B-Man in VIP making it rain, poppin' bottles, stuntin' hard.

Outside they spotted B-Man chillin' on the hood of his whip. It didn't look like he was about to mash out. A little while later, from inside their whip, they spotted one of the strippers get into the car with B-Man. The driver crunk up his engine, planning to follow B-Man. Fifteen minutes passed and B-Man's car had not moved.

"Drive by that nigga's shit, shawdy. Let's see what the business is," instructed his accomplice.

They drove pass B-Man's whip, but could not see through the limo tint. They noticed B-Man's Chevy slightly bouncing up and down.

"I think they off in that bitch cuttin' something, shawdy," one said to the other. "Drive around the lot, let me see where Security at."

"Hurry up, baby," cooed Sinnamon.

"Turn over, let me hit it from the back," said B-Man.

"Un-uh," she refused. Tricks got it straight missionary style, fuck doing acrobatics for three-hundred dollars. She was a pro, not some part-time ho tricking just to add a little spice to her life. If she was going to do acrobatics, the nigga needed to spend a stack or more, anything else would be disrespecting the game.

B-Man was on that X and shit, so his staying power was incredible tonight. He was gettin his money worth. He was

tryna break the elastic up in that pussy, when the front door of his Chevy snatched open.

"Nigga, you know what it is! Let me see ya hands!" barked the burner-toting intruder.

"Bitch, don't move or say a word or I'ma slump ya ass!" Sinnamon was threatened.

B-Man, with his naked ass in the air, recognized the twins right away.

"Y'all doing it like dat, my niggas?"

"Shut da fuck up, pussy nigga fo' I split ya wig!"

They robbed B-Man of his money and jewels, and the burner he had stashed under the front seat. Sinnamon got jacked for three hundred dollars B-Man had paid her and a few pieces of jewelry she'd been wearing. The robbers also took B-Man's and Sinnamon's clothes, leaving them butt ass naked so they couldn't hop out the car and run to security for help.

B-Man quickly used his cell phone to call Bed-Stuy, who was still partying inside the strip club, and told him to come out to the car. His next call was to Khalil.

"Fam, those bitch niggas DeShawn and DeWayne just jacked me and one of ya girls!" B-Man uttered excitedly as soon as Khalil answered.

"Yo, calm the fuck down and tell me what happened." Khalil was already heated and B-Man hadn't yet given him any details. He got even hotter once his brother told him how the robbery had gone down.

"Is Sin okay?" he asked.

"Yeah, she good," B-Man informed him.

"Aight. Just chalk it up for tonight, we'll get at the twins in due time. Right now I'm with Q; we're going to visit Rapheal. I'ma hit you back."

Khalil hung up and told Q what had happened.

"Them niggas must think this shit is a game," Khalil said to Q as they rode in Q's whip, on their way to Georgia Baptist to visit their pops.

Q was laughing as he imagined B-Man getting jacked and left butt-naked, trying to run up on some pussy.

"And he say I got a tender head on *my* dick!" Q quipped.

"That shit ain't funny," Khalil said, laughing nevertheless. "They robbed my ho, too. They gots to pay for that."

"What B-Man doing trickin' with Sinnamon, anyway? That nigga be on some other shit," Q remarked as he pulled into the hospital's parking lot.

Rapheal, who had suffered a punctured lung and damage to his stomach in the shooting, had been moved from ICU to a private room. As soon as he was off the ventilator the cops had questioned him about the incident, including the identities of his assailants. Rapheal wasn't brand new nor was he some model citizen wanting to cooperate with the police. He threw the two detectives who questioned him, curve ball after curve ball. To their question, "Do you have any idea who shot you?" Rapheal had answered, "Not the slightest."

That was a lie.

"What it do, pops?" asked Khalil.

"Caught a hot one," Rapheal made light of the incident, though inside he was seriously asking himself if it was possible that the person he suspected of shooting and robbing him could indeed be the culprit. If so, shit was more serious than the slug he took.

"What don't kill you can only make you stronger," Q added.

Sophie could've set up the robbery," Khalil said with anger etched on his face.

"No, she ain't have nothing to do with it," Rapheal said with certainty.

"We gonna check it out anyway," Q said.

"You'll just be wasting your time."

Unbeknownst to them, he had a damn good reason why he didn't suspect Sophie.

"When you gettin' up outta here?" asked Q.

"Doc says it'll be a week to ten days."

"I already told Elisse to look for y'all a new spot to lay y'all heads," Khalil said. "Me and Q gon' handle the finances, don't worry about that."

"And don't worry 'bout paying me for that last bird I dropped in ya lap, pops. Just build ya strength back up. I'ma fuck wit you again," Q promised.

Rapheal felt blessed to have two sons willing to hold him down through thick and thin. Shit was real, 'cause in the hood most niggas don't fuck with their pops, and vice versa.

"Have y'all talked to B-Man?" asked Rapheal.

"Yeah, pop, but he on some other shit," Khalil confessed.

Rapheal just nodded his head.

The other shit B-Man was on at the moment was huntin' down DeShawn and DeWayne. "Those pussies had the nerve to jack me without masks on! I'ma show em' I'm not one to be fucked with," he ranted to Bed-Stuy, who didn't wanna get involved in any personal beefs. B-Man felt a certain way about that but pushed it to the back of his mind and decided to handle the twins' dolo.

They must ain't checked my street credentials. Niggaz know I'll set it off! How da fuck these fools gon' play me? Like they folks don't live in the hood no more.

The twins grandmother still lived in Thomasville. B-Man went to the hood and snatched up their granny. He took old girl back to his and Gwen's crib and made her call her grandsons.

"When y'all niggaz bring me back my shit I'll let her go. Put po-po in it and I'm slumpin' her! Fuck the rest. I'll go out dumpin' on they asses too!" B-Man threatened.

"Just be easy, man. We'll bring ya shit back, just don't hurt my granny," DeShawn said. "You know we don't fuck wit po-po like dat."

"I'm telling you, nigga, if po-po show up on the scene I'm going all the way out, and I'm slumpin' grandma first!" B-Man vowed.

"It ain't gon' even go down like dat," DeShawn assured him.

"Just keep ya cell phone close by; I'ma call you back in a day or two and tell you where to take the money."

"Fool, what da fuck you snatch up Mrs. Freeman for?" Q admonished B-Man when he told him what he had done.

"Khalil, talk to this stupid ass nigga—he done lost his damn mind," Q said passing the phone to Khalil.

"What the business, bruh?" Khalil asked.

"Them niggaz wanna play foul, I can play foul, too," replied B-Man

"Fuck it, what's done is done," Khalil sighed shaking his head. "How you wanna play this?

"I'm going all out!" B-Man told him.

"Is it worth all that?"

"To me it is."

"Damn, bruh, I wish you would've had a little patience. We coulda handled this another way. Mrs. Freeman good people."

"Y'all ain't gotta ride. I can handle mines by myself!"
Click.

"B-Man be buggin'," Khalil commented to Q, staring at the blank screen on his BlackBerry.

"I think that nigga fuckin' with that glass dick, for real."

"Come again?" Khalil said.

"For real, shawdy. You know the streets talk. I got that from a junkie bitch who say B-Man smoked crack with her and tricked off. Shawdy ain't gonna lie about no shit like that.

"*Whaaat?*"

"No lie, Khalil—And I heard Gwen on that shit too."

"B-Man ain't going out bad like. I can't say the same for Gwen. I know shawdy fuck with them woos."

"Shid, they fuck wit' more than woos. Both of 'em. I done seen a million and one smokers, fam. I'd bet my last breath B-Man done let that bitch turn him out."

"You think so?"

"Is a pig's pussy pork?"

Before Khalil and Q could get back in touch with B-Man and assist with his situation, concerning the twins, B-Man moved on his own. He called the twins and told them, "You know that lil' ho in Thomasville who Q be fuckin' with?"

"Corlette?" asked DeShawn.

"Yeah. Drop the shit off at her crib. When I know it's all there, I'll release ya grandmother."

B-Man headed over to Corlette's house to advise her of the agreement, but he didn't tell her the whole story.

Corlette asked, "Why DeWayne and DeShawn gon' drop something off over here? I don't mess with them like that."

"It's just business, lil' mama. Just do me this one favor. Q know how it's going down," he lied.

Later that evening, Corlette called B-Man to let him know that the twins had dropped off some money and jewels for him. Miss Jean, Corlette's money-hungry moms, agreed to meet B-Man with the guap since he offered to pay two hundred and fifty dollars.

B-Man met Miss Jean at a convenience store a few blocks from his crib. Once he was back at the crib, and had assured himself that all his shit had been returned, B-Man dropped the twins' grandmother off on the other side of town. He'd made her lie down on the floor, in the back of his Chevy, so that she wouldn't know where he lived, the same way he had brought her there.

When Q found out what B-Man had done he snapped. "Nigga, why you involve my shawdy in that shit?" Q pushed his way into B-Man's apartment. Khalil was on his heels.

"M.O.B. nigga!" B-Man said.

Q scooped B-Man up and body slammed him. *Dayum, this nigga light as fuck,* he thought as he tussled with his brother.

"Stop 'em, Khalil," cried Gwen, who was looking a hot mess.

"Let 'em get it off they chest," Khalil said.

"They gon' break something!"

Khalil ignored her. As he watched his brothers tussle, he was eyeing Gwen in his peripheral, thinking she was already broke the fuck up, why worry about the furniture.

Q got the best of B-Man, for the first time that Khalil could recall.

"*What nigga? What?* You can't fuck with this no more!" boasted Q after Khalil separated them.

Embarrassed at getting his ass whooped in front of his woman, B-Man hauled off and punched Q dead in the eye, violating the pact the brothers had made way back. Q's eye swelled up instantaneously.

"Oh, you doing it like dat, nigga?" he spat at B-Man.

Then his hand went to his waist.

Khalil tried to grab Q's arm.

Gwen screamed just as the gun went off!

The single shot echoed in their ears. B-Man fell to the floor clutching his leg.

"Shit, man! Shit! What the fuck wrong with y'all? We family!" Khalil screamed.

He snatched the nine from Q and shoved him in the chest with two hands.

"You trippin', shawdy!" he said, pushing Q again, hard. Then he went to B-Man.

"Damn, bruh, we gon' have to take you to the hospital. Ain't this some shit!" he was shaking his head in disbelief. "Q, you dead the fuck wrong!"

"I'ma kill dat nigga!" B-Man winced, holding his leg and rocking back and forth.

Gwen jumped in Q's face. "What the fuck you do that for?"

"Back up out my grill, bitch!" Q barked.

Gwen glared at Q. "I'm calling the police!"

"No, you not," Khalil interjected sternly. "This family BI, Gwen. We gon' handle this, me and my brothers."

Anger was etched on Khalil's face. He had seen this shit bubbling between B-Man and Q ever since he came home from the joint, but he never thought it would reach this level.

"What happened to bonded by blood? Huh?" he asked.

Q wasn't saying nothing, but he was already regretting what he'd just done.

"My bad, shawdy. For real, though," he finally said, directing his apology to B-Man.

"Fuck dat! Y'all niggas ain't my fam, and Rapheal ain't my daddy! Ask him, he'll tell you."

Khalil and Q weren't giving any weight to B-Man's words. He was mad, talking out of his head.

"And Q, while you riding around acting like you *The Last Kingpin*, nigga, I was running dick up in ya lil' wifey! Yeah, ask Persia what's up with that. *Real talk, bitch nigga!*"

Q's mouth dropped open and his brows furrowed. His face twitched with fury.

Khalil said, "Go on home, shawdy. Me and Gwen will take B-Man to the hospital. You done fucked up, bruh. Damn!"

Q bounced. Khalil and Gwen helped B-Man out to his Chevy drop and eased him into the back seat. Several towels were around his thigh to catch the blood from the gunshot wound. B-Man was talking shit, still stressing that Khalil and Q wasn't his fam, and telling Khalil, "I don't need your fucking help, nigga."

Khalil let B-Man's words bounce right off him. Whatever B-Man was stressin', Khalil's love for his brother was bigger than that bullshit.

While Khalil was trying to get B-Man settled on the back seat of the car, he noticed a baby doll wrapped in a real baby's blanket. *Elisse said something about that bitch that set up the robbery carrying a doll,* he recalled.

Q walked into the condo with a mean unit on his face. B-Man's words played in his mind. *I was running dick up in ya lil' wifey... Yeah, ask Persia what's up with that... Real talk, bitch nigga!* Q wanted to believe that his brother was lying, saying crazy shit just to hurt him, like that shit about Rapheal not being B-Man's pops.

In a way, Q was glad Persia wasn't at home; he didn't wanna confront her with accusations. He smoked a Newport, showered, changed clothes, and then drove to Georgia Baptist Hospital to see Rapheal. Immediately after taking a seat at his

pop's bedside, Q questioned him about B-Man's claim. Rapheal confirmed that he was not B-Man's biological father.

"Damn, pop, why you or Black Girl ain't tell us," said Q, shaking his head in disbelief.

"After your mama had Khalil I went to the joint to serve a short bid on some misdemeanor shit. While I was away Black Girl hooked up with a square nigga. She came to visit me and told me that she was gettin' out of the life, no more prostituting. By the time I got out six months later, she was pregnant by the dude, but she wanted to come back to me. The nigga had caught feelings and didn't wanna let go so I had to do what I had to do. Don't even ask what I did because you already know. After that was handled, I accepted ya mama back and tried to accept B-Man as my own. Khalil was too young to remember and you was still in my nut sac," explained Rapheal.

The story fucked Q's head up, but it explained why B-Man didn't really resemble him and Khalil. They had the same mother, but B-Man had a different pops.

"I wonder how B-Man found out," Q said.

"Black Girl probably told him," guessed Rapheal. "She always said she would tell him one day."

"Dayum!" Rapheal said, "Your mama would be real hurt if she was alive to see how y'all beefin' with each other. She probably turning over in her grave."

"Yeah, I know, pop. I don't know why I did that stupid shit."

"Y'all still *blood brothers*—y'all got the same mama. Go make up with your brother," suggested Rapheal, keeping another secret to himself.

Q didn't know which hospital Khalil had taken B-Man to, he'd find out later then go make peace with his fam. He was feeling so bad about wettin' his brother, the fact that B-Man had blacked his eye didn't even matter. *Damn! What the fuck I shoot him for?* Q was chastising himself as he drove home. Shit was fucked up, he had shot his own brother, Khalil was heated at him, and he had just found out that it was true that Rapheal wasn't B-Man's pop. And that wasn't the least of it.

The Newport dangled from the corner of Q's mouth as he called Persia on her cell phone.

"Where you at?" he asked as soon as she answered.

"At the hair salon," Persia replied. "What's wrong? You sound upset."

"Come home, A-fuckin'-SAP!"

"What's going on, baby?"

"Come home, now!"

Persia came through the door with an attitude.

"What's the big emergency?" she spewed, setting her Hermes bag down on the cocktail table.

With her hair freshly done she looked delicious. But Q was now seeing past her beauty and sex appeal.

"What happened to your eye, boo?" she asked, startled when Q came out of the master bedroom, where he'd been packing her clothes. "Oh my god, baby, what happened?"

"You fucked with my brother, huh?"

His tone was cyanide.

The unexpected question caused Persia to damn near lose her breath. In those few seconds of silence, any slight chance that the accusation wasn't true evaporated like a drop of water in the desert's sand.

"What are you talking about?" Persia tried, to buy time to formulate a lie.

Whap!

Q slapped wifey so hard her pearly white teeth rattled.

"Don't even fix your mouth to try to lie about it, bitch!" Q backhanded Persia, knocking her on her ass. She balled into a knot and cried and screamed her head off.

"Low down, rat bitch. I oughta kill you!" *Whap.* "I treat you like a queen . . . " *Whap!* " . . . buy you a new whip, clothes, jewels . . . " *Whap!* " . . . and you fuck my muthafuckin' brother!" *Whap! Whap! Whap!*

Q was pummeling her with his fist, out of control in his fury of heartbreak. He was punching Persia in the face, the shoulders, the back of her head, any spot she left unprotected. Tears were streaming down his face by the time he caught himself and stopped.

"Get your shit and kick rocks, ho!" he spat, standing over her, chest heaving in and out.

Persia lay curled up on the living room floor. Her freshly done hair was all over her head in a tangled mess. She tasted blood from a busted lip and her head throbbed. Her body rocked with sobs.

"When I get back you better be gone, bitch. You can take all the clothes and shit I bought. Fuck dat shit. I don't want none of it left here to remind me of your dirty ass. Just leave my door keys!"

He stormed out the door, slamming it behind him.

B-Man was lying in a hospital bed, with his leg elevated and heavily bandaged. Khalil had met Q right outside the doorway as he came toward the room. They dapped hands and gave each other a brotherly hug.

Q whispered what Rapheal had confirmed. Khalil took the news in stride. It didn't matter. In his eyes, they all were still fam as much as before the revelation.

"So how is he?" Q asked about B-Man's condition.

"He good, but he heated as a muthafucka. Ain't said a word to me since he came out of surgery," replied Khalil in a hushed tone so that their voices wouldn't carry into the room where Gwen was at B-Man's bedside.

"I'm going inside to see him," Q said as one of the surgical doctors left out of the room.

"He ain't gon' wanna see you," warned Khalil.

"I know. But I wanna see *him.*"

"Brace yaself then, 'cause you know how stubborn B-Man is."

"It don't matter. I was wrong to take it that far, so he has the right to go off on me. I'm not even mad about him and Persia. The bitch was poison anyway," conceded Q as he stepped inside B-Man's room.

Gwen started grillin' Q as soon as he entered the room. He wasn't studyin' her junkie ass, though. What was between fam was between fam.

"Gwen, step out in the hallway for a minute, let me talk to my brother," Q said.

"You wanna talk to him, baby?" she asked B-Man, not budging.

"I ain't got nothin' to say to that nigga—him or Khalil."

The bitterness in B-Man's voice was thick, as if it had been coagulating for years. "Them niggas ain't my brothers!"

"Step out the room, Gwen," Khalil firmly instructed. "This family business. I ain't in no mood to tongue wrestle."

Reluctantly, Gwen got her itty-bitty ass up and stepped out into the hall.

"I'll be right outside the door," she said over her frail shoulder.

Khalil closed the door.

"Check it, shawdy," began Q with remorse in his voice. "My bad, for real, bruh. Man, I wish I could take that slug back, undo *that* and whatever it is I've done to make shit so bad between us. For real, fam . . . I love you, nigga. Why we always beefin', shawdy?"

B-Man didn't respond.

Q continued, "Just tell me what I gotta do to make shit right with us again. What, bruh, you still salty 'cause I didn't split them bricks more evenly between the three of us? 'Cause all the bricks in the world ain't more important to me than you and Khalil. Real talk, you can have *all* that shit. Them thangs don't mean more to me than fam do, shawdy. I ain't even salty with you' bout Persia, pimp. A ho gon' be a ho; if it hadn't been you it woulda been some other nigga. The bitch just a rat. It's good I found that out now instead of later, before I wifed that bitch for real."

"Real talk," Khalil intoned. "Blood thicker than water. And about this thing with Rapheal, man, that don't change shit between the three of us. So what? Just 'cause Rapheal ain't ya biological, he the only pops you know. The three of us still came out the same coochie."

"Y'all niggas through?" B-Man finally spoke. "Cause if so, y'all can get da fuck up outta here. We ain't brothers. We ain't fam. We ain't nothin'! Not as far as I'm concerned."

"You don't mean that, bruh," said Khalil.

"Shid, I mean every word I just said. As for you Q, nigga you betta stay da fuck outta my way, 'cause if we ever bump heads again I'ma dump on ya ass like I'd do any other nigga."

CA$H

Chapter Twenty two

Because family BI had him stressed, Khalil had been short tempered with his hoes lately. Last week he had pimp smacked the shit out of Sinnamon, for nothing really. When he realized that he was in the wrong, he simply said, "Charge it to the game, ho," and left it at that.

Rayne and Cha Cha was getting on his last nerve with their petty ass bickering back and forth. He had made them both stand in opposite corners of the living room, their noses pressed against the wall, like two school children. Then he had them write, "I will not bicker with my wife-in-law", one thousand times each.

"Y'all wanna act like little children, well, that's how I'ma treat you, unnastand?" he explained.

"Yes, daddy," Cha Cha replied, obediently finding paper and pen and doing as she was told.

"Khalil, let me see you in the bedroom," Rayne requested. "We need to talk."

"Nah, bitch, *we* don't need to do shit. *You* need to get a pen and some paper and handle your business, before I have to snatch a hole in your ass!"

When Rayne turned in her written "assignment", each page was streaked with tears.

Emily hadn't been spared Khalil's wrath, either. Snow Bunny had went on a two-day date with one of her usual "friends", without letting Khalil know where she was at. It didn't matter that Emily called Khalil up and handed him six thousand and five hundred dollars upon her return. He accepted the trap then promptly boxed her muthafuckin' ears.

Q had pulled up in the projects. His whip was immediately swarmed by kids as usual.

"Back up, shorties. I got y'all," he smiled. He was never stressed when the kids bum rushed him for ice cream and candy money. He took time out to pass out a few dollars to each of them before continuinig about his business.

When Q finally made it to Corlette's door, she met with a kiss.

"What it do, shawdy?"

"I'm good, baby." She smiled.

"Y'all ready?" he asked.

"Yeah, let me go get Alize out the bedroom."

Corlette handed him their daughter's diaper bag and her own overnight bag.

Q was taking Corlette and the baby home with him to spend a few days with him at his new crib. Before he had copped a new spot Corlette refused to go with him to the old one that he and Persia had shared. Now that he had the new spot, Corlette was happy, but Persia hadn't walked away meekly.

Two days after he had kicked Persia's ass and put her out, Q came home and got swarmed by po-po. Persia had sworn out a warrant against him for domestic violence.

"Vindictive bitch!" Q had cursed after he was cuffed and on his way to jail.

He called Corlette to bail him out and she didn't hesitate. She and Miss Jean stepped right to their business, and Q was back out the next day. Miss Jean had been taxing him ever since.

Bonded by Blood

Q strapped his infant daughter into the baby seat in the backseat of his new 600 series Benz he'd just copped two weeks ago. The new whip was just to let Persia know he wasn't faded. Corlette settled into the passenger seat and immediately ejected T.I. out of the CD player and replaced it with Monica—that was her girl.

"Let's compromise, shawdy," said Q. "How 'bout we listen to some John Legend?"

"I'm feelin' him," said Corlette.

So Q slid in the CD *Get Lifted*.

John Legend's melodic voice filled the inside of the Benz. Corlette closed her eyes and let the peanut butter, soft leather seats wrap her in a sweet embrace.

The windows were up and the air was on low. The smell of the brand new interior was accentuated by the coconut air freshener emitting from the vents. John Legend was singing: *Baby when I used to love you ... there's nothing I wouldn't do ... I went through the fire for you ... anything you asked me to ...*

Corlette reached over and held Q's hand, affectionately. She hoped like hell he realized how much she loved him. She knew that he was probably still hurting over Persia. That didn't worry her, though. She would help him get over the pain of Persia's trifling infidelities.

"I love you, Q."

The words came from her heart.

Q affectionately squeezed her hand, as he came to a stop sign, about to leave Thomasville Heights. A car pulled up beside them and the window slid down.

All of a sudden, without warning, the Benz was sprayed with a burst of gunfire. *Splacka! Splacka! Splacka! Splacka! Splacka! Splacka!* The car screeched away. Q followed, bustin' back with his nine.

Corlette was screaming. She had been shot in the face! But those screams were nothing compared to screams of agony that came from her when she looked in the back seat to check on baby Alize. The car seat was covered in blood. It seemed unreal that so much blood could've come from an infant.

Sadly, though, it was real. Alize had been hit by two slugs.

With Corlette screaming hysterically, Q drove like a mad man, rushing his lady and their daughter to the hospital. Alize, just four months old, was pronounced dead on arrival. Corlette, in addition to having been shot in the face, had gone into shock.

Police and news hounds were thick outside the church where the funeral was held. At the service Corlette was inconsolable. "They killed my baby! They killed my precious little baby!" Her face was disfigured and swollen, from the hollow point she caught in the jaw. It had gone through her jaw, knocked out several teeth, and severed the tip of her tongue. So when she talked it was with a discernable lisp.

Q held Corlette throughout the entire service. The whole hood was there. Most of them genuinely grieving over the senseless loss of life. Silent tears streamed down the mourners' faces as they watched Corlette jump up screaming, "Why Lord? Why did you let them kill my baby? Please take me instead. I don't want to live without my precious daughter," she bellowed tearfully.

In the days following the funeral, Corlette spent hours just sitting at home on the couch staring at a collage of Alize and fingering her baby's clothes. Her body rocked with loud sobs. She felt that she could not go on living.

Corlette repeatedly cried. "I wanna be with my baby."

Bonded by Blood

Q and Miss Jean tried their best to console her, but Corlette's grief was immense. As soon as they left her alone in the house, she took an overdose of painkillers. Q came home and found her passed out on the bathroom floor. He rushed her to the hospital where she had to have her stomach pumped and was committed for twenty-four hour suicidal observation.

When Corlette was no longer on suicide watch and released from the hospital, Q moved her in with him. Miss Jean moved into the new high rise apartments that had been built where the notorious projects called Carver Homes once sat. The Housing Authority had threatened to evict her from the old place, accusing her and Corlette of harboring drugs for Q. So Q just moved Miss Jean to avoid the drama.

Word on the street was that the twins had been responsible for the shootings. Snitches in the hood dropped dime to po-po, and the twins got snatched up and arrested during a roadblock set up in the projects, close to where their grandmother lived. But the police didn't have any evidence on which to hold them beyond seventy-two hours for questioning. DeWayne was released. DeShawn was held on a warrant for aggravated assault in an unrelated case.

As soon as Khalil heard, he was on his way to Q's crib. "Shawdy, you gotta get yaself back on point. For real, bruh. This ain't accomplishing shit," Khalil said.

He was at Q's crib. Since the funeral, Q had been surviving on Newport's and Seagram's VO. Dozens of ashtrays ran over with cigarette butts, and empty vodka bottles were everywhere. Corlette was barricaded off in the bedroom. She wasn't suicidal but she was still drowning in grief. Add to that, she had shattered every mirror in the townhouse, unable to face her own image. Her once beautiful face was hideous. But plastic surgery could correct that if she and Q would pull themselves together and handle their business.

Khalil brought Rayne and Sinnamon along with him to scrub and clean Q's crib. While they went about that task, Khalil poured out every drop of liquor he found. Q was sitting on the couch in a near catatonic state.

Khalil went upstairs and knocked on the bedroom door.

"Corlette," he called out. "Shawdy, you don't have to open the door or come out of there, just come to the door, close enough to hear what I have to say."

He heard no sound or movement.

"Please, Corlette. Just give me five minutes, then you can get back in bed and I'll go away. This is Khalil."

He heard moving around in there.

"Go away, Khalil. I don't want to talk. I just want Alize back."

She was at the door. Khalil could feel her weight pressed up against it. And he could hear her crying.

"Corlette, I'm not gonna lie to you," he said soothingly. "Nobody has the power to bring Alize back. She's in God's arms now, shawdy. Can't nothing harm her no more. Me and Q gotta step to them niggaz who hurt y'all, shawdy—that's the street law. But he can't do nothing in the condition he's in. If you don't pull yourself together, both of y'all gon' keep going downhill. But you stronger than that, baby girl. Q needs you to be strong for him, shawdy. I never liked that bitch Persia. I always knew she was only around for the money. For real, Corlette. Pop peeped that, too. We both peeped that you are genuine, and got real love for Q. Well, shawdy, now is the time to show how official you are. I know you hurtin', but you're strong. Q needs you, shawdy."

After a while there were no more sounds of movement in the townhouse. No sounds of Khalil's or his women's voices. Corlette knew that they had gone.

Corlette saw that the mirror over the bedroom dresser had been shattered into one huge cobweb. She knew that she must have done it, but could not remember having done so. In the bathroom, she found the mirror over the sink cobwebbed, too. The same for the full-length mirror on the bathroom's door. Seeing her reflection distorted in the cracked mirrors amplified the hideousness of the scar on her face left from surgery. With the mangled tip of her tongue she felt the gummed spaces in her mouth where her teeth had been shot out.

Corlette had never been vain or conceited, though she had always known that her looks were much more than average. Now, she felt, Q might not find her desirable any longer. She certainly didn't feel beautiful anymore. But Corlette was determined not to add to her grief by drowning in self-pity anymore. She would just have to make herself as beautiful as circumstances would allow, and trust that Q's desire for her was more than skin deep.

Corlette stepped into the shower and turned the water on full blast, as cold as she could stand it. The cold shower invigorated her. She wiggled into a tight pair of low riding Apple Bottom jeans, and pulled on a baby tee. She combed her hair into a ponytail and applied gloss to her lips.

Q sat on the couch, refilling his glass with liquor that had somehow avoided Khalil's eyes. He looked up to see Corlette coming down the stairs. He immediately noticed that she had fixed herself up. When she came up to where he sat, he saw that for the first time in weeks there was life in her eyes. She kneeled down on the floor, between his knees, and gently took the glass of Seagrams from his hands.

"No more of this, baby," she said softly but firmly. "We're going to be okay." Her lisp was pronounced, but she was not self-conscious of it. "We have to pull ourselves together . . . for the memory of Alize."

At the mention of their baby's name Q hugged Corlette, leaned his head down on her shoulder and said, "I'm sorry. I was slippin'. I should've never had y'all in the car with me. I knew the twins had beef because of what my brother did to their grandmother. I should've moved y'all away from Thomasville . . . "Q said.

"It's okay, boo," Corlette soothed, kissing his tears.

"No, it ain't. I wish I would've caught those slugs instead of you . . . and . . . my . . . sweet . . . baby . . . girl."

"She's in God's arms now; no one can ever hurt her again," Corlette said with conviction.

For the next five minutes they held each other and cried. When their tears subsided
Corlette kissed her man with the emotion of all that they were going through together. Later she bathed Q, and washed his dreads.

When Corlette was done, Q took her to bed and made slow, passionate love to her. He kissed her deep, paying no attention to the severed tip of her tongue. When he placed soft kisses all over her face, he was tryna assure her that he still desired her despite her scar. They made love to each other slow and long. Later, when they lay spooned together, they both knew that they were ready to pull themselves back together, aided by a bond to each other that they vowed never to let anyone or anything come between.

Chapter Twenty Three

Q bounced back with a new focus and determination that was born out of all that he'd been through lately. If he didn't know the streets wasn't nothing to play with before, he definitely knew it now. He was on a mission to get it like never before. Either he was gonna claim the streets or the streets was gonna claim *him*. Wasn't no in-between anymore, it was all or nothing. He couldn't lose now because he no longer feared death. He believed that God would judge him by his heart, not so much his deeds.

With all the heat that came behind Alize's murder, Fazio had cut Q off.

Because his name was good in the streets, it wasn't difficult for Q to plug into a new connect. The prices weren't as sweet as Fazio's, but the quality of the product was comparable, so Q rolled with it. He no longer fucked with consignment, so he was definitely his own man. Fuck Fazio, Q was glad he had robbed that nigga now. Fazio had shown there is no loyalty in the game.

Q stepped his game up even larger than before. Niggas saw in his eyes that he wasn't taking no shorts. In the hood they said he was chasing death, so only a fool would test his guns.

Q had sent Corlette to a plastic surgeon in Miami, recommended by Cha Cha's lady friend, to have her grill fixed. Now, he was tryna locate that bitch nigga DeWayne. He had heard the twin be creeping through Thomasville sometimes to visit his grandmother. He had been staking out the spot, hoping to catch twin slipping, but hadn't had any luck.

Q pulled up to B-Man's spot in an incognito whip. He got out and went to B-Man's front door.

Gwen answered his knock.

"Where my fam at?"

Gwen stood in the doorway, like she wasn't gonna let him in. He pushed right on pass her. He hadn't talked to B-Man since that day in B-Man's hospital room.

His eyes grew large when he saw B-Man at the kitchen table sucking the glass dick. The smell of burning crack was unmistakable. Q had cooked an assload of that shit in his young lifetime, plus the smell of crack being smoked remained imprinted in his memory from way back when Rapheal and Black Girl used to get high around him and his brothers.

"I didn't let him in!" cried out Gwen. "He pushed right pass me, like he the police or something!"

"Shut up, bitch! You got my fam smoking this shit," Q checked her junkie ass.

"Don't be callin' my lady no bitch," said B-Man.

Then he put the glass dick back in his mouth; there was no sense in tryna hide shit now.

"Fam, let's go. Walk out this muthafucka with me, and let this junkie ho make it the best way she know how. Real talk, B-Man, she ain't doing nothing but dragging you down in the gutter with her crackhead ass!"

"Kick rocks, nigga!" replied B-Man.

"Nah, pimp, I ain't leaving without you. You better than this, shawdy. Fuck the shit that went down between us; it ain't even about that no more."

"I said, *kick rocks, nigga*! Do you, and let me do *me*!" B-Man snapped.

"I can't do dat, shawdy, we fam! What, I s'pose to turn my back and let you go out bad? We blood, fool! I love you, nigga. I ain't finna' let this shit take you out like it did Black Girl. Fuck dat! Let's bounce, nigga."

B-Man was quiet, as though he was considering leaving with Q. Gwen went over to him, threw her arms around him as if he was her life raft.

"Don't leave me, baby!" she pleaded through parched lips. "How he gon' come over here and tell you I'm bringing you down? If he got so much love for you why he shoot you?"

Her words seemed to make B-Man reconsider. Q saw their effect on his brother.

"Check it, pimp," Q softened his voice and switched strategy. "You can always come back. Just leave with me now, to get your head together. Let's go fuck wit' Khalil for a minute."

Then he said to Gwen, "If you love my brother you'll encourage him to go."

Gwen refused to do that, though. Without B-Man, who was jacking to support their drug habits, she would be ass out.

"I ain't goin' nowhere," B-Man said.

Q wouldn't give up. "Bruh, I need you to ride wit' me on that nigga, Twin. Your head gotta be right to handle that. For real, shawdy, you the only nigga I fucks wit' like dat."

"I told you, I don't fuck wit' you no more. Ain't shit changed, nigga."

"Bruh, that pussy ass nigga killed my daughter."

"So what? That's *yo'* loss not mine!"

B-Man's callousness hit Q like a slug to the chest.

"Fool, if you hadna involved Corlette in that bullshit, none of that shit would've jumped off!"

"Charge it to the game, nigga," B-Man replied. "You a big-money nigga, go buy yourself another daughter."

Q reached under his jacket, pulled out his burner, ready to nod B-Man *and* his junkie bitch. As he was about to squeeze the trigger, Black Girl's words came to mind. *"Believe it or not, home is often where the hate is."*

"I'ma let you have that, shawdy," Q told his brother. He tucked his burner back into his waistband, turned and walked out. A hot tear slid down the side of his face as he got into his car.

Khalil and Rapheal could only shake their heads when Q related things to them.

Khalil said, "I can't believe B-Man let that punk bitch trick him on the dope."

"Believe it," Q reiterated. "Real talk, I almost slumped his stupid ass. I mean, when he said that shit about I can go *buy* myself another daughter."

"That dope got him talking out of his head," concluded Khalil, not wanting to believe there was any other explanation for their brother's coldhearted words.

The next day Khalil went by B-Man's crib himself, to see if he could talk some sense into their brother. He had to bang on the door for damn near twenty minutes to get an answer. He knew someone was at home, he'd heard voices inside when he first walked up to the door.

The weather had changed; it was now cool outdoors so Khalil sported a thick leather jacket, with a matching leather fitted cap.

Finally, the door opened.

"What you want?" B-Man asked.

"Step aside."

Bonded by Blood

When B-Man didn't move Khalil said, "Don't test me, bruh, or one of us going to the morgue today."

"It ain't gon' be me."

"Maybe . . . maybe not," Khalil responded.

They stood nose to nose, neither of them batting an eye. B-Man wanted to punch Khalil in the face; smash his nose in for the many times he felt Khalil had chosen Q's side against him. But he felt sure that Khalil was strapped. He had seen a bulge under Khalil's jacket.

"Like I said, *step aside*, nigga!" demanded Khalil.

B-Man blinked first. He stepped aside to allow Khalil to come inside.

Khalil saw several glass crack pipes and straight shooters on the cocktail table. A large chunk of crack and a razor blade lay on a hand-sized mirror between the drug paraphernalia. Gwen watched over it all; seated on the couch, looking tore the fuck up. Khalil eyed her with contempt thick enough to choke a whale.

He turned to B-Man. "Bonded by blood! If that still means anything to you, let's get up out this bitch."

"I'm a tell you like I told Q . . . kick rocks, nigga!"

"That's how you want it?" asked Khalil.

"That's what I said, ain't it?" B-Man snapped.

"You know me, playboy—I ain't gon' baby you. You's a grown ass man now. If you salty about some ole bitch shit, get over it. Men talk shit out, bitches deal with emotions and shit."

"You callin' me a bitch?"

"Naw, bruh—you's a Jones boy, you could *never* be a *bitch*. We ain't bitch-made. What I'm stressin' is this: let bygones be bygones. It's still love, fam."

"Miss me wit' dat *fam* shit! Like I told dat nigga Q, I don't fuck wit' y'all two niggas no more. As far as I'm concerned, y'all niggas dead."

"That's how you feel? You put it on Black Girl?"

"I put it on Black Girl," B-Man swore.

Khalil looked him in the eye and told him he was sorry to hear him say that. Then he said, "In that case, me and Q wash our hands of you." He opened his jacket and retrieved the bulge from within the oversized inside pockets. It was two kilos.

"These are from Q."

Khalil let the two bricks plunk down on the table, right between two crack pipes.

"You can let this shit bring you up, or you can let it take your weak ass all the way out. It's on you."

Gwen was sweating the two kilos of cocaine, licking her dry, cracked lips and rocking her body back and forth.

Khalil stabbed the bitch with his eyes. He reached inside his breast pocket and pulled out ten stacks in hundred dollar bills. He tossed the grip on top of the mirror where the razor blade and chunk of crack lay.

"That's from me and Rapheal. You on your own from here on out, stupid-ass nigga."

"Fuck you!" B-Man spat. "I don't want shit from none of y'all. Rapheal ain't shit to me. You ain't shit, but a Rapheal wannabe! And Q, he always thought it was all about *him*. He pussy, though!"

Khalil was surprised by the depth of his brother's jealousy and envy.

"Get out my crib, nigga. And take all this shit wit' you! I don't need nothin' from y'all hos!" spewed B-Man.

Gwen flung herself on top of the kilos and the money. "No, B-Man, don't give it back to 'em! They owe you more than this, baby."

Khalil leaned over her and hocked a glob of spit dead in the junkie bitch's face. B-Man took a step toward him, but froze when Khalil whipped out a burner.

"You feel like a frog?" growled Khalil. Then he backed out of the apartment, burner ready to set it off if B-Man had made a break toward him.

When Khalil drove off, several gunshots could be heard coming from B-Man's doorway, but they didn't come close to penetrating Khalil's Hummer.

With Khalil's and Q's help Rapheal and Elisse had moved into a new luxury apartment near downtown. Sophie had entered a rehab program on her own. Rapheal had visited her at the clinic and found out that she'd checked herself in two days before he was robbed. It turned out that Sophie had been breaking into trick's cars on her old ho stroll, while the tricks were off inside the whorehouses getting served. She had gotten lucky when she broke into a trick's car and found five thousand dollars and nine ounces of crack. She admitted smoking some of the dope before deciding to surprise Rapheal by checking *herself* into rehab, and paying for it *herself*.

"I'ma get myself back fine again, daddy," she vowed, "and come back to you."

"You know I have Elisse," Rapheal reminded her.

"It's not like I'm not used to sharing you, daddy," She smiled, showing some of the vitality she had before life and drug abuse choked it out of her.

Rapheal returned her smile, then said easily, "I doubt if Elisse would go for that,"

"Aw, c'mon, daddy," she said, dismissing his remark with a flick of her hand. "Can't no young thing tell you how to handle your business. Once a mack, always a mack—ain't that what you used to tell us, daddy? You just think I'm old and broke down. But wait until I come home from here, I'ma be back thick and fine just like I was when I was one of the baddest hos on Auburn Avenue. Just wait, daddy, you'll see."

"Just concentrate on getting yourself together. You hear me?"

"I will, daddy," promised Sophie.

B-Man and Gwen had been smoking like two chimneys for the past month. B-Man was selling small weight out of one of the two bricks they had, while he and Gwen was doing their best to bloop every last gram of the second brick. Bed-Stuy came through and got high with them frequently, but he didn't fuck with the glass dick; he snorted.

Today they were at B-Man's crib getting high, as usual. B-Man had his big lips wrapped around one end of the glass dick, sucking on it like a ho sucks her man's dick. Bed-Stuy, was chiefing on a blunt, silently appalled by B-Man's quick addiction to the pipe. He had lost love for B-Man over the time they'd been cliqued up. He was especially salty about the way B-Man had played him with the money they got for slumpin' Lamar.

Though Bed-Stuy had shitted on B-Man, too, cuffing money sometimes when they pulled licks, he didn't consider that to be the same as what B-Man had done to him. Cuffing money during a lick was just part of the game. There would always be opportunities to get some "get back" on other licks. But slumpin' a nigga was a whole 'nother story.

He hadn't risked that for the chump money he'd been paid. He hadn't even stepped to Q about it because he knew that it was B-Man who had put shit in the game. So now he didn't give a fuck if his man smoked so much crack it busted his muthafuckin' heart! As long as B-Man was on point when they picked up that steel and pulled on those ski masks, Bed-Stuy ain't have shit to say to him about his glass dick addiction.

"Yo, money. That kid, Shawn, who we jacked for that dro and shit running his mouth like he wanna see us," Bed-Stuy said, after finishing off the blunt of cush.

"Shawdy, don't want no drama," B-Man sat the pipe down long enough to remark.

"He must do, he in the streets barking and shit."

"What you wanna do, go see him again?"

"I'm sayin', yo. I ain't waiting on him to come see me."

"I'll handle dat lil' pussy nigga, I know where he be hangin' out at."

"I'ma roll with you, son."

Bed-Stuy got up and went to the bathroom to take a piss. From the hallway he could see into the bedroom, where Gwen was asleep across the bed in nothing, but a bra and panties. The panties were up the crack of her ass. *Ma done fell way off,* he observed, shaking his head as he closed the bathroom door.

Gwen was in a deep slumber. Before finally laying down and going to sleep yesterday, she had been up seventy-two hours without sleep. Much of that time had been spent getting high. She and B-Man hadn't bathed in three days. Nor had they eaten anything. Finally, Gwen's sleep and food deprived body had shut down. She'd been out like a light now for more than twenty-four hours with no sign of waking up anytime soon.

"Yo, B, you back fuckin' with your fam yet?" Bed-Stuy asked B-Man, having returned from the bathroom.

"Hell, naw, I told you I ain't got no holla for them niggas no more."

"Shid, Q doing big things, that nigga's name is hot in the streets."

"Fuck that nigga, shawdy," B-Man replied with distaste. "Q be on some mo' shit. Dat nigga can eat a dick for all I care!"

"He gettin' at the money, though, son. You might need to make the peace and reap some of those blessings. Everywhere I go niggas screamin' his name. Son, dropping work all around this muthafucka," Bed-Stuy went on.

He could sense that B-Man didn't like being reminded of his brother's success. Which is exactly the reaction Bed-Stuy was hoping for.

"But I feel you, dawg. Q is on some other shit. When Khalil was on lock, Q needed you to hold him down, 'cause niggas would've been looking to touch him without a killa on his team. Now since Khalil is home, Q switched up on you. Yeah, that's some fool shit, after all the work you put in."

B-Man said, "It's all good," but his expression said something quite different.

Bed-Stuy decided not to press on. There was plenty of time to subtly influence B-Man into jacking his own brother. Bed-Stuy knew that it wouldn't take much.

Later in the week, B-Man just so happened to run into Shawn outside Stroker's, a strip club frequented by many hustlers. Shawn was sitting on the hood of his whip, kickin' it with two other niggas B-Man recognized. The three men were sharing a blunt while discussing a new stripper that had only been working at the club for a few weeks. B-Man crept up on them from behind, and before anyone knew what was going down, he had a Desert Eagle pointed in Shawn's face.

"You looking fo me, bitch nigga?" B-Man asked, with menace.

"Nah, pimp. I ain't got no beef with you." Shawn quickly copped deuces, raising his hands in the air.

"Put your hands down, nigga!"

"Ah'ight, pimp. You got that lil' bit."

He lowered his hands to his side.

"What's the business, homie?" asked one of the dudes Shawn had been burning the blunt with.

"This ain't got shit to do wit' you, Nut," stated B-Man. Then he returned his attention to Shawn. "Nigga, you don't look for me, I look for *you*!"

He cracked Shawn across the head with the steel, drawing blood.

Shawn crumpled to the ground, moaning like the bitch nigga B-Man knew him to be. He had been barking in the streets, acting like it was gon' be do-or-die the next time he locked eyes with either B-Man or Bed-Stuy. But like many niggas, his bark was bigger than his bite.

Shawn tried to curl up to ward off some of the punishment being inflicted on him.

"You got that, pimp," he kept crying as B-Man repeatedly cracked his head.

When B-Man grew tired of pistol-whipping him, he snatched the platinum chain off Shawn's neck and took the watch off his wrist. Then he went in the nigga's pockets and removed his money.

"I ain't hard to find!"

He kicked Shawn in the face.

CA$H

12 3 6

Bonded by Blood

Chapter Twenty Four

Corlette had undergone the last of three surgical procedures a few weeks ago, including the orthodontal work to insert permanent partials in her mouth. Now she was inside her plastic surgeon's private room anxiously waiting for him to remove the bandages from her face.

"You ready to have a look?" Doctor Weinbaugh asked

"Yes," Corlette said nervously. She could hardly control her breathing.

Doctor Weinbaugh handed her a long-handled mirror.

Corlette closed her eyes. Then she held the mirror in front of her face, keeping her eyes shut. She took a deep breath, slowly exhaled, then just as slowly opened her eyes.

When she saw the reflection looking back at her, a tear trickled from her eye, and a smile instantly enveloped her, now flawless face.

"Oh my god! Thank you so much," she cried.

"You approve?" the plastic surgeon asked.

"Oh yes, doctor. I love it!" she could hardly believe that the person in the mirror was *her*.

The surgeries to repair her face hadn't changed her appearance much from how she used to look before getting shot, and that was just perfect in Corlette's book. She was pleased that she looked like her old self again. Maybe a bit more symmetrically perfect, about the face, but definitely the same as before.

Q was waiting for her at the airport when she arrived back in Atlanta from the plastic surgeon's clinic.

"*Dayum*! I almost didn't recognize you," he kidded her.

The smile on his face was as wide as Corlette's.

"Now I'ma have to keep niggas out your face."

"Neva dat. You're the only nigga for me," Corlette declared.

Everyone was impressed with the wonderful job the surgeon had done to restore Corlette's original look. They were amazed that no scars or disfigurement remained. When they commented on it, Corlette did not hesitate to show her thirty-two pearly whites. Only the skilled eye of an orthodontist could detect that she had partials. Corlette thanked Q over and over again for paying for everything, and for loving and desiring her while she went through it all.

"There ain't nothing I wouldn't do for you, shawdy," Q said.

Now that his shawdy was back looking like Keyshia Cole, Q knew that she would be much happier. The tragedy they'd gone through together had bonded them much closer than what had been between him and Persia. He knew that he would never love again the way he had loved Persia. Q was cool with that; he never wanted to love blindly again anyway. What made this love *better*, though, was that he knew Corlette loved him back.

Corlette's love comforted him, and it allowed him to handle his business in the streets without having to worry about shit being raggedy at home when he was away. Now that he was plugged in with a new connect, and po-po had backed up off of him some, he was back on the grind. He had toned down his shine a lot lately. He was just trying to stack chips. Khalil was constantly reminding him to keep his mind on his money and his money on his mind.

Fazio was pressing Q to fuck with him again, but Q wasn't thinking about doing business with his old connect no more. When the heat was on, Fazio had cut him off, without a second thought. He hadn't showed Q any loyalty. So, *fuck Fazio*! That's how Q felt. If Fazio kept pressing him, he'd get the same thing Q was about to serve to DeWayne.

Q, Khalil and Rapheal were strapped and ready. Q just got the call he'd been waiting for.

"He just went up in his grandmother's crib," the caller had whispered into the phone. "Hurry up. I'ma stay here and watch the place. I'll call you if he leaves," the boy said, and Q knew that he could count on shorty to do just that.

As they were entering Thomasville Heights, Q hit lil' shorty on the cell phone he had given him. Vashon answered the first ring. "Yeah?"

"What's the business?"

"He still there."

"Aight, shorty, go on home. I'll get at you in a few days."

"You need me to roll witchu?"

"Naw, lil' nigga. Take yo' butt in the house."

Q checked his watch and saw that it was almost midnight. The street was quiet and still at that hour. Q drove past the apartment then parked around the corner. One by one they exited the car, at two-minute intervals. Q, who had gone first, was posted on the side of Mrs. Freeman's building. He was slouched down on the cold ground, leaning against the building like a bum. The only thing that would've betrayed his disguise was the thick jacket he wore, and his sneaks. They were too new to belong to a bum. Q didn't plan on letting anyone get up close enough to him to peep that.

Khalil posted up across the street, near where Corlette used to stay. Rapheal walked up and down the block,

portraying the actions of a crackhead, late-night-shuffling, a role he played well from personal experience. An hour passed before luck broke their way.

From the side of the apartment building Q heard a door open and close. He jumped up when he saw Khalil moving with swiftness from his post across the street.

Q had his TEC-9 locked and loaded as he ran from around the side of the building. DeWayne had his back to Q, so he didn't see him coming but he heard the hurried footsteps. Then he noticed the figure coming toward him from across the street. It was dark out, but the streetlight revealed the burner aimed at him right before it went off. *Blocka! Blocka!*

Khalil squeezed two shots, but both missed. DeWayne jumped two feet in the air. When his feet touched concrete he dodged to the right, half running, half reaching for his own strap. The glock slipped out of his hands, smacked pavement, and he accidentally kicked it further away from him. When he bent to pick it up he felt a hot explosion in his ass. He yelped and grabbed where he'd been shot, before snatching his burner off the ground.

Q was letting the TEC-9 spit. He knew that he had hit the nigga at least once; he'd heard the nigga yelp like a bitch. Now the nigga was tryna run, with a limp, occasionally bustin' back over his shoulder. Q and Khalil were side by side now, tryna run DeWayne down, but not carelessly because they had to respect his wild shooting. Anyway, the fool was running right toward Rapheal and his choppa.

DeWayne tried to stop in his tracks when he ran into the choppa that was leveled at his chest. Rapheal didn't hesitate to avenge his granddaughter. The choppa coughed angry, loud, and repeatedly.

DeWayne was blown backwards from the inpact of the choppas deadly ammunition. He smacked the pavement and died in a puddle of his own blood.

Q pulled up in his Ford Explorer. When Vashon saw him pull up to the curb, he hopped off the hood of the broke down hooptie, and walked up to the driver's door of Q's whip.

"What it do, lil' pimp?" Q smiled down at him from inside the SUV.

"Slow motion," replied Vashon.

"Hop in, let's ride, lil' nigga."

As they drove out of the projects, Q said to Vashon, "Good lookin' out lil' man. But you know you can't mention nothing to *nobody* about that."

"Man, I ain't slow, and I damn sho ain't no snitch I'ma take dat to the grave wit' me," replied Vashon, with a realness beyond his years.

The hood breed 'em official like that, at an early age.

"You know, you gotta walk the walk, you can't just *talk* it."

"I gotcha, big homie. You gonna see."

"Aight. I'm a hold you to that," Q said. "Check it, I'ma break bread witcha for handling that business, but I don't want you to be running around the projects flashing the money I'ma give you," he warned.

"You don't owe me nothin' for what I did, big homie. You looked out for me and my sister plenty times. But I do wanna ask you to put me on your team?"

"What?"

"Yeah, big homie—man, you know my mom's is on dope and me and my sister ain't got shit. Rats in the gutter living better than us. I ain't asking you to give me nothin', Q. Just put me under your wing so I can grow up to be just like you."

How the fuck could Q say no to that?

Over the next month, Q schooled young Vashon on every aspect of the dope game that can be taught without the student having to actually live it to learn. That included weighing dope, cooking it, whipping it, the whole nine. He talked to Vashon about the necessity of having a solid name in the streets.

And, above all else, "Never shit where you sleep," Q advised him, amongst many other jewels he dropped on the lil' soldier, who was about to turn thirteen.

"And," he added, "don't have a loose tongue around bitches. Most of 'em can't help but to gossip, putting a nigga's business all in the streets. Even if they don't mean to get a nigga cased up, they will."

"Check dat, big homie," acknowledged Vashon, listening attentively to every jewel being passed on to him.

"Don't trust niggas no farther than you can see 'em; even then, expect the worst. Niggas can't stand to see another cat rise up. Jealousy is a dangerous emotion; envy, too. Muthafuckas like crabs; they'll pull you down in order to rise up themselves. Fake right at they ass and go left."

Vashon rode shotgun with Q everyday soaking up game. As far as going to school, he deaded that. He already knew how to read, write, and count money. The rest of his education would have to come from the streets.

For Vashon's thirteenth birthday, Q took him to Teaser's and let him stunt in VIP. He paid Sinnamon, and another stripper to leave the club with his young protégé and break him off at the mo-mo, all night long. The next morning, when Q scooped Vashon up from the motel, he told him,"You official now," half smiling.

"His young ass like ta wore us out!" Sinnamon's couterpart said.

Q became to Vashon, like Baby is to Lil' Wayne, and vice versa. Soon Vashon was handling grown man weight; making drops alongside his mentor; strapped—eyes always open to detect any funny-style shit.

At five-ten, Vashon was tall for his age and could easily pass for seventeen. So when he whipped through Thomasville Heights in his Tahoe, the cops weren't more likely to pull him over than they would any other young black male.

It was an unseasonably warm day for January in the "A" so the hood was live. People were out on the block doing what hood niggas and shawdies do when the weather is nice.

"I'm a hustler" by Pimp C was bumpin' through his speakers. The flip-flop paint on his whip was killing 'em, and the twenty-six inch rims sparkled as Vashon parked in front of his mom's crib and hopped out. He was rocking Roc-A-Wear from head to feet with a phat chain around his neck, wrist froze. When he waved back at an astonished shawdy and smiled, his new platinum grill set his profile the fuck off.

Q had put youngin' in the game.

Vashon went inside to holla at his people. He had been staying with Q, and hadn't seen much of his fam for the past few months.

Gloria hugged her son. "Hey, baby! Whose car is that I saw you pull up in?"

"That's me, ma."

"Take me for a ride, Vashon!" six-year-old Val asked excitedly.

"Next time, lil' stuff," he promised, bending over and scooping her up. "You been a good girl?"

"Yep."

"Humph!" Gloria shook her head.

"I have!" Val refuted her moms.

"It don't matter, you still my heart," Vashon said, kissing his little sister's forehead.

He kicked it with mother and little sister for a minute, gave them both some money and headed out the door. Back in his whip he switched Pimp C to T.I. turned on all four TVs, with the press of one button, just to stunt on niggaz. When he was eating nothing but hope sandwiches, he used to pray for the day he could be ballin' like the Big Dogs in the hood. He had to floss a little bit now. He owed himself that.

Vashon saw her standing outside with her girls. Every one of them, but the one that mattered was going crazy over the whip as he pulled up to the curb, even though they couldn't see past the tint to see who was driving.

"*Vashon!*" one of the shawdies screeched with excitement when he rolled down the window.

"What it do, Cierra?" he spoke.

"Boy, whose whip you done stole?"

"Girl, don't insult me like dat. This my shit."

"You lying!" accused another shawdy.

"Whateva. I ain't tryna prove nothin' to y'all silly asses. Anyway, back up off my whip before ya breath ruin my paint!"

"Naw, you didn't just try to clown me!"

"Chill out Cierra, I'm just fuckin' wit you, homegirl," Vashon said, smiling platinum.

"Damn, nigga, you done came the fuck up."

Cha-ching! Cha-ching! Her sixteen-year old eyes saw dollar signs.

"I'm just tryna build my weight up," he replied with a bit of modesty. "Yo Jaid, let me holla at you fo' a minute," Vashon called past Cierra and 'em, to the object of his interest.

Jaid was a super thick sixteen-year old redbone whom Vashon had always wanted to holla at. But back when he was busted, he didn't have the confidence to step to her. Jaid had a baby, but she wasn't out there like that—shit happens sometimes. She had always had an easy smile for Vashon when he spoke to her. She knew that he liked her, but like any sixteen-year old shawdy, especially one with a child, she considered a thirteen-year old a little boy, despite Vashon's height and maturity.

"Hey, Vashon," Jaid spoke from where she stood, on the sidewalk.

Seeing that she probably wasn't going to come up to his whip, Vashon opened the door, and got out. Cierra and 'em stepped closer to admire the leather seats, the wood grain dash, and the four small flat screens. Their teenaged pussies throbbed.

Vashon strolled up to Jaid, his platinum chain matching his smile. His Roca-Wear gear was crisp and new.

"What's up, Vashon?" Jaid asked, looking like she was tryna keep her cool, even though she couldn't believe her eyes. Shawdy looked super thick today.

Vashon's confidence wasn't phased. Not anymore. He was no longer *busted*. These days his swag was turned all the way up. He fucked grown-ass women twice his age. So he wasn't lacking confidence as he replied, "I came to claim *mine*."

"What?"

"Damn, what I gotta do, spell it out? You know I been wanting you for a long time."

"You ain't but thirteen or fourteen, boy—how you gon' be wanting anybody a *long* time?" Jaid brushed him off.

"Oh, you got jokes, huh?"

He smiled back at her.

"I see I'ma strike out if I try to holla at you around your girls," he said.

"They don't influence me."

"Well, I wish they *could*. Look at 'em! Over there acting like they ain't never seen a phat whip before."

"That's their business. The whip don't make the man—or boy, in your case."

"What a boy know 'bout dis?" Vashon flashed the weight on his wrist.

"That don't impress me. You ain't gon' be able to take it to prison with you."

"Prison? Ha! Shawdy, me and prison go together like two dicks—a bad mix. It ain't happenin'."

"I hope not, Vashon. Nice seeing you. I gotta go in the house and check on my baby."

Jaid bounced.

Vashon was walking back to his whip, head down in defeat—about to tell Cierra and 'em to get out of his goddamn whip when he heard Jaid call his name from her porch. He turned to hear what put down she would hurl at him this time.

"You are looking damn good though, lil' daddy," she yelled to him. Then the door closed behind her.

Q and Vashon had just dropped two bricks off to a nigga on Fulton Industrial Boulevard. Q had fucked with Slim a coupla times before, serving him four and a baby the first time, a half a block the second time. Apparently Slim had been really stacking his chips to jump from a half a block all the way to two of them guys. Slim had explained that he and a friend were going in together to cop the two bricks. Q hadn't wanted to meet Slim's partna; he just served Slim the blocks for twenty stacks apiece and told him to get at him when he needed to re-up.

At Q's stash crib they began counting the stacks Slim had given them. In total the money added up to just twenty-six thousand and five hundred dollars! Q called Slim on his cell phone, heated.

"What it do, homeboy?" Slim answered.

"*What it do*? Nigga, this paper is short!"

"What?" Slim dummied up.

"You heard me, *nigga*?"

"How short is it?" asked Slim, as if he didn't know already.

"Thirteen and a half stacks!" barked Q.

"Damn, nigga—who you hollerin' at? I ain't no bitch. Tell you what, folks! Whateva I owe you, get it like you live!" Slim hung up.

"Check," Q said to himself . Then he said to his protégé, "How deep you in with me in this shit, lil' soldier?"

"Ten toes down, big homie," vowed Vashon.

Two nights later Vashon caught Slim coming out of the poolroom over on Fulton Industrial. Vashon creeped up on the careless nigga before he could react.

"Rock-a-bye baby, bitch nigga!" *Splacka! Splacka! Splacka!* "Get it like we live, huh?" *Splacka*!

Corlette was visiting her moms, so Q and Vashon were at the townhouse by themselves. Two days had passed since Vashon nodded Slim. They was just chillin', staying out of the streets as a precaution against whateva. Q still couldn't figure out why Slim tried a monkey stunt like that. Somebody should've told him that Quantavious Jones was no longer taking any shorts!

Still, there was a lesson learned.

"From now on, we ain't hittin' nobody off until we check the money," Q told Vashon.

They were eating buffalo wings and chili cheese fries and playing video games. Switching subjects Q asked, "What's up with that shawdy you fiendin' for? What's her name again?"

"Jaid."

"What's the business? She still won't give you no holla?"

"Naw, shawdy straight won't come in. I went through there again yesterday. I got her number from her girl, but when I called, Jaid still stressin' I'm too young for her. Plus, she talkin' bout I'm throwing bricks at the penitentiary."

"Shid, I done already told her ain't going down like that. I'ma stay two steps ahead of a downfall, in case I slip. I'll still be one step ahead. Ain't dat what you taught me, big homie?" said Vashon.

"Fo, sho."

Q gave him a pound, and was dropping jewels on him when the doorbell chimed.

"What it do, bruh," Q spoke, letting Khalil and Sinnamon in. "What's up, Sin."

"Hey, Q. Hey Vashon," Sinnamon spoke. "Vashon, you ain't been ripping them lil' girls' coochies up, have you—with your big dick, young ass."

"Oh, shawdy packin' like dat?" Q laughed.

"Shid, that young nigga gon' catch a murder case with that shit between his legs if he put it up one of them lil' young virgin pussies," Sinnamon declared, half-serious, causing them all to laugh.

"Nigga, you can't trick with my ho no more. Fuck around and steal my Number One," joked Khalil.

"Neva dat, daddy," Sinnamon jumped back in.

Q, to the embarrassment of Vashon, told them of Vashon's failed pursuits of Jaid.

Khalil said, "Shawdy, don't be taking advice on females from Q. Holla at me for that; you see how I'm doing it."

"Tell him, daddy!" Sinnamon tossed gas on it.

"Check this, shawdy. You got this lil' ho's phone number. This Jaid girl, who can't recognize a thorough young nigga when she's in the presence of one?"

"Yeah. I got her number."

"Call the lil' hooker up and tell her your uncle wanna holla at her."

Vashon pulled out his cell phone and punched in Jaid's digits.

"May I speak to Jaid? Hey, shawdy, this Vashon. Can you talk? Ain't nothin' up—not really. My Uncle Khalil wanna holla at you. Huh? I don't know; he just wanna holla at you."

Khalil accepted the phone from Vashon.

"*Watch this*," he whispered.

A half hour later he passed the phone back to Vashon.

"Yeah, shawdy, what's up?"

"You can pick me up Friday night around eight o'clock. Don't stand me up, either," said Jaid.

"What she say?" asked Khalil, with a knowing grin, when Vashon got off the phone.

"She told me to pick her up Friday night at eight."

When Friday came Vashon arrived at Jaid's crib at 7:45, not wanting to chance being late. He waited downstairs in the living room, talking to Jaid's mother, while Jaid put her fourteen-month old son to bed and finished getting dressed. When asked his age, Vashon said that he was eighteen. As for the expensive whip parked outside, he said that it belonged to his uncle. He didn't like lying to Jaid's mom, but there was no way in hell he was gonna tell her the truth about his age or his hustle.

They went to the movies, and then afterwards chilled at Jaid's crib for a while. Vashon's maturity had all but extinguished Jaid's apprehension. The only hurdle left for him to get over was her reluctance to get involved with someone who was throwing bricks at the penitentiary. She had heard that he was cliqued up with Q. Her baby's daddy used to be in the streets like that. Now he had a life sentence. Though they had already broke up when he got cased up, after her baby's daddy got sent away, Jaid had shied away from dating hustlas. The uncertainty of a hustlaz fate was more than she could handle.

"Everything in life is a gamble," Khalil told her, when he had convinced her to give Vashon a chance. Jaid could feel him on that, and she was beginning to feel Vashon.

When they locked tongues on the couch, cuddled and tongued some more, Jaid was saying to herself, *I can't believe I'm sitting here kissing a thirteen-year old!* By their third date, though, Vashon's age no longer was an issue. That night they rented a hotel room and made love for the first time.

After trickin' with Sinnamon an 'em, Vashon had learned a lil' something to put on Jaid. Plus, listening to Foxy Brown spit on that cut "Big Bad Mama", featuring Dru Hill, one day while rolling with Q, Vashon had heard Foxy rap: *got 'em strung, let 'em know I'm like an ICEE, for the best effect you got to use your tongue.* So he gave Jaid some of that, too. Though it was his first time getting down like that, he knew to search for that little button, with finger and tongue. Jaid directed him to the pace that pleased her most, and after twenty minutes of this foreplay, she was calling out her ecstasy. A few minutes later when she covered Vashon's erection with a Magnum condom,

Jaid wasn't sure if she was going to be able to handle all of him. But that young pussy had stretched wide enough for a baby to come out of it, so it damn sho' adjusted to what Vashon was packing.

After their first night of love-making, it was a wrap.

Q noticed the similarities between the way he had fiended for Persia, before finally getting her, and the way his young protégé followed the same course with Jaid. He took note of it, but he wasn't too concerned. Jaid didn't seem all that materialistic. Besides, Q had bigger concerns occupying his thoughts.

Bonded by Blood

Chapter Twenty Five

A Dude; Q dropped weight to on consignment, had just called saying that he'd gotten jacked. Usually, it wouldn't have mattered that the niggas got jacked for the product; once the work touched their hands, they were responsible. *Fuck dat! Pay me!* Q would've said. But what the dude told him caused Q concern.

"It was your brother and that New York nigga he be with."

This was the third time in two weeks it had happened. Q knew it was on the up and up, 'cause the three cats who'd claimed to have been jacked by B-Man and Bed-Stuy didn't know one another. Q knew for sure that B-Man knew that he fucked with them niggas, on the work consignment tip. B-Man had rode with him more than a few times to hit 'em off with work.

"What's that nigga's problem?" Q asked, exasperated. "What, he wanna war with his own fam?"

Rapheal offered no answer to the conflict. He knew that there was no such solution as the right one. Q had to either war with his brother, or let B-Man's violations go unchecked. B-Man was a bully-type nigga, the type that preyed on any sign of weakness, Khalil pointed out.

Natural instinct was to advise Q to do whatever he had to do, but for Khalil that meant telling one brother to body the other. Bonded by blood, Khalil reminded himself. That meant he couldn't just have Q's back, he had to hold B-Man down, too. But the hell if B-Man wasn't tryna make that an impossible.

"Let me try to talk to that stupid ass nigga," Khalil advised Q.

"*Somebody* better talk to dat fool! He gon' make me treat him like we really *ain't* brothers!" threatened Q, biting his bottom lip in frustration.

"That nigga talkin' crazy," Khalil announced after he had called B-Man and tried to get some understanding re-established between them all.

Fire was in Q's eyes.

"What you gon' do?" Rapheal wanted to know.

Q exhaled. Then he fired up a Newport, inhaled, blew smoke rings up in the air. For a while he said nothing. Finally he spoke.

'I'ma chalk these violations up. Just charge 'em to my heart. Fuck it."

He dialed B-Man's number.

"Gwen put my brother on the phone!"

"Yeah?" answered B-Man coming on the line.

"Look, bruh, I don't know why you stepping on my toes like dat. That's *three* of my people you done jacked. Now I'ma charge those to my heart and wipe the slate clean 'cause I love you, nigga. But if you bother *any* of my people again, it's gonna get ugly," Q warned before ending the call.

The stress B-Man was purposely causing Q wasn't the only drama that was pressing on Q's nerves, making him wanna go the fuck off. Persia was being vindictive now that he didn't fuck with her no more. At court, for Q's preliminary hearing for the domestic battery charge Persia, showed her ass.

As soon as Q walked into the courtroom, accompanied by his lawyer, his pop and Corlette, Persia, went into a hysterical fit, frontin' like she was deathly afraid of Q. She was frontin' so hard the judge ordered the bailiff to stand next to Q, to assure Persia that he could not get to her. Q just shook his head. *This bitch clowning like a muthafucka in front of these crackers! I had to be blind not to be able to see through this fake bitch.*

In the middle of the precedings Persia asked the judge if he could order Q to pay her some type of alimony.

"No, ma'am. This is not a divorce hearing," replied the judge.

"Your Honor, my client and Persia Atkinson were never *legally* married," interjected Q's attorney.

"Well, she could pursue financial support under the laws of *palimony*," the judge said. "However, this is not the proper place for that."

"Anyway, your Honor, my client is presently unemployed."

"He ain't *unemployed!*" yelled out Persia. "Judge, he got plenty money! He's a drug dealer, and—"

"Your Honor, I object!" screamed Q's lawyer.

His face was as red as a ripe tomato.

The judge smirked, "Calm down, Counselor. You opened the door for that. Be that as it may, Miss Atkinson I won't allow you to blurt out accusations such as that in my courtroom. We are here on charges totally unrelated to the road we've somehow veered down. Will counsel for both parties please approach the bench."

Q didn't chance looking at Persia, for fear that he'd be unable to stop himself from running over there and knocking the bitch's teeth out. Corlette was mean-mugging the punk bitch, though. As they left the courthouse Q had to grab Corlette and pull her away, to keep her from going after Persia.

"Boo, let me kick that bitch's ass!" Corlette pleaded.

"She ain't even worth it, shawdy," he said.

"Let her go!" screamed Persia. "I'll tear that ho a new asshole."

Q had to practically drag Corlette to the car.

On the way home he admonished her for letting Persia get to her. But deep down he was feelin' the way Corlette was ready to represent him.

If he didn't already have enough drama in his mix, more was added when his cell phone rang.

"What it do, pimp?" began Fazio.

"Who dis?" asked Q.

"Oh, since you a big-timer now, you don't recognize my voice no more?"

"Oh," recognizing the voice now. "I'm good, folks. How you?"

"Could be better."

"I heard that."

"You ready to start back shopping with me?" asked Fazio.

"Naw, I'm good where I'm at, folks. 'Preciate it."

"Who put you on your feet, Q?"

"You helped me up," conceded Q, "and I 'preciate dat."

"You ain't acting like it."

"Damn, man, what you want from a nigga?"

"Loyalty."

Q half-laughed. "Dat shit gotta go both ways, don't it? You ain't showed me none when I was stressin' dat."

"After all I done for you; that's how you gon' do it?"

"Yo, man, this conversation ain't going nowhere. I'ma get at you another time," said Q.

"You gettin' too big for your G. You know you not built like that."

Q caught the threat *and* the insult, but he let them both slide.

"Whatever dawg. I'm just doing me."

"Get at me soon or I'ma get at you," Fazio said, his implication apparent. "For real, though."

Q wasn't faded. What Fazio didn't know was that Q had elevated to that other level. The game had brought out the killa in him when the twins killed his innocent baby. It didn't even matter now.

The next day Q went and got "Alize" tatted over his heart. Now, let Fazio and the rest of 'em *bring it on*!

Corlette was over in Thomasville Heights at a baby shower for a friend that she had grown up with. It was just coincidental that B-Man was cruising through the projects when Corlette came out of the apartment where her friend's baby shower had just concluded. B-Man spotted her and pulled up to the curb and parked.

"What's up, shawdy?" he spoke to Corlette, getting out of his hard-top Chevy, the '64 he had before he copped the drop.

It wasn't until he was right up on her that Corlette recognized B-Man. *Damn, he's looking bad!* She said to herself, frowning at B-Man because she held him to blame for Alize's death.

B-Man drawed back and stuck a burner to her head.

"Take off all your jewelry, and give it to me!" he barked, eyes looking crazy.

"B-Man, why you doing this?" she cried as she began removing her jewels.

"Gimme that purse, too, bitch!"

After he removed the money he found inside her purse, B-Man tossed it on the ground at her feet.

"Tell your nigga if you want to, you just gon' get him killed!"

Several girls had seen the robbery going down, from the doorway of the apartment where the baby shower was held.

They had been afraid to intervene, but they had called the police.

Of course, B-Man was long gone when po-po pulled up.

Corlette refused to file a complaint despite being pressured to do so.

After po-po left, one of Corlette's friends asked, "Wasn't that Q's brother, B-Man who robbed you?"

"Looked like his car," one whispered to another.

Corlette didn't respond. She got in her car and drove straight home, crying all the way there. When Q came home, later that night, he could tell something was wrong with his lady. When he asked what was the matter, Corlette lied to him.

"My stomach hurts," she said.

But she knew it would be just a matter of time before he noticed she wasn't wearing her necklace, watch and rings. Still, she didn't wanna get anyone killed.

Sinnamon hurriedly raced down to the dressing room and threw on her street clothes. She was crying and shaking so bad she could hardly button her blouse. B-Man had showed up at the club to come and get her and take her to Khalil. Her man had been shot in the head in an altercation with the police. He was holed up at the Days Inn, off of Cleveland Avenue, and had sent his brother to bring her to him.

She didn't realize she had been tricked until the hotel room door closed behind them, and Khalil wasn't there.

Smack! B-Man knocked her on the bed.

"Get naked, bitch!"

The gun was inches from her face. Sinnamon was a pro; she didn't panic. Becoming hysterical might get her killed.

"We can do this, baby boy, without all that."

She undressed.

"Let me give you a condom to put on, to protect us both, baby."

"Naw, bitch! Open your mouth. And if you bite my shit I'ma pull this trigger!"

B-Man made Sinnamon suck him until she thought her jaws might permanently lock. Then he punished her with the dick. He fucked her ass and pussy with a violence that was maniacal. He tore poor Sinnamon's ass guts to shreds. Left her leaking like a dripping faucet.

Khalil was furious! Q was, too. Early that morning Corlette had tearfully told him truth.

When Q and Khalil shared information about what B-Man had done to their ladies Khalil recalled seeing the baby doll wrapped in a blanket in the backseat of B-Man's whip. He remembered that Elisse had said that the woman who set up the robbery seemed to have a doll wrapped in a blanket, disguised as a real baby.

"Fam, I think it was B-Man who robbed and shot pop. And I think Rapheal has known it all along."

Q nodded his head, he concluded that they couldn't put nothing pass B-Man.

"I got *this*!" Q angrily insisted Khalil let *him* handle it.

"I'll be back tomorrow night. Me and Bed-Stuy going to Savannah to handle some business," B-Man told Gwen, as he bent down to lock the small safe in the bedroom closet.

"Okay. Did you leave me something out?"

"Yeah."

He tossed her a half-ounce of crack.

"Thank you, baby," beamed Gwen. "Be careful."

B-Man wasn't going to Savannah; that was aight. He was going to spend the night with Amore. He hadn't gone out much

the last three days. He'd been staying at the crib expecting his brothers to come over there talking shit.

The young boy saw B-Man get in his '64 Chevy and drive off. When the car's tail lights could no longer be seen, he waited fifteen minutes then walked up to the apartment door and knocked.

"Who is it?" Gwen asked, vexed that someone was interrupting her smoking.

"Is B-Man home?"

"No, he's not."

"Well, I'm s'pose to drop off some money I owe him. I'm Bed-Stuy's nephew."

Money? Gwen peeked through the peephole and saw a tall young boy. He didn't look threatening so she opened the door.

The gun appeared out of nowhere. Its tip was deathly cold against her forehead. "Back all the way into the kitchen and you bet' not scream, bitch!" his voice was as cold as his eyes. Gwen did as he instructed. In the kitchen he made her kneel down as if she was praying.

Boc! Boc!

The next day, when B-Man returned home, he found his girl face down, with two holes in the back of her head. And the safe was missing. He removed all the guns and drug paraphernalia from the apartment before calling the police.

As soon as he was able to get away from the po-po and their accusatory questioning, he called Bed-Stuy and told him the business. He needed to gauge whether or not his jack partner was somehow responsible.

"Fuck outta here!" Bed-Stuy uttered, in genuine disbelief. "Yo son, that's fucked up! Who you think did that shit?"

"Maybe, Shawn," guessed B-Man, before reconsidering. "Naw, he too pussy."

"I hate to say this, B, but . . . nah fuck it."

"Say it, nigga."

"What about one of your brothers?"

"Maybe Khalil," he allowed. He was still underestimating Q.

When B-Man called him talking a lot of gorilla shit, Khalil said, "Nigga, miss me with all them threats. I ain't slump ya junkie bitch. But karma is a mafucka."

B-Man hung up and called Q, just on a hunch.

"Touch mine. I'll touch *yours*!" Q simply said. "Now, let shit go, shawdy. Oh, it's gon' get ugly."

"It done already got ugly, bitch nigga," B-Man snapped.

Q went to visit Black Girl's grave. This was the first time he had been back since they put her in the ground. He sat down on the ground, next to the small headstone with her name inscribed on it.

"Hey, Ma," he began slowly. "If you're somewhere watching over us I know you're ashamed of what's going on between your boys. We promised you on your deathbed that we would never let it come to this. But Ma, it's like B-Man don't want it no other way. I don't wanna kill my own blood but I don't wanna let him kill me either. Tell me what to do, Black Girl, 'cause I don't have the answer." Tears dripped from Q's eyes. "What I gotta do? Move away? Ma, I don't understand why B-Man so angry at me and Khalil. What we do to him? So what if Rapheal ain't his biological? Me and Khalil are still his brothers—bonded by *your* blood."

Q stayed for more than an hour. It felt good to talk to his mom.

Before getting ready to leave, he said, "Oh, Black Girl, what you think about Corlette? She's the one, ain't she? Well, I'ma

bounce now. Word is bond, Ma. Ain't nothin' gon' make me kill my brother, even if that means he'll end up killing me. On another note Pop doing good, huh? Yeah, he done bounced back. Gotta go, Ma. I love you. Kiss Alize for me."

The tears were still falling when Q reached his whip.

Chapter Twenty Six

K halil had no complaints with the way Q chose to respond to the foul shit B-Man had done lately. An eye for an eye. He had no tears to shed for Gwen. The junkie bitch had been killing *herself* slowly anyway, and taking B-Man down with her.

Khalil was glad he had let Q handle that because had he handled it, B-Man might've been on today's obituary page in *The Atlanta Journal-Constitution*, instead of Gwen. That's how hot Khalil had been when he found out what B-Man had done to his top ho. Sinnamon was fucked up. She was wearing a diaper like a twenty-seven year old baby. It would be at least another two weeks before she would be able to go back to work.

To make up for Sinnamon's lost wages, he had to push his other hos to fill her quota as well as their own. Emily had no problem stepping up her game; she had a list of wealthy clients that could be counted on to come through for her. Rayne, who didn't enjoy her line of work anyway, wasn't pleased to learn that she would have to turn extra tricks. Nevertheless, she complied. Cha Cha wasn't agreeable, though. But she quickly changed her attitude when Khalil tapped that hard head and threatened to send her back to Roco. Cha Cha didn't want that; she knew if she was sent back to her ex man, ass whippin's would become regular. With Khalil they were few and far between.

Khalil moved Rayne and Cha Cha out of the apartment in Riverdale as a precaution against anything B-Man might be planning to do to them. Khalil couldn't figure out what his crazy ass brother might do next. It seemed that B-Man was determined to force his hand. Unlike Q, Khalil wasn't willing to grant their brother immunity from his gun. If it came down to him or B-Man, he wasn't going to his grave just to uphold his promise to Black Girl. If B-Man didn't back the fuck up off him, Khalil was prepared to do what he had to do.

Rayne was especially shook up over what had happened to Sinnamon. She couldn't understand why Khalil's own brother would violate one of them like that.

Another thing she couldn't understand was Khalil being so tight with Q these days. They were thick as thieves, as far as she could tell. Just seeing them together, the bond between them was obvious. All of which didn't add up to Rayne. She thought back to when Khalil was desperate for money to pay off that gambling debt. She had called Q to plead with him to help Khalil out and Q had rejected her pleas with an indifference to Khalil's problems that was in contrast to the love she saw between them now. She didn't say anything to Khalil about it because she had vowed to believe in him. However, doubt had begun to creep into her head.

B-Man was fucked up. Gwen was dead, and the apartment manager refused to allow him to continue the lease. Bed-Stuy hadn't come through for him. After all the shit they had done together, the nigga hadn't even offered him a place to lay his head until he could get his own. That bitch Amore had said, when he asked to rest at her spot, "We aight, baby boy, but I ain't tryna do it like *that*."

B-Man punched the bitch in the goddamn face.

Then he hit Persia on the hip to see where she was resting at. Maybe she'd let him rest with her, if for no other reason than to get back at Q for kicking her to the curb. Once he rested with her for a minute, she would fall in love, and he'd finally have her. He'd also have to fake her out like he had bank 'cause she definitely wouldn't fuck with a broke nigga.

"I'm glad you called," Persia said when B-Man rang her phone. "Yeah, we can meet. I need to talk to you, too," she said.

Yeah I knew she missed the dick! B-Man said to himself. If he would've had money for a room, he would've told her to meet him at the Hyatt. But since he'd been wiped out when they killed Gwen and took his safe, B-Man asked Persia to meet him in the parking lot of South DeKalb Mall.

If Persia had fell off, haters couldn't tell by her appearance. Q's ex pulled up in her freshly washed and waxed Ford Escape SUV. She parked beside B-Man, got out and slid into his passenger seat. The black suede pants she was rockin' hugged her thighs and tapered down, where they disappeared into the top of calf-high leather boots. A suede and leather jacket set off the hookup. Her hair was in long curls, one of which she had to keep tossing out of her face. The femininity of the movement had B-Man craving to have her as his. Persia was still shining, looking like a star. *I'll rob banks to keep this bitch happy, if she'd just be mine.*

"So, what's up, baby boy?" she asked. Her sexy red lips were hypnotic.

"Oh, I'm good. What's been up with you?"

"Nothing, really. Just missing the hell out of your brother."

"Oh, yeah," replied B-Man, dejected. He had thought she was about to say she'd been missing *him*!

"For real. Look, B-Man, tell Q that you lied about us sleeping together. Please. Just do me that one good."

"It's too late for dat. He ain't gon' believe me. Anyway, I don't fuck with him and Khalil no more."

"Why'd you have to tell him in the first place?" she asked angrily.

"Fuck that nigga. We can hook up—you and me."

"That ain't happening, B-Man. I should've never fucked with you like that no way," she said. Now that her well had run dry, she missed her water.

"What, I ain't good enough for you?" B-Man asked.

"You want the truth?"

"Yeah."

"No, you don't," she assured him.

"It's like dat?"

"Life's a bitch, baby boy."

She sounded so heartless B-Man realized that it would've been futile to ask her for a place to rest his head. What the fuck did she care about him? Everything was all about her.
Persia offered him five hundred dollars if he'd help her straighten things out with Q.

"Tell him I'll drop the assault charges against him," she added.

"You got the money with you?"

"Yeah, but you gotta call him right now." Persia looked inside her purse for her cell phone. When she looked up, she was staring at a burner.

"Empty that purse, bitch! And come off those jewels—all of 'em."

B-Man rented a motel room for a week with part of the money he took from Persia. The rest he smoked up, the jewels, too. When the money ran out, he was back to having no where to stay, sleeping in his Chevy drop. Somebody had stolen his '64 the week before.

Today that crack gorilla was on his back large as hell. He was desperate to come up with a lick, but wasn't shit working out. Bed-Stuy claimed that he wasn't fuckin' with the steel no more. B-Man knew that the nigga was tryna fake him out. He had the feeling that Bed-Stuy just didn't wanna fuck with *him* no more. It was all good. *Fuck dat nigga!* B-Man told himself.

Bed-Stuy was feeling the same way about B-Man. *Fuck, he think I'ma let his crackhead ass rest at my spot? Shid, ain't no way, duke! He was already a sheisty-ass nigga before he got on that shit. Ain't no way I can fuck wit' son no more. Really, I need to slump that nigga before he try some dopefiend shit. Nigga might get cased up and flip on a nigga. One thing's for certain and two things for sure—a nigga can't put nothin' past a crackhead. Word! That crack done made that nigga turn on his own brothers. What da fuck he care 'bout me? Shid...nothin'! Yeah, I'ma slump his ass,* Bed-Stuy decided.

B-Man had been sleeping in his Chevy drop for the past two and a half weeks. Shit was so bad; he had been renting the drop out to young trap boys for a couple of rocks an hour. He hadn't bathed in more than a week, and the funk had begun to insult even his own nose. The only things he still had, besides the Chevy drop, were a cell phone and a burner. The young trap boys had offered to buy the burner, but he hadn't sold it because if he sold his gun, he wouldn't be able to jack anybody. He felt his luck begin to change when he received a call from Bed-Stuy.

"What's poppin', son?"

"Shit. What's up wit' you, shawdy?"

"Got this sweet lick set up. You wit' it, B?"

"Fo sho'. Do I know the nigga?"

"Nah, I don't think so. Check it, son. Fall through my crib so we can chop it up."

"I'll be through there in 'bout an hour," said B-Man.

"One," replied Bed-Stuy, ending the call.

B-Man checked his Desert Eagle. He only had four rounds in the clip. That would have to do. He put one round in the chamber and slid the burner back under the car seat. He got out, locked the doors, and went inside the Moreland Avenue crackhouse where he usually did business.

"Yo Tone, let me get an eightball on credit. I gotcha later on tonight, shawdy," B-Man said to one of the young trap stars that ran the crackhouse.

"No money, no dope. You know da rules, pimp."

"Damn, nigga. All the money I done spent up in this bitch, you gon' act like dat?"

"Don't take it personal, pimpin'—house rules."

"What, you don't trust a nigga?"

"Trust?" laughed Caesar, Tone's partna. "Nigga, in God we trust. Er'body else gotta pay up front!"

"Check it, shawdy. Hold this as collateral."

B-Man held out his cell phone.

"Nigga, I don't want that shit. Anyway, dat bitch probably 'bout to get cut off!" Tone clowned him.

B-Man fought back the urge to snap on these half-pint wannabes. He wanted to remind the quarter kilo-buying young jits that his brother had enough cocaine to bury them *and* their crackhouse under! Had he had the Desert Eagle with him, B-Man might've *took* their shit.

Calming himself down, B-Man assured them that the cell phone was pre-paid, and good for another month.

"I'ma get my phone back, man."

"Gone give him four and a half," Caesar said to Tone. "If you don't come straighten your face, we takin' your whip— wherever we see you."

These niggas must think I'm pussy, B-Man said to himself. *Later for them, though.* He picked up the eightball of crack that Tone tossed on the floor at his feet.

"Y'all don't give *me* no credit!" complained a smoker named Tweety Bird.

"Naw, bitch, 'cause you don't know how to pay your debts," Tone checked her.

"Well, can I suck your dick for a dime sack?"

"Hell no! I just got my dick sucked an hour ago by a fine ass bitch."

"What about you, Caesar?"

"Fuck, no! Your headgame is wack! You da only crackhead ho I ever met that don't know how to suck a dick!" Tone cracked up.

B-Man dropped a fat chunk of crack on the pipe. He had the other end of the pipe in his mouth and was putting the lighted torch to the bowl end, about to take a blast.

"You gon' let me hit it, baby?"

Tweety Bird slid next to him on the floor, where he sat with his back against the wall.

B-Man unzipped his pants with his free hand. Tweety Bird stepped to her business. Tone and Caesar bent over with laughter when they heard her exclaim, "*Dayum*! This junkie ass nigga got a big donkey dick!"

Bed-Stuy patiently waited for B-Man to show up. His mind was set; he was gonna do what he had to do. He planned to play him the same way he had played his man, Universal Sun, up in the Boogie Down.

Bed-Stuy and Universal had been best friends since elementary school. They had done petty crimes together, coming up. When they were older they started jackin' niggas; mostly dope boys. One day they had slumped a dope boy and his wifey during a robbery. Po-po came with major heat, cause wifey was a white chick from a prominent family. Bed-Stuy got worried that Universal might flip on him if they got connected to the murders, since Bed-Stuy had been the triggerman. When a dope boy named Caprice put out an open hit—worth four and a half ounces of crack and ten thousand dollars—on Universal becauseUniversal had been robbing his crack houses, Bed-Stuy figured he might as well collect on the hit since he planned to nod Universal anyway. He'd never have to worry about a dead man flippin' on him.

Bed-Stuy told Universal that he knew of a sweet lick. A stash house where nobody lived.

It was so dark outside that Universal couldn't see that the house they were about to run up in was abandoned. When they kicked down the door, Bed-Stuy, who was behind Universal, quickly raised his arm and squeezed the trigger of the burner in his hand. Universal slumped to the floor, twitched two or three times and it was a wrap. Bed-Stuy collected on the hit then moved to the "A".

Now, as he awaited B-Man's arrival to his crib, he anticipated running the same game on him. He had already chosen the vacant house where he would do what he felt he had to do.

The pipe had B-Man so preoccupied that he hadn't realized that more than an hour and a half had passed since he started smoking the ball. The clock on his cell phone told him that he was running late; he'd told Bed-Stuy he'd be there in an hour. That was at nine o'clock, it was now ten-thirty. He took one last hit of the pipe and told Tweety Bird she could have the last hit left.

"I'll holla at y'all in a few," he promised Tone and Caesar, heading for the door.

"Naw, pimp, that stays," Tone stopped him, removing the cell phone from B-Man's waist.

When B-Man stepped outside into the winter's night air, he was dripping with sweat and his mouth was dry. He licked his lips a hundred times before he reached his whip.

When he pulled up in front of Bed-Stuy's apartment on Jonesboro Road, he parked, reached under the seat and got his strap. Outside the car, he slid the Desert Eagle in the back of his waistband, where it was hidden by his jacket.

"What up, B?" Bed-Stuy said, opening the door for B-Man.

"Same ole shit," B-Man responded.

Bed-Stuy gave him a pound. "Damn, duke stank like a muthafucka!" he said to himself, stepping back away from B-Man.

When B-Man went to sit on the couch, Bed-Stuy hurriedly said, "Let's go sit in the kitchen, yo."

He didn't want B-Man sitting his smelly ass on his couch. The kitchen chairs were made of plastic, he could easily wash the smell off of them.

Bed-Stuy handed B-Man a glass then brought out a bottle of gin. B-Man, who was already paranoid from the crack he had smoked, was watching Bed-Stuy's every move. He declined the gin. Hard liquor would fuck up his crack high, would throw it all the way to the curb. He didn't want that.

"You got a beer?"

Bed-Stuy got a beer out of the fridge and handed it to him.

B-Man drank two beers while listening to bed-Stuy explain about a stash house, somewhere out in East Point, where there was supposedly a lot of drugs and money stashed.

"And ain't nobody living there, to keep an eye on it," Bed-Stuy pointed out. "No pit bulls, nothin. The shit gravy."

"Whose spot is it?" asked B-Man.

"One of them New Orleans niggas."

Hurricane Katrina had fueled the migration of thousands of Louisiana hustlaz to the "A".

"Who put you up on the lick?"

"A lil' bitch that moved down from BK. Nigga took her by there, tryna show off that shit. Ma say it's at least fiddy of them birds up in that bitch. Plus mad fetti."

"Aight. When we gon' hit it?"

"Tonight, son."

"I'm wit it," said B-Man, finishing off a third beer. "Let me go take a piss and I'll be ready to do this."

"That's what I'm talkin' 'bout, son," smiled Bed-Stuy.

This nigga must think I'm a fool, B-Man was thinking as he pissed. If the money, and them thangs is at a house where ain't nobody there, what he need me to go wit' him for? It ain't even no jack, it's a simple burglary if it's like he says. But the shit ain't on the up and up 'cause we ain't never did a lick the first night we spoke on it. Fuck naw!

B-Man stepped out the bathroom with the Desert Eagle in his hand. Bed-Stuy was sitting at the kitchen counter when he came back into the kitchen. As soon as he saw the look on B-Man's face, and the burner in his hand, Bed-Stuy reached for his own burner.

Five shots rang out in the small kitchen. B-Man stood over his dying partna, his Desert Eagle aimed down at him, but empty of shells. He had got the jump on Bed-Stuy; had squeezed off four shots, two of which caught Bed-Stuy in the chest. Bed-Stuy managed to squeeze off a single shot before he had tumbled over, but it was just reflexive, it had no aim, and missed B-Man by two feet.

B-Man didn't realize that his clip was empty until he pointed the Desert Eagle down at Bed-Stuy's head and heard the click when he squeezed the trigger. He saw that Bed-Stuy's own burner was lying on the floor, two or three feet away from. He bent down and picked it up, aimed it down at his once-robbing partna.

"Yeah nigga, you thought I was slippin'. Never underestimate a Dirty South nigga!" *Blocka!* B-Man shot Bed-Stuy point blank in the forehead and didn't even blink when his man's brains oozed out onto the floor.

He hurriedly searched the apartment but found only five stacks, some lightweight jewels, and a couple of burners. He stuffed it all in a pillowcase and dipped. When he got back to the crackhouse on Moreland Avenue he paid Caesar and Tone and got his cell phone back. Then he bought another four and a half grams and left to go get a motel room, Tweety Bird in tow.

Bonded by Blood

Chapter Twenty Seven

pring stiff-armed winter to the side much in the way Q was doing the competition; never forcefully, just with a subtle, natural way of exerting it's season to reign over the others.

Q's street lieutenant was young Vashon. The boy had watched closely and soaked up everything since they cliqued up. He had a mind like a sponge when it came to drug business. He had been no more than an average student in school, but in the streets, Vashon showed the potential to become valedictorian.

"I'ma be the youngest kingpin, big homie," he vowed.

Q had copped Vashon and Jaid a three-bedroom condo not too far away from where he and Corlette rested at, and the two couples were constant companions. Q sold Vashon his Corvette and Vashon had it tricked out and sitting on all black rims. His girl Jaid usually pushed the Tahoe. Shawdy was holding him down like a true thoroughbred.

Her only demand of him was that he not bring drugs, around her and her son. Vashon had no problem with that at all he had been schooled not to shit where he slept, anyway. The last thing he wanted to do was endanger his girl and his step-son.

The only other demand Jaid placed on Vashon was one that was a lot more difficult for Vashon to honor. She demanded complete faithfulness.

"If you say I'm the one you want then it shouldn't be hard to do," she'd said. "Now if you ain't ready for this just let me remain living with my mama; we can still kick it and neither of us won't lay no claims on each other. But if we move in together I'm not putting up with no cheating nigga. I ain't playing, Vashon. The first time I catch you, I'm leaving, and I'm not coming back. I put that on my son's life."

"I feel you, Jaid," he'd said, hugging and kissing her. "You ain't gotta worry about me creepin' on you. You're the only girl I've ever wanted, for real, shawdy. But you gotta stay true to me, too."

"Oh, I'ma do that," she'd vowed.

So far they both were keeping it thorough, which for two hood-raised, young teenaged lovers, it was something to be admired. For Jaid, faithfulness wasn't hard to maintain. Though she'd had a baby at a very, young age she had never been promiscuous. Vashon was only her third lover and she truly hoped that he would be her last. Niggas tried to push up on her whenever she went anywhere without Vashon. Especially, when she visited her peeps in the projects, or when she was at GED class. But she was too in love and committed to Vashon to do anything more than say hello to another nigga.

For Vashon, faithfulness wasn't quite as easy to maintain. Now that he was getting' to the money, and his swag was magnificent, shawdies wouldn't let him breathe. They stayed up in his grill tryna get him to cut something with 'em. What kept him from falling weak to a young nigga's natural lust was the recollection that when he was busted, none of those hos had any talk for him. When he was at the strip club with Q, ballin'—all the variety of grown ass pussy was tempting as fuck to a young nigga. But Vashon, who had an analytical mind far more advanced than his age, thought about the consequences versus the rewards. One night of pleasure could cause him to lose his girl for a lifetime. At the end of the day a shot of pussy wasn't worth the consequences.

Q was exposing him to all levels of the game, preparing him for the day he graduated from under his tutelage. Q wasn't the type of selfish nigga most muthafuckaz in his position usually were. He wanted to see his lil' nigga doing big things. Q's way of treating Vashon earned Vashon's complete trust and loyalty.

Q had begun to play the background more and more lately as he became comfortable allowing Vashon to handle things. Of course, Q still remained the HNIC, but niggaz didn't see him so much these days. Naturally, street niggas underestimated Vashon's age as well as his gun. But a few incidents that left those who violated leaking, convinced the streets that Q's young protégé wasn't to be trifled with.

The formidle duo were together in Q's new big boy Benz, bumpin' "Street Life" by Rick Ross. Q was smoking a blunt. The windows were down, allowing fresh air to carry the smell of the purp away because Vashon didn't get high. Q had just spent a week on Saint Thomas island with Corlette, treating his boo boo to a little R & R.

"That nigga Twin s'pose to get out soon," Vashon told Q, after catching him up on the past week's business.

"DeShawn?"

"Yep. That's what I heard."

"I thought he caught a dub for an aggravated assault?"

"I thought so, too. But niggas say he gave that time back to them crackers; got his shit overturned on appeal," explained Vashon, letting Q know to be on point. "We gon' have to deal wit' dat nigga, big homie. You know he gon' want some straightenin' for his twin getting slumped.'

"I'ma handle it; I been waiting on this day," Q said with morbid anticipation.

"Put me in the game, coach," Vashon begged for some gunplay.

"Sit this one out, lil' soldier. Me and Khalil gon' handle it; this one is family biz."

"*I* ain't family?" Vashon looked hurt.

"Fo sho. You know you my lil' brotha from anotha." Q gave Vashon a pound. "But I need you to hold down the streets while I handle this. Feel me?"

"Yeah, I feel you, big homie. You know I'ma play my position, whateva is best for da team," Vashon responded with sincerity.

Chapter Twenty Eight

Q checked his safe and saw that it was sitting on swole; he could get out Of the game now. It made sense to get out before the inevitable fall came. Fazio was hating on his rise, threatening to take him to war because he was getting' crazy cake and wouldn't shop with his ex connect no more. Besides money, Q had a wifey that he truly adored and could trust. Maybe it really *was* time to get out.

Corlette couldn't have been happier when Q told her that he was thinking about getting out of the game. She had found out last week that she was pregnant, but she hadn't shared the news with him yet because she wasn't sure if she wanted to have the baby. For one, the loss of Alize had hurt so deeply, Corlette knew that she could not endure the death of another child. She believed it would always remain a possibility as long as Q was in the game. Life had already proven that the violence that hovered over a drug dealer had no mercy on the innocent lives of children. Corlette knew that she was too devoted to Q to leave him. If the violence that surrounded him claimed *her* life, so be it. She'd rather die with him than live *without* him. But she could not bring another child into this world and expose it to the unpredictable violence that was a part of their lives.

As the weeks went by, Q was readying himself to retire from the game. He considered himself lucky when he thought about it. Yeah, he had been fuckin' with work since he was thirteen-years old, but he had been fucking with major weight only four or five years. Not many niggaz, he knew had stacked the kind of chips he was now sitting on, in such a short time. A month short of twenty-two years old, he was sitting on three mil.

Q wasn't a fool, he knew that three mil tickets might seem like a lot, but it would not last a lifetime unless he found a way to flip it once he went legit. Then, too, he wanted to bless Khalil and Rapheal—and even B-Man—with some grip if he was calling quits. He figured he would split a mil ticket between the three of 'em, break Vashon off proper. Then, he'd be left with a little less than two mil tickets. *Nah, that ain't enough to walk away with. I'ma make one more large ass re-up.*

B-Man was doing bad. His ass was nothin' but a straight smoker now. He had sold his Chevy drop, bought some weight with the money, with the intention to come up. But he had ended up smoking more dope than he sold. A nigga had jacked him for the rest. Muthafuckaz knew he had fell all the way off when he traded his burner for some crack, which Tweety Bird helped him smoke up. Now that he had no more money or crack, the junkie bitch had ran off with another smoker.

B-Man was so fucked up, his hustle now was stealing steaks and shit out of supermarkets, and trading the meat for rocks. Or he washed Caesar and Tone's whips for a rock or two. When they wanted a laugh they gave B-Man and a junkie ho a couple rocks to put on a freak show. It amused the two young dope boys to watch B-Man punish those hos with his donkey dick. They gave the hoes *three* rocks to let B-Man stick that donkey dick up their asses. Then Caesar and Tone laughed like crazy when them hoes shitted all over the place. When they stopped laughing they'd throw a coupla rocks at B-Man's feet, saying "Clean dat shit up!"

Q and Khalil heard about how niggas was handling their brother. Bonded by blood ran through both of their minds.

"Let's go see what the business is, shawdy?" Q suggested.

Q, Khalil, Rapheal and Vashon pulled in front of the crackhouse in two whips. Caesar and Tone was outside, clownin' B-Man for not wiping all the wax off their whips when he detailed the cars just a while ago.

From inside their own whips Q and 'em heard the two lil' jits handling their fam like a straight J. Q and 'em were out of their whips, business in hand, before Caesar and Tone could react.

"Go ahead, test my muthafuckin' G, nigga!" barked Vashon at Tone. The nine Vashon gripped convinced Tone not to try him.

"What about you?" Rapheal echoed, talking to Caesar.

Q and Khalil patted down the two jits. Caesar was strapped; Tone wasn't. Q took Caesar's burner, removed the clip and, the round in the chamber, and then slung the burner down the block.

"You know who I am, lil' nigga?" barked Q, all up in Caesar's grill.

Caesar nodded his head. Q was well known in the streets.

"Well, if you know who I am, then you know B-Man is fam, right?"

"Uh-huh," muttered Caesar.

"Well, why you got my brotha out here, chumpin' him off?"

"Aw, man, he—" *Whap*! Q slapped him in the mouth, with his burner, knocking him to the ground.

"Fuck you think, shawdy—you can disrespect my fam!"
Whap! Whap!

"You got something to say about it?" Vashon asked Tone.

"Naw, man."

"You just said somethin', nigga!" *Whap! Whap!*

Khalil and Rapheal then joined in the beat down. The four of them pistol-whipped Caesar and Tone damn near to death.

Q, tried to help B-Man get off the dope, but he was too far gone. Q got him an apartment, but it quickly became a crack den. Q didn't know what to do with him. They tried to get him to go to rehab but B-Man wasn't hearing it.

Khalil had lost his first ho. Cha Cha had left to go shopping one morning and never came back. At first Khalil thought that B-Man had snatched her up. He armed Sinnamon and Rayne with .25 automatics. Then, a week later Cha Cha called. She told him that she was living in Miami, being taken care of by Eva.

"Cop and blow," Rapheal reminded him.

Khalil digested the advice and vowed to tighten up his game while Q, who was at his side, was thinking differently about his own hustle.

Q had spent a mil and change on one last re-up. After he flipped this weight, he was getting out of the game, he promised himself as he dressed for his birthday party.

Q's twenty-third birthday celebration was held at the Level Three nightclub, the same spot where they had Khalil's welcome home party almost two years ago. The place was packed.

Q and Corlette were dressed in matching colors; he was rockin a cream Sean John two piece suit and chocolate gators, accessorized with an iced-out Jacobs watch and bracelet.

Corlette wore a form fitting cream colored strapless dress by Donna Karen. Her jewels sparkled around her neck, wrists, and from her fingers.

Khalil was stuntin' hard in his light gray Armani suit and matching bossilini. Rayne, Sinnamon, and Emily were on his arm looking well worth the price it would cost another nigga to get some holla.

Rapheal was there with Elisse and Vashon was there with his boo Jaid. Even B-Man was in attendance. He had cleaned himself up for the occasion. Persia was outside the entrance showing her ass because she was not allowed inside. Security had been given pictures of her and were told not to allow her admittance.

"I still can't figure out what I ever saw in that rat bitch!" Q said to Khalil. They were posted up at the bar.

"A big butt and a smile," cracked Khalil.

"Yeah I guess so."

"You got you a winner now with Corlette."

"Fa sho, and the game been real good to a nigga, that's why I'm about to get out before it turns cold," revealed Q.

"Happy B-day, nigga!" Jimmy wished Q.

"Thanks homie," Q replied. He looked at Jimmy suspiciously and Jimmy peeped it.

"Homeboy, me and you have always been good—I fuck with you the long way. Whatever problem my uncle got with you don't involve me, I'm just here to celebrate your birthday with you."

"Fam, you got a problem with this nigga?" asked Vashon who had just walked up and was already aware of Jimmy's relation to Fazio.

"Naw, it's all good," Q quickly assured him.

"I'ma fuck with you later man," Jimmy said and touched fist with Q. Then he grilled Vashon before bouncing.

"You don't want no drama," Vashon called out behind him.

Q shook his head at his young protégé cockiness.

B-Man eased off and caught up to Jimmy on the other side of the floor. "Yo, Jimmy lemme holla at you, dawg."

"Yeah, what's up?

"A while back Fazio's stash got robbed right?"

"Yeah, what do you know about that?" asked Jimmy with furrowed brows.

"I know who did it. Call your uncle up and find out how much that information is worth to him."

B-Man followed Jimmy outside where they made the call to Fazio.

"He says he will pay you a half a brick and ten stacks but the information has to be concrete," related Jimmy to B-Man.

"Oh, its concrete but tell him it'll cost him two bricks and twenty-five stacks, nothin' less," negotiated B-Man. "And he need to have it delivered to me within the hour. I'm not giving up any information until I have what I asked for in my hand."

Jimmy relayed B-Man's demands. A few minutes later he said to B-Man, "The stuff is on its way."

While Jimmy waited outside in his Nav' for Maldanado to arrive with the drugs and money, B-Man went back inside to the party. He stopped Rayne as she was on her way to the lady's room.

"You don't have to be afraid of me," he said softly, reading the apprehensive expression on her face. "I think you're too good of a woman to be doing what Khalil has you doing. And trust, it was never about him needing you to help him get out of a gambling debt—that was game. Rapheal coached him on how to turn you out."

"I don't believe you," replied Rayne.

"Real talk, the drugs you got busted with were never intended to go to Khalil's homeboy. Khalil set you up. He needed for you to lose your job so that you would lose your independence and have to move up here and depend on him. It's the same dirty ass game Rapheal ran on my mother back in the day."

Rayne knew that B-Man wasn't lying. What really hurt her was that it had been Khalil's plan for her to get caught carrying drugs into the prison where she'd worked. B-Man told her that it had been Khalil who'd placed the call to the prison to alert them that she'd have drugs on her that day.

"And that shit about him owing a huge gambling debt— please! Khalil don't gamble. When have you known him to gamble? Believe me, a gambler can't just quit gambling overnight. It's like a drug addict. Besides, Khalil wouldn't have been afraid of no loan shark! My brother ain't afraid of shit."

Rayne listened to B-Man go on and on, and though she knew B-Man was a crackhead who was capable of all types of treachery, she knew that in this instance he was telling the truth. When she thought back on everything, it all added up. She looked across the room and saw Khalil and Q laughing— thick as thieves. *Q was in on it too, they played me*, Rayne realized. She ran back to the ladies room in tears.

Twenty minutes later Rayne slid into the booth that Khalil shared with Sinnamon and Emily. She had dried her eyes and gathered her emotions. "You okay?" Khalil asked.

"Yes, daddy," she answered in a sweet voice and leaned over and kissed him. Thanks to him she had become good at pretending. They drank champagne and watched Q bend down on one knee, in the booth next to theirs, and propose to

Corlette. Sinnamon and Emily rushed over to get a closer look at the huge diamond engagement ring.

"Khalil, I feel sick. Can we please leave?" Rayne asked.

"Let me go over here and congratulate Q then we'll bounce."

A half an hour later, Khalil left with his three ladies, they had rented the Executive Suite at the Hyatt-Regency in Buckhead for the weekend.

B-Man eased outside to collect the blood money and drugs that Maldanaldo had arrived with.

Chapter Twenty Nine

Q and Corlette left the party hand in hand. Q was sober but Corlette was giddy with drink and the excitement of knowing that she would soon become Mrs. Quantavious Jones. They said goodnight to Vashon and Jaid then slid into the back of the chauffeured limo that Q had rented for the occasion.

Not long after the limo pulled out of the club's parking lot a van full of Mexicans pulled in traffic behind it.

High on the top floor of the Hyatt hotel, in the bedroom of the Executive Suite, Khalil was propped up in bed with his back against the headboard. He had on brown silk boxers and nothing else. Emily was on his right and Sinnamon was on his left side cuddled under him. Rayne was in the bathroom.

David Hollister played in the background and the bedroom lights were dimmed. Khalil looked up to see Rayne standing at the foot of the bed holding the .25 automatic that he had given her for protection. Here eyes were vacant and her jaw was stiff.

"You slimey-ass bastard!" she hissed.

Khalil's forehead wrinkled. "Say what?"

"You heard me, nigga—I called you what you are, a slimey ass bastard!" Rayne raised the gun and cocked one in the chamber. Emily scrambled off the bed and scurried underneath it.

"Baby Love, what are you talking about?" asked Khalil, very poised.

"When was the last time you gambled, Khalil?"

"Huh?"

"You've never been a gambler, have you? It was all just a scheme to turn me out, wasn't it?"

Pow!

She fired a shot pass his head. Khalil jumped and Sinnamon screamed.

"Put down the gun, baby, and we can talk," Khalil said softly. But Rayne was not trying to listen to anymore of his lies.

"No, Khalil, there's nothing you can tell me that will give me back my innocence. I loved you, but it was never about love with you. You were just playing the game. Well, pimp muthafucka, you played the wrong chick!" *Pow! Pow!*

The first shot struck Khalil high in the chest. The second one hit him in the neck and ruptured his esophagus.

Sinnamon screamed at Rayne. "You stupid country bitch!" she covered Khalil's body with her own, willing to take the next bullet for him, but Rayne lowered the gun to her side and wept as her whole body trembled at the sight of what she had done.

Sinnamon was covered in Khalil's blood. She screamed for Emily to call 911. Tears poured down her face as she cradled Khalil's head in her lap. "It's okay, daddy. I promise I'm not going to let you die."

TO BE CONTINUED

Coming Soon...

CA$H

TRUST NO BYTCH
BY CASH
CHAPTER ONE

Brazen stood face to face with his cell mate and mentor with a heavy heart that was in contradiction with the ruthlessness that was reserved for others.

In the thirty-six months that they had shared a cell at the federal prison in Hattisburg, Pennsylvania the man that he affectionately called Unc had become a surrogate father as well as a best friend to him. Though anxious to return to the streets of Cleveland, Ohio and apply all the things that Unc had taught him, he felt strong emotions about leaving his enlightener behind.

"I wish I could take you with me." he said with unbridled sincerity. Devin's stoic expression did not crack. He appreciated the thought but it did not change his circumstances; he had twenty years remaining on a thirty year sentence for drug racketeering and related crimes.

"Don't worry about me, I'm built to last. Go out there and put your hustle and murder games down like the street general I've trained you to become. Remember, leave no enemy alive or they'll seek revenge. Never forget that those around you are the ones that can do the most harm to you. No matter if it's friend or family you must execute them at the first sign of treason . . . no exceptions. They violate. . . you bury them. Let God be the one to forgive 'em." Brazen nodded his understanding as Devin continued. "Fuck what you've been told before. Self-preservation is the only code of the game that does not get broken." He wished he had adhered to his own advice ten years ago when the Feds began snatching up his

clique and pressuring them to testify against him, he repeated what he had told Brazen on many occasions.

"I let certain niggas live because I thought they were built like me and would stand on the code Death Before Dishonor. When the government started snatchin' up their family members and seizing their assets muthafuckas saved their own asses and left me for dead."

I feel you. That's why I'll have no mercy on anyone who shows that they have a flaw. Thought Brazen.

"It's like I've been preaching to you for three years, it's imperative that you get in and get out. If you overstay your time in the game you'll end up in a coffin or right back in here. Go at it hard so that you can stack your money before anyone realizes that you're doing the type of numbers that you're doing. Because once it's known that you're a made man everyone will come after you. Take no prisoners and spare no feelings. You can trust yourself and you can trust my daughter. Absolutely no one else!"

"Yes sir." he respectfully replied.

Devin took a step closer. Brazen could smell the prison issued toothpaste on his breath. They both stood six-feet two. Devin's bitter black eyes bored into Brazen's optimistic brown eyes. His chest heaved up and down. "Son, my daughter is all I have left in this world. She's been trained by the best. She is comfortable wearing stilettos or a bulletproof vest but I don't want her in the line of fire. And you are not to fuck over her. If any harm comes to her I will reach out from prison to touch you, by any means necessary." He issued a stern warning.

Brazen respected him but he feared no one, so the threat didn't rattle him. He had no plans to do Devin's daughter wrong. He put a mitt on the older man's shoulder. "Relax Unc. I would never shit on Jazz," he promised. "I put it on all that I love. . . I won't ever betray you."

The two men embraced then Brazen saluted him.

"Go take over the city the way I once did." said Devin.

"With all due respect to your legend, Unc, I'ma do it bigger and better. With Jazz by my side there's no stopping my rise." Vowed Brazen.

His mentor smiled. "Go on. My daughter is probably outside waiting."

Brazen turned and walked towards freedom and a destiny that was no longer in his control.

DISCUSSION QUESTIONS FOR BONDED BY BLOOD

1. Should Black Girl have disclosed to all three of the boys that Rapheal wasn't B Man's father, instead of only disclosing it to B Man?

2. Why do you think B Man so envious of his brothers?

3. Should Black Girl's maternal instincts have trumped her street instincts and led her to point her sons in legitimate directions instead of illegal hustles?

4. What do you feel made Q steal from Fazio?

5. Would things have turned out differently had Q slumped Fazio after stealing from him?

6. Should the two brothers have allowed B Man to get away with so many transgressions against them?

7. Should Rapheal have told who robbed and shot him? Would that have changed anything that transpired later?

8. Did Khalil love Rayne?

9. Would young Vashon had found his own way into the game, even if Q hadn't put him on?

10. What do you anticipate transpiring in the *Bonded by Blood* sequel?

WAHIDE CLARK PRESENTS
BEST SELLING TITLES

Trust No Man

Trust No Man II

Thirsty

Cheetah

Karma

The Ultimate Sacrifice

The Game of Deception

Karma 2: For The Love of Money

Thirsty 2

Country Boys

Lickin' License

Feenin'

Bonded by Blood

Uncle Yah Yah: 21st Century Man of
Wisdom

Life 4 A Life

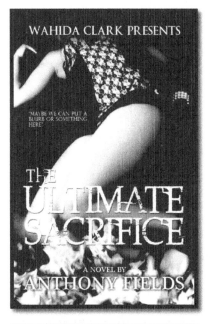

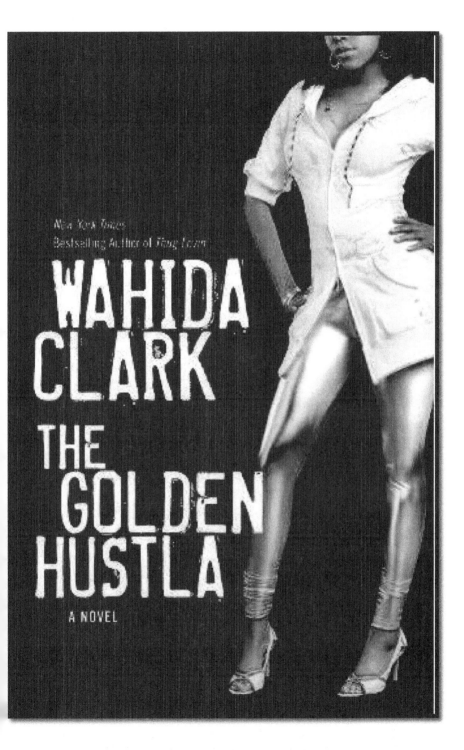

New York Times
Bestselling Author of Thug Lovin'

WAHIDA
CLARK

THE
GOLDEN
HUSTLA

A NOVEL

COMING SOON!

WAHIDA CLARK PRESENTS

BONDED BY BLOOD

Three Brothers, One Promise.

CA$H

WAHIDA CLARK PRESENTS

LICKIN
From Lust to Love to Deception and Death
LICENSE
A NOVEL BY
INTELLIGENT ALLAH

WAHIDA CLARK PRESENTS

THIRSTY

MIKE SANDERS

WAHIDA CLARK PRESENTS

COUNTRY BOYS
TRUE STORY

Leon "Pop" LASSITER   Sidney "Coo" SMITH

WWW.WCLARKPUBLISHING.COM

FICTION Cah

Bonded by blood

X

Ca$h.
$15.00   9/14   **3201200110907**

CPSIA information can be obtained at www.ICGtesting.com
Printed in the USA
BVOW08s0824170714

359450BV00010B/153/P